"What else besides cards do you do well, Miss Hillcrest? You seem the kind of woman with other secret talents a gentleman might be interested in."

Ah, so they were back to flirting again. She had wondered if she'd imagined it the other night. "A lady never tells," she said primly, but then fluttered her lashes in an exaggerated fashion.

He grinned. "Neither do I, no matter how bold the lady might choose to be."

Sylvia had to admit she enjoyed the occasional flirtation. There was no harm in it with Wharton. He would never be a client of the Hillcrest Academy. He was much too self-assured to need any help courting a wife.

But might Wharton be something else to her? Something a little scandalous, perhaps? His eyes and smile hinted at wicked thoughts.

Heather Boyd

Desire by Design

Distinguished Rogues

The characters and events portrayed in this book are fictitious. Any similarity to real persons, living or dead, is purely coincidental and not intended by the author.

DESIRE BY DESIGN
Copyright © 2020 by Heather Boyd
Edited by Kelli Collins

Cover Design and Formatting by Heather Boyd

Chapter One

Mayfair,
February 1816

"The problem with not having a mistress is that everyone believes I have time on my hands and must be entertained," Alexander, Marquess of Wharton, confided to his good friend, Lord Carmichael, in a whisper as they strolled into the latter's dining room. "I have been besieged by invitations from those who feel I need to be amused."

"Did you believe you could not refuse us tonight?"

"I did not say I didn't agree with them," he promised with a laugh. Alexander found great enjoyment from his friends. This particular one was now no longer a bachelor, unfortunately, and had to be shared.

He glanced at the four chairs and the place settings. "Is your wife joining us tonight or is it to be a gathering of men?"

"My wife and her good friend, Miss Sylvia Hillcrest, will join us directly, I'm sure. Do forgive them for not being present when you arrived."

"Of course," he murmured. He did not feel at all slighted, but was satisfied to have a moment to talk alone and uncensored with his friend before he had to watch his words. He always had fun with Carmichael. Often at his own expense. "Do I know Miss Hillcrest?"

Carmichael rolled his eyes. "She attended my wedding, you've sat down to several dinners with her sitting near you, and I think you even shared your sled at Christmas."

Alexander hid a smile as he shook his head, denying everything. "Can't place her."

Carmichael growled in exasperation. "These little games of yours work best on people who don't know you as I do. You don't forget anyone. Ever."

He grinned then. Carmichael used to fall for it once upon a time. "How is the little woman treating you these days? Has she forgiven you for falling down drunk New Year's Eve yet?"

"She acts like she has forgotten, but I'd rather you didn't mention that night again for a while," Carmichael said in a low warning tone.

"Exceptional night, that. We should do it again soon."

"Not if you expect another invitation to dine with us."

Alexander grinned. "Ah, she's coming into her own. Asserting herself. Excellent. She was much too retiring when you first married. I'm quite looking forward to seeing her take on the *ton* this season."

"I'm not," Carmichael said with a shake of his head.

"Carmichael, you always worry too much." Especially about how society would treat his wife because she lacked connections and a distinguished pedigree. "She'll do fine. Didn't she win over those attending Exeter's Christmas party?"

"I suppose," Carmichael grudgingly agreed.

Alexander had heard enough gossip about the new Lady Carmichael to believe his friend's fears were unfounded. "The ladies took her under their wings, and I'm sure she soaked up their teachings, or at least pretended to be like them while they were around."

"As long as she doesn't become them."

Alexander shrugged. "They adore you, so they'll help her. Lenore is a sensible woman and will see through any false friends very quickly."

"Hush," Carmichael warned, and then quickly turned toward the door as his wife joined them. "Ah, there you are, my love."

Lady Carmichael glided into the room, followed by her good friend, Miss Hillcrest. The former practically glowed when she met her husband and kissed him. The latter wisely looked the other way.

Carmichael hooked his arm through his wife's. "Darling, you remember my friend, Lord Wharton."

"Hmm, I'm not certain I do," Lady Carmichael said, squinting at him. "Have we met before, my lord?" And then she laughed, teasing him. Using his own tactics against him, no less. The change in her was quite marked, and he utterly approved.

He put his hand over his heart and played along. "I am wounded."

"Of course I remember you." She dipped a curtsy. "How are you this evening?"

Alexander bowed deeply. "Not in as good a mood as you appear to be."

She retreated to her husband's side and clung to him. "Well, you're not married to a wonderful man."

"And likely will never be," he joked. He turned to Miss Hillcrest and inclined his head. "A pleasure to see you again," he murmured.

"Likewise," she murmured before taking a step back.

Since most women, especially the unmarried ones, tended to throw themselves into his path, he found her apparent disinterest in him unusual.

It made him want to make her look his way again.

Foolishness.

They sat down to a companionable dinner. Carmichael had been home to his country estate recently and had much to tell. His wife nodded a great deal, and Miss Hillcrest smiled at her plate.

Oblivious that he had monopolized the conversation thus far, Carmichael continued. "So we'll be returning before the season ends to see the result."

"I see. Are you going to tell us all what you had for breakfast this morning, too?" Alexander teased, keeping a straight face.

Carmichael looked around the table. "I beg your pardon?"

"I asked what you had for breakfast. That's really the only facet of your life since we last met that you've failed to share with us tonight."

Miss Hillcrest muffled a laugh into a napkin. Her eyes flickered up to his and sparkled with amusement. She returned her eyes to her plate as she spoke. "I'm sure it was a very interesting breakfast."

Carmichael scowled. "You only had to say I was talking too much."

"I was hoping you'd stop on your own," he confessed. "I've always been utterly fascinated by your innermost thoughts. I assume we all are."

"Excuse me," Miss Hillcrest spluttered, and then quickly fled the room.

Alexander hid a smile over her fast retreat. He pasted a concerned expression on his face and turned back to Carmichael. "I do hope nothing is wrong with her."

"I'm sure there isn't," Lady Carmichael reassured him, but she too was on the verge of losing her composure.

Lord Carmichael really only talked incessantly when he was very nervous or worried.

Alexander flicked his eyes over his friend, and then his wife, looking for similar signs of distress in her. But all he saw was a wife who practically glowed with good health and happiness.

He sat up a little straighter as an idea struck him hard. The Carmichaels had been married for a while now. Was the woman increasing already?

Carmichael, who was terrible at keeping good news to himself at any other time, would certainly be nervous about impending fatherhood.

Miss Hillcrest returned, calmer but with her eyes downcast as she sat. She glanced only toward Carmichael, as if she didn't dare look at Alexander again. "Did you ask him yet?"

Carmichael glanced Alexander's way then. "I didn't have a chance. My friend was too busy making fun of me."

"Well, you make it so easy." Alexander wiped his mouth with a napkin, prepared to say yes to becoming a godfather or guardian to the Earl of Carmichael's first offspring. He'd been expecting it for some time. There was no one better qualified to bear the responsibility. Carmichael certainly couldn't ask their friend Scarsdale to do the job. "Ask me to what?"

"You don't have to, if you don't want to." Carmichael cleared his throat. "We wondered if you might consent to play cards."

That wasn't the question Alexander had expected. "We play cards all the time. Why the special request?"

"Tonight. Here."

He gestured toward the door. "Lead the way."

"Ah," Carmichael said, drawing out the sound too long, "you'll be paying against Miss Hillcrest. Not me."

Alexander wanted to groan. Playing against a novice, unused to high-stakes games, was a bore. He didn't want to insult their friend, but it wouldn't be a pleasure to trounce her in the first game. "No offense intended but wouldn't it be wiser to pick someone of equal skill to play against her?"

Carmichael grinned. "That is the point."

The woman in question regarded him evenly, not offended, and not excusing him either from the challenge. He saw no gracious way to spare her the humiliation of the loss, since she seemed quite willing to go along with their host's idea of entertainment.

He nodded reluctantly, foreseeing future awkwardness when they met again another time. He followed the ladies to the morning room where a table and cards, money too, had already been set up. Determined to get it over with, he dealt the first hand quickly.

And then lost.

And lost.

And lost again.

Alexander put his fourth losing hand down slowly, utterly perplexed. He usually won against seasoned players. This tiny fiend sitting opposite had hidden depths he hadn't expected. "That is," he said, searching for the right word, "extraordinary?"

Carmichael laughed. "Surprising, isn't she?"

"Quite." Alexander wasn't angry to have lost to a woman. There were undoubtedly skilled card players of either sex in the world, and he had played against the very best and lost before. However, Alexander had seriously misjudged his opponent. He shifted in his chair and studied the deceptively benign figure more closely.

Sylvia Hillcrest looked like the dullest wallflower in existence, but when she picked up the deck, her fingers were nimble as she shuffled the cards to and fro, preparing for the next game to start. The best card players tended to have a bit of flare about them, but this woman had none.

And then she met his gaze…and allowed him to see through her little disguise for a brief moment.

She was amused by his confusion. She had expected to beat him.

Alexander sat back, noting his hosts were grinning. They obviously had expected this outcome, too. Only Alexander had underestimated his opponent.

He adjusted his opinion. The woman was intelligent and cunning and *acted* the part of a wallflower very well.

He'd overlooked the spinster, assuming to know her worth and skill, because she'd *wanted* him to do so. And the rest of society, too, had unwisely looked the other way.

"I hope you're not angry with us for not warning you," Carmichael said, breaking the silence.

Miss Hillcrest's eyes dipped, as if she was expecting him to berate her at any moment—which wasn't his intention.

He smiled slowly. "Not at all. Everyone has good nights where luck lays down like a lover or flees into the night. I'm sure another round will prove I'm right."

"It's not luck," she protested, eyes flashing with outrage.

He picked up the cards and reshuffled them slowly, studying Miss Hillcrest as she hurried to lower her gaze again. Now there had been a *true* glimpse of her nature. It made her more interesting to him, too. "Are you suggesting you would beat me every time we play?"

"Oh, she has against us," Lord Carmichael promised, cutting in. "We played many a hand on our journey back from the Duke of Exeter's estate. I lost five and thirty hands in a row before she had emptied my pocketbook, and I had to concede defeat."

Alexander set the cards back down quickly. Carmichael was a skilled player, and he'd never known the earl to have so long a streak of bad luck.

"Nearly every time," Sylvia Hillcrest assured him as she piled up the winnings in neat stacks around her.

Everything about the woman was neat and unexceptional, from the top of her mousy brown hair, to her sensible and dull blue evening gown. Her appearance screamed for a man to look somewhere else. No wonder she'd bested him tonight. He hadn't heard a whisper of Miss Hillcrest's talent, and she hadn't presented much of a threat on first glance.

So he lingered in studying her now.

She fluttered her hands, obviously discomposed by his scrutiny. "I can choose not to win, too. That's why I hardly ever play in public. Unless my opponent can afford the loss of funds, it soon becomes a sore point between friends. I always intended to give Lord Carmichael his money back, but he wouldn't hear of it."

Alexander shook his head. "I was hardly expecting a challenge in you. Well done."

A cheeky smile played over her lips momentarily, and then she sighed. "Lord Carmichael wanted me to play against a worthy opponent. You play very well."

"Not well enough to beat you."

"By rights, I should give my winnings back to you, too." Then she started to pick up her winnings—or rather, his losses— prepared to hand them back. Miss Hillcrest had made a tidy sum off of him tonight. The amount was nothing he would miss in the long run. But he could understand how others in society might not be so forgiving when they lost to a wallflower. "Keep the money. It was fairly won, but I promise you the next time we engage in such a battle, I shall not underestimate you again."

That made her smile grow and, sensing he'd said the right thing to reassure her, he slapped his hands on the table and looked around at everyone. "It has been a delightful evening. Thank you."

"I'm so glad you could join us tonight," Lady Carmichael murmured, rising.

"I am too." He stood when Carmichael did, and bid the ladies a good night.

Before they could leave, Carmichael rounded the table and kissed his wife soundly, "I'll see you soon."

Lady Carmichael agreed and led her friend back toward the drawing room. But Miss Hillcrest glanced over her shoulder at the door—and winked at him before disappearing.

Alexander felt as if she'd just knocked him off his feet. Cheeky wench!

Tonight was the first time he'd truly paid attention to her, and it seemed he'd missed a lot.

"Are you coming," Carmichael called.

"Yes, I suppose," he agreed, although he was tempted to follow the women, and particularly the unexpectedly bold Miss Hillcrest. He clapped Carmichael on the shoulder and they strolled in the opposite direction. "I see you and your wife are still so very polite to each other," he teased.

Carmichael's smile softened. "I promised we'd see Miss Hillcrest home together. I just wanted to make sure she didn't go out without me."

"Ah," he murmured, disinterested in having Carmichael launch into the benefits of his recent marriage again. Carmichael was quite changed since he'd wed. He was rarely out without his wife and spent much time engaged in *her* interests instead of his old ones. He absolutely refused to attend scandalous parties if his wife couldn't attend them, too, and he had hardly shown his face at the club this year.

Still, he was a good friend and confidant. Alexander would adjust to the loss of his frequent companionship in due time, he expected.

They made their way into the library and shut the doors. "You're not offended I didn't warn you, were you?"

Alexander found a chair and made himself comfortable. "About Miss Hillcrest's skill? No, why should I be?"

Carmichael sighed with obvious relief. "I must admit it was a bit of a test. You are the best player I know, and obviously the best at keeping a secret. Sylvia dabbled a bit and won at Exeter's one night, and got snubbed for it the next day. She couldn't be persuaded to play after that, other than alone in the carriage with us, and here tonight."

"No one likes to lose to a wallflower," Alexander noted, and then shrugged. "I wonder how she'd fare against the likes of Lord Pulling and his circle."

Carmichael shook his head quickly. "He doesn't have your sense of humor. He would not be amused if he lost to a spinster."

"It would be enjoyable to see them brought low, though. If she were married or engaged, she might not risk reprisals, but as she is a spinster, I'd advise against it."

Carmichael winced. "The lady is decidedly not interested in men, courtship or marriage for herself, so I suppose we'll never see that day come."

One detail had stuck in his mind about Miss Hillcrest. "Doesn't she run some sort of school for gentlemen?"

"With her two cousins, yes. The Hillcrest Academy. They help gentlemen polish up their manners before they attempt matrimony. We were lucky she could join us tonight, actually. Since her visit to Exeter's estate, the Hillcrest Academy has been overrun with younger sons in need of tutelage."

Alexander blinked. "Are there so many gentlemen deficient in seduction techniques?"

"Lacking in polish to impress the parents, perhaps," Carmichael corrected. "But Exeter's stamp carries great weight, so…"

"Since Miss Hillcrest and the new Duchess of Exeter became close over the holiday, her value to society is greater than ever, I take it?"

"Indeed."

Wharton nodded. "She accomplished a feat many titled women of our acquaintance couldn't claim for themselves. She has the duchess' ear, and the duchess has the duke's. Quite the coup."

"It wasn't as coldly done as that."

"Oh, but that will be what everyone thinks." Alexander shrugged. "Her grace's cautious nature shows how wise a choice Exeter made in his wife. Now, on to the real reason I came."

"What's that?" Carmichael asked, blinking.

"Our little problem."

Carmichael looked confused. "What problem?"

"Norrington," Alexander reminded the earl.

The clouds cleared in Carmichael's eyes. "Ah, yes. Norrington."

"Did you find out anything more over the last week?"

"Nothing we can use to free him from his own error in judgment. He's still gambling as if he's wading in funds."

"Damn. We shall need to have him followed. See where he goes, who else he owes."

Carmichael shook his head. "Isn't espionage a bit extreme? Just ask him."

"Would you admit you were in danger of losing everything not entailed? No. I'm sure you would not. Besides, the damn fool is avoiding me."

"Because of his wife."

"It's nonsense." Alexander scowled, recollecting a rumor about himself that was causing him problems again. He had once favored Lady Norrington, but that had been before she'd wed Lord Norrington. "I have no intention of making Lady N my mistress this season, or any other."

"Glad to hear it." Carmichael threw himself into a chair. "I'm not sneaking around to low places spying on the man for you, then. I won't embarrass my wife when people claim I'm bound for ruin again."

Carmichael had nearly drowned himself in grief over another woman nearly a year past, but he'd found his way, married and settled down, and was perhaps about to become a father soon. And possibly too busy for an old friend with a pressing problem he needed help to solve. "I've someone in mind for the task of following Norrington about, or a few someones, perhaps. I'll be using an intermediary so it won't come back to him that I'm looking into his affairs. Norrington has damn sharp eyes, but his wife is miserable."

"And he has a prickly disposition." Carmichael nodded. "How is it that you even found out about their problems?"

"I happened upon husband and wife in the park. They'd just argued, and Norrington had stormed off. She was obviously upset, and she just blurted it all out to me," he admitted. "Swore me to secrecy of course, when she'd realized how it would seem. But I could help her. I've managed to buy up some of the debt so others couldn't."

"He won't see it that way," Carmichael warned.

"Would you allow a friend to become insolvent if you could stop it?"

"No. I suppose not." Carmichael pulled a face. "Are you going to tell them what you've done?"

"Of course I will not. Norrington would only get in another huff," Alexander warned.

"You should tell *her* what you're doing, at least. She attends St. George's every Sunday when in Town."

"If I presented myself at St. George's for any reason, my mother would return to Town expecting a wedding. I'd rather not stir up trouble in that direction if you don't mind."

"Speaking of your mother, where is she this season?"

"Home."

"And your brother and sisters?"

"Obviously elsewhere, or I'd be in a very bad mood." He shrugged. His family knew better than to trouble him when he was in London, which was often. "My sisters are with Mother in the country, my brother is probably off somewhere drinking again."

"Toby does have other interests, and you know it."

Alexander pinched the bridge of his nose. Just thinking about his brother gave him a megrim. "It pains me how little he cares about the fate of our country."

"His interests lie in living," Carmichael noted. "At least he's not underfoot. That might upset all your plans to run our lives for us."

Alexander lowered his hand. "There is that, I suppose. I had such hope for him once."

"When was this?"

"I was twelve, and Toby eleven. I'd started my training for taking Father's place. Practicing speeches and such. Learning all I could. Toby used to help me write them but then he started looking out the door at the prettiest housemaids. I foolishly blabbed to Father instead of handling the matter myself, and that was the beginning of the end. When Toby came of age, he started spending every day away from home, in the tavern or at the races. Father was encouraging his vices by that time, I'm afraid to say. He moved into the dower house and kept a woman there, too, I later found out. Till I inherited, anyway, and put a stop to it."

"Ah, brothers." Carmichael put his hands behind his head. "How troublesome they must be."

Alexander studied Lord Carmichael a long moment and pulled a face. Carmichael had no living family, other than his wife…and perhaps their expectation he hadn't mentioned yet. Alexander was curious if his suspicion was correct. "I suppose it won't be long before you have a squalling brat underfoot."

Carmichael's grin grew slowly. "I wondered if you'd notice."

"Hard to miss that you and your wife were beaming all night." He nodded, pleased that he'd guessed correctly. "Congratulations to you both."

"Thank you. We were planning to tell you before we return to the country. We won't be back this year."

"Ah, I'm sorry to hear it but I do understand." Everything was changing. Alexander would have to rely on other friends for amusement soon.

Carmichael squinted at him. "I've been meaning to ask. Did you change your mind about getting yourself a wife?"

Alexander spluttered. "Good God, no. I've no patience for my existing family, and you want to saddle me with a wife?"

"You'd have company while I'm away in the country tending my wife and first child."

"I hardly need a keeper," Alexander complained sourly. "Why on earth do married men always try to hamstring their bachelor friends with a permanent woman? A wife would only get in my way."

"Perhaps she could help you."

Alexander snorted. "I doubt there is a woman I've ever met who can keep as many secrets as I do, or help me with any of them." A woman was a distraction and a complication he could happily do without this season.

Chapter Two

Albemarle Street
London

"So it is all very satisfying, don't you think? We are booked solid for two months at least, and there are more gentlemen hinting at coming to see us, too." Sylvia Hillcrest glanced at her two cousins lying on her bed, noting they were both captivated by her ceiling. She nudged them with her foot. "Are you even listening to me?"

"Indeed we are. You've done so well in society, and as a result, business in booming."

"You don't sound very enthusiastic," she noted, growing concerned that her efforts had fallen short of their expectations.

"Forgive us, dear cousin. But we both returned very late last night," Eugenia explained.

"I couldn't sleep at all," Aurora lamented.

Sylvia hadn't, either. She had spent a lovely evening with her friends and, when she'd come home, a lovely night counting her winnings from Lord Wharton. And then her thoughts had strayed into scandalous territory about him. "If you're so tired, then why did you come into my room and wake me so early?"

Eugenia smiled. "I felt the need for your company."

"I did too," Aurora murmured. "No one talks better sense in the morning than you, Sylvia, and I am not thinking with a clear head at all."

Eugenia adjusted a pillow under her head. "Indeed. I had the most remarkable encounter last night. It's quite overset me."

Sylvia turned onto her side and rested her head upon her hand to look at her cousin more closely. Encounters with handsome men were the highlight of her life. "Ooh, do tell?"

Eugenia pressed her hand to her brow. "He's simply much too young to speak of but so horribly appealing I cannot help myself. I cannot seem to put him from my mind."

"Who was he?"

"I've no idea. We passed each other in a hall. A chance meeting. My shawl slipped from my shoulders, by accident not design, and he gallantly returned it. We spoke barely a dozen words, and yet…"

"And yet…" Aurora and Sylvia said in unison, and then sighed, too.

Aurora turned on her side, tracing the pattern of Sylvia's coverlet before she spoke. "I heard the most marvelous man sing last night. His beautiful voice sent such a thrill through me, I had to apply my fan and pretend my blush was simply the overheating of the room."

Aurora was fascinated by dancers, musician, and actors. There was a new man on her mind nearly every week.

"What was the song?" Sylvia asked.

"I've no idea." Aurora laughed helplessly and put her hands to her cheeks. "I was too intent on him. How wicked of me."

They joined in laughing.

London held all sorts of interesting sights for a broadminded lady who understood passion, even if they, as spinsters firmly on the shelf, were not supposed to admit such things out loud.

Sylvia, too, had a recent encounter that had set her heart aflutter.

A man had truly seen her intelligence last night, and for a change had not been offended or threatened. The intensity of Lord Wharton's gaze had sent a ripple of sensation through her, quite unlike anything she'd ever experienced before. Sylvia was well versed in attraction and the need to fight it for the sake of propriety. However, last night, she'd thrown caution aside and let her own show, too. She'd winked at him!

Likely nothing would ever come of the flirtation but it was nice to imagine the possibilities. The Marquess of Wharton was far above her on the social ladder and could have anyone he wanted, most likely. They could hardly have anything in common, and his morals when it came to women were rumored to be quite broad. But oh how nice it had been to imagine more—for just a little while.

"What of you, Sylvia? Did anyone catch your eye?"

"Every single day," she complained, deciding not to share her encounter with Lord Wharton because he was known to them all. "I really worry that this business we're in of advising gentlemen will prove ruinous for our composure in the long run. We cannot use the image of them all farting in bed as a deterrent to finding them attractive."

"London is a challenge for all of us in different ways," Eugenia warned, thrusting out her hand.

Sylvia caught it up, as did Aurora. "We'll do as we promised each other when we first moved in together. Discretion. Always. All we can rely upon is each other."

Eugenia flopped onto her back. "I'm glad we can talk together like this. Imagine trying to hide how we feel about handsome gentlemen forever."

"I'll never keep secrets from either of you," Aurora promised.

"I don't think you could keep any at all, Aurora."

They all laughed again because it was true. Aurora was the most vocally, passionately, attracted to men of the three of them, and the least likely not to admit it. Sylvia wasn't quite as eager to share her encounters, for fear they never quite measured up to her cousins' grandly passionate experiences.

They lay quietly for a while until Aurora stirred. "Who is coming today?"

"Lord Sullivan at ten, Scarsdale at four, and there might be a new man coming at two for a quick conversation," Sylvia said, ticking them off on her fingers.

Aurora scrunched up her face. "I promised to call on Lady Bisley at ten. She sent me a pretty letter saying she missed my company. If I am to keep her happy, I shall not be available to help with Lord Sullivan today."

Eugenia sat up. "We'll manage if you can be back for Scarsdale in the afternoon. Sylvia has to prepare for Lady Norrington's evening soiree today."

Sylvia studied her fingernails. "Yes, ten hours of preparation might just be sufficient to turn me into a ravishing creature men clamor to dance with. I wish it might be a masked ball so I can pretend to be someone other than me."

"If you're ravishing enough, they might want more," Aurora teased. "Feel free to borrow anything you need from my wardrobe."

"And from me, too. These little excursions of yours into society have finally turned the tide for us, but you must look your best. Make the most of this chance for new introductions while there are so many returning from the country for the season."

"Thank you, I will if I need anything," she agreed, biting her lip. Society was notoriously fickle, hard to please. Popularity in London came and went like a fitful breeze. At the moment, this season, Sylvia was receiving a greater number of invitations to some of the best society events, but there was always the underlying worry that they might stop if she offended anyone by being too much like herself. That was why she did not gamble very often.

With the day planned, Sylvia's cousins left her alone with her thoughts. Yes, her visit to the Duke of Exeter's country estate with her friends had given them all credibility and introductions beyond their wildest dreams. Because of that, Sylvia had decided she would not pursue any amorous liaisons, should the opportunity arise in the near future. Her cousins counted on Sylvia to maintain their reputation, not destroy it with an unwise affair with the wrong man who might talk later about having her in his bed.

She got out of her own, her thoughts returning to her encounter last night with Lord Wharton. He was quite fine to look at, and she admired confident men. The Marquess of Wharton was undoubtedly that and more.

He wasn't excessively handsome, but proud of his looks and appeal. He wasn't even really that scandalous or a libertine when compared with some other rogues she'd met in society so far. He seemed to have a healthy respect for women, and that only increased Sylvia's fascination with him.

They had met at Lord and Lady Carmichael's wedding last year, though she doubted he even noticed her then. It had been many months since she'd found the marquess invading her dreams. In those, he took what he wanted and left her well pleasured and weak. It was almost disappointing to wake up some mornings to the truth and her empty bed.

But wake she must, because she had a very busy day ahead. First on her agenda after dressing was to take a brisk walk to Berkley Square and back for the exercise, and to purchase sweetmeats from a shop there, too.

Sylvia took a maid along with her so she was not seen walking alone and set off at a brisk pace.

Berkley Square was an enclosed garden, one of many in the better parts of London. It was a far cry from the rambling country walks she'd enjoyed in her youth in Marlow, Berkshire. But long walk or not, Sylvia felt all the better for the short exercise. The extra inch of flesh around her hips warned Sylvia to disregard any advice that suggested she ought to be still at her age.

They dodged carriages and crossed into the park and began their circuit. After one turn about the square, Sylvia noticed a lady sitting by herself on a park bench. The woman was unfamiliar to her, and she looked away as she skirted the perimeter of the quiet park a second time. The day was fair and other pedestrians few. But there was something in the way that lady sat so still that kept Sylvia's attention returning to her.

The woman must have been older than fifty, with white-blonde hair styled in ringlets at the back of her head. Her clothing was first-rate fashion and she wore it with the ease of someone accustomed to only the best. Sylvia looked for a companion of the woman, or perhaps a footman or groom lingering nearby. But the woman was utterly alone, and that was unusual in this neighborhood at this time of day.

Sylvia's walking path around Berkeley Square took her near the woman again, and as she drew closer, the lady glanced her way. Pale silver eyes stared at her and then lowered to her clasped hands. Those eyes had been weeping recently, or were trying not to now.

Rather than boldly approach the woman and ask what was wrong and if she could be of service, Sylvia paused nearby, pretending she had a stone in her shoe.

Her maid helped hold her up, and Sylvia smiled apologetically as she hopped up and down. "There is nothing worse than a stone in ones shoe, is there?"

The woman smiled tightly. "No, I suppose not."

She winced, tried to walk on, and then shrugged. "Do you mind if I share your bench a moment?"

The woman inclined her head. "Not at all.

Sylvia hobbled to the bench and sat down, fiddling with her shoe. She pretended to find her rogue stone and put her footwear back on slowly. "What a lovely day it is turning out to be," she gushed.

The older woman huffed. "For some, perhaps."

"Not for you?"

"Obviously." The woman sighed. "That's why you sat down, isn't it? You saw an old woman alone and upset and came over to question her."

"I wanted to ask if I could be of any service," Sylvia admitted quietly.

"Not unless you can work miracles," the woman said, and then pressed her lips tightly together. She looked about to cry again, too.

"Not miracles, I'm afraid, but I'll do my best," she promised, worried for the old woman. "What do you need?"

"Time. I need more time in this world."

"We all do."

The woman turned to her suddenly. "What do you know of the creeping of time? You're young. You have your whole life ahead of you."

Sylvia leaned toward the woman. "I am a woman who never married and probably never will. Believe me, I've plenty of time to consider my mortality."

The older woman huffed. "What are you? Twenty?"

"Six and twenty. Society considers me ancient."

The woman peered at Sylvia. "My word, you're hiding your age better than most. Better than I did. By your age, I had all my children and was weary to the bone."

Sylvia would have liked children of her own. She would have enjoyed the making of them, too. "I'm sorry to hear that."

"Why did you not marry? You've a pretty enough face to capture a man's fancy."

Sylvia shrugged. "I wanted to wed but never quite got around to it, I suppose."

The old woman's gaze grew hard. "A lack of acceptable suitors?"

"That and lack of a dowry," Sylvia confessed, being completely honest about her past for once. "When I did have funds from a small inheritance, my choices were between a much older gentleman, and a man nearer my age with nine children."

"So you chose neither. Very shortsighted of you."

Sylvia smiled at the rebuke. "It's not so bad, not being married. I live with my cousins very happily. I come and go as I please and have time to spoil other people's children."

"And strike up conversations with sad old ladies in Berkley Square, too." The woman laughed softly. "Having your own children is better but I warn you never to spoil them. They will all forget the sacrifices you made for them when they were young and ignore you when you are old and gray."

Oh, how that must hurt every mother. Impulsively, Sylvia caught the other woman's hand and squeezed. "I'm sorry they don't appreciate you," she told her. "I would give anything in the world that my mother was still alive to listen to. She died when I was very young. I never had another."

The other lady blinked several times and then patted her hand. "Perhaps my ungrateful children will miss me when I am gone."

Sylvia was starting to feel a little maudlin now herself. She did not know this woman's name but she doubted she'd ever forget their conversation today. Part of her had always wondered if she'd made a mistake turning down her two suitors—when she'd had them—for a life of liberty and adventure with her cousins. Their time together hadn't always been smooth sailing. There were silly little aggravations at times. Sylvia wasn't so sure either path would have been better for her.

"Well, I should be getting back. Heaven knows what those daughters of mine have been up to while I was gone." The lady inclined her head to Sylvia. "Thank you for the conversation, young lady. I hope some fellow sees beyond your age and lack of dowry."

"If not, I'm sure I will be fine on my own," she promised the woman.

The lady hurried away, and Sylvia took note of the house she entered. It was one of those places frequently let to different families during the season.

Sylvia stood and, with one last glance toward the distant townhouse, urged her maid to join her in a brisk walk around the square before they returned home.

Chapter Three

The card room at Lady Norrington's soiree was full to the brim when Alexander strolled in around midnight. He was late, as usual. He preferred to make a discreet entrance instead of an early one, especially here, where his welcome could be decidedly cold. He probably only had Lady Norrington to thank for this unexpected invitation.

A servant was quick to deliver him a glass of wine while he studied the ballroom and guests, then quickly grew bored. He turned his attention to the sidelines, noticing where old friends stood together, and where new acquaintance stood looking dazzled by the novelty of the gathering.

He was surprised to see Miss Hillcrest in the former group. She really had ingratiated herself with the *ton*, given how much a part of the conversation she seemed to be with some of the high sticklers. They must approve of her business, too, which made no sense to him. A man should not need the guidance of three unwed women on how best to propose marriage to anyone.

He wouldn't need that sort of help when the time came—far from now. He was the Marquess of Wharton. That alone recommended him to just about anyone—and he was rich, too, in his own right. That probably mattered more to any family than his pretty face.

He strolled the perimeter of the room, and then left to slip into the card room, watching fortunes won, and some lost. The poor losers slunk away fairly quickly and returned to the ballroom, while the winners boasted their skill to those watching and kept playing.

He came upon Lord Norrington at a table and paused to watch the game.

Norrington was particular and only played with certain lords, and tonight he was losing to those same lords yet again. The earl should give up throwing his money away and make economies.

Alexander drank sparingly, his heart sinking as another game came to a conclusion with Norrington losing, by his count, hundreds of pounds. Probably not his last loss of the evening, either.

The man was too stubborn to help himself, and his wife would undoubtedly suffer for it later. He looked about, hoping to find Lady Norrington in the card room. She alone might have a chance to distract her husband from throwing their future away.

He found her engaged in conversation with Miss Hillcrest. He wasn't aware of their connection, or when it had started, but she was on the guest list so, of course, it stood to reason that they were friends of sorts.

Perhaps they had played cards together at another party.

Perhaps Sylvia Hillcrest was helping to ruin the Norringtons.

No. Not deliberately, at any rate. She had said she applied her skills carefully, hiding her real talents to avoid giving offense.

And then Alexander thought of how he might make use of Miss Hillcrest's talent at cards to help a one-time friend get out of a sticky situation.

Miss Hillcrest had said she could win and lose a game at will. The only person Alexander particularly wanted to be the recipient of money tonight was a Norrington, lord or lady. He didn't care which.

But how to arrange it? He couldn't just walk over there and offer to fund Miss Hillcrest in a game himself. Any sensible person would be offended and turn him down. But there really was no time like the present. Tonight, they were all under Norrington's roof. It was worth the risk in his opinion. Alexander would need to be extremely discreet when he explained his scheme to help the Norringtons; meet Miss Hillcrest alone somewhere, and extract a promise from her to keep her mouth shut about it later.

He also didn't want Miss Hillcrest to misunderstand him when he tried to arrange their meeting. She might fear he meant to seduce her. He was hardly interested in that, of course. She was far too buttoned up and proper for him to consider taking to bed.

But then their eyes met across the room for the first time that night—and he remembered several things about her. She was attractive in her own way, and she had smiled at him very boldly the last time they'd met. Winked at him, too, but only when their hosts had been looking the other way.

He winked at her now.

Miss Hillcrest's brow slowly creased in confusion then she nodded to him, before turning back to her conversation with Lady Norrington. That conversation needed to end, but he couldn't be the one to interrupt. He didn't want Lady Norrington to pay attention to him talking with a spinster when he was known to avoid them like the plague.

He moved away from Norrington's table and watched another game for a few minutes, keeping track of Miss Hillcrest.

When her conversation ended, she made her way out of the card room and into the entrance hall. He followed her slowly, noticing she did not rush to turn into the ballroom, as he suspected she might. She ambled, fan open and cooling her face as she walked directly for the open terrace doors.

Anyone who saw her might assume she was venturing out for a breath of fresher air. Spinsters of her age were not usually pursued by scoundrels or watched over very closely, either. Their age, and the absence of a sizable dowry, made older women such as Miss Hillcrest much less interesting. They certainly had never interested *him*.

Until tonight.

He waited a few minutes and then stepped outside, too, via another set of doors farther along the room. He strolled the terrace, keeping to the shadows until he came upon Miss Hillcrest looking up at the stars.

She stood in plain sight of the ballroom guests, though. Her gaze slowly lowered and then she turned slightly in his direction, revealing she was aware of him. "It's a beautiful night, isn't it?"

"I suppose." Alexander answered but he clung to the shadows still. He couldn't stand at her side without causing tongues to wag inside.

"What do you want?"

"Who said I wanted anything?"

"You looked at me twice tonight. Of course you must want something. Have you come to get your money back without Carmichael finding out?"

"Of course I did not," he exclaimed, highly offended. "Actually, I had something else on my mind."

Her breath hitched, and Alexander nearly groaned. Why did all women think he intended to seduce them when he only wanted a moment of their time? "Nothing scandalous," he hastened to assure her. "Well, perhaps it is, but nothing too arduous for you. I have a question."

She shuffled a little farther along the terrace towards him, though not all the way into the shadows. "Then ask it."

He checked to see no one was on their way out to the terrace before he spoke. "Can you specifically lose a hand of cards to just one person at the table and not have them realize it was done deliberately?"

She was silent a minute, and then she lifted one delicate shoulder in a shrug. "That is harder, but I have done it with my cousins a few times. Why?"

"Can you keep a secret, too?"

She glanced up at the sky. "Yes, I normally would."

Alexander debated the wisdom of sharing his plans with this woman. He was taking a risk confiding in her, but it might be the only way to make headway with his scheme to prop up the Norringtons' failing fortunes. "There is a lady inside who's in a bad way, financially. She hides it well but I wish to ensure her happiness continues. Discreetly, of course."

"If she is such a *good* friend, why not just slip her the money yourself the next time you meet her alone?"

"It's not that way between us." He pulled a face. Everyone assumed his interest in Lady Norrington was romantic. "Her husband would never accept charity, and I wish not to cause discord between husband and wife. But if she won at cards..."

"It would not be charity," Miss Hillcrest finished for him. "Very clever. They would believe it to be luck and never suspect the money came from you."

Alexander risked a peek inside the ballroom. So far they were alone on the terrace but he doubted that could continue all night. "So?"

She sighed. "I've not the funds to gamble tonight."

"I do, of course."

Her smile showed amusement. "Of course you do."

He put his hand into his pocket and withdrew a handful of notes. "Why don't you come over here, into the shadows to get it?"

She remained where she was and looked up at the stars again, lifted her arms and then danced into the shadows. Anyone who saw her would have laughed, thinking her an odd old duck, but they also wouldn't question why she had disappeared from sight. Not immediately.

She blinked a few times as her eyes adjusted to the darkness, and then smiled up at him, her eyes alight with interest. "All right. Who is your mysterious lady friend?"

He leaned close to whisper in her ear and caught the scent of her perfume. Roses. The soft scent unexpectedly stirred him. "Our hostess," he whispered.

"No!"

He grabbed her upper arm quickly. "Keep your voice down," he hissed. "I don't want to be found alone with you."

Miss Hillcrest jerked back a step. "That was rude."

Worried that their voices may have carried, he gripped her by the waist, lifted her up, and set her farther from the doorway. He stared down at her, hemming her in. "I don't want anyone getting wind of this," he warned in a whisper.

"I'll keep your secret," she promised. "I like her very much."

He pressed the money against her belly. Their fingers brushed as it changed hands, and Miss Hillcrest squinted as she tried to count the money in the dark.

Meanwhile, the scent of her perfume worked on him still...and he began to think of the fun of stealing kisses far too much.

"This is a fortune," she whispered, unaware of his reaction to her.

He shrugged away her wonder. He'd do more if he could get away with it. "It's hardly anything I'll miss."

He heard a noise and, instead of fleeing alone, he drew Miss Hillcrest farther along the terrace with him into deeper shadows. Now they would really cause a scandal if they were found alone together so far from everyone. Society would certainly misunderstand.

The money crackled as she clenched it tighter in her hand. "Maybe to someone like you it is, but a woman of my modest means wouldn't ever carry about this much in funds on such a night. It would draw attention."

He hadn't truly thought of who he was handing his money to, just the need to get it into the right hands. He was briefly annoyed that he'd chosen the one woman who couldn't do as he asked immediately. Or was haste unnecessary if success was inevitable?

He did want to be discreet with his generosity. There were those waiting to watch a proud man like Norrington fall and be forced to sell valuable property to cover his mounting debts. "Then lose as much to her as you deem prudent tonight, but get the rest to her within a week."

Miss Hillcrest's eyes widened. "You'd trust me to hold this much money for you?"

"I will be watching you closely, Miss Hillcrest. If you fail me, I'll ruin you."

A funny sound escaped her as she stuffed the money into her reticule. "Would you really?"

"I am not joking, Miss Hillcrest."

She looked up slowly, and the corners of her mouth lifted into a wicked smile. "I didn't think you were, but your mistake was believing a woman like me wouldn't like the sound of ruin—the *other* kind—very much. Oh well."

He blinked. "I beg your pardon?"

"Oh, dear. I've gone and shocked you, haven't I?" She raised one shoulder and sighed. "Few ever want an old spinster to flirt with them."

She spun away before he could respond, dancing into the light from the ballroom as if she hadn't just met with him and taken five thousand pounds with her. When she walked back into the ballroom, chin high and serene, he stood there gaping like a fish for several moments.

He shook his head and then hurried to another doorway and returned to the ballroom, too.

Miss Hillcrest was just full of surprises. He really had been a fool about her. She was a cut above average. Women like her might be fascinating but in the end, worth steering clear of. They easily tangled a man up in their affairs and distracted him from his own.

But tonight, Alexander had a good reason to follow her around Norrington's townhouse discreetly for the rest of the evening, taking note of her behavior toward the other guests and keeping an eye on her rather plain reticule.

She seemed well liked, particularly by gentlemen—both married and unmarried, too.

Every now and then, Miss Hillcrest caught him watching her, and that impish smile of hers returned. If he didn't know better, he'd swear the woman was enjoying having him follow her about. *Saucy minx.*

Of course, over the years, many women had wanted him to dangle after them. He was well versed in deflecting unwanted admirers. His last mistress had tried hard to make him love her, of all things.

His lips curled into a relieved smile as Miss Hillcrest took another man's arm and strolled away toward the card room. He couldn't quite see who it was, though.

Since Miss Hillcrest had left the ballroom, Alexander saw no good reason to remain if he didn't intend to dance with anyone. She could be on her way to the card room now, but he didn't want to follow too closely. He trusted her skill at cards but he did want to be on hand to witness her accomplishing his goal. From what he'd heard, this little event had been paid for wholly on credit.

He turned for the card room, but then Lord Carmichael materialized before him. "Going somewhere?"

"Not really." He pointed ahead. "Who was that fellow walking with Miss Hillcrest? I cannot for the life of me remember his name."

Carmichael stretched to see then rolled his eyes. "For heaven's sake, that's Lord Sullivan."

Sullivan. Widow. A man on the hunt for a bride to please his family. "So, is he a client of the Academy like Scarsdale pretends to be?"

"I suspect so."

"Poor man, to resort to such drastic measures."

Carmichael looked at him with amusement. "Your day will come, too, I expect."

Alexander bristled. "I will not have to set one foot in that establishment to find the right bride for me."

"No, women will be beating down your door to catch you in the parson's trap, no doubt," Carmichael teased.

Alexander turned a withering glance on his closest friend. "Shouldn't you be with your wife? Where is Lady Carmichael tonight?"

He jerked his head to the far side of the room. "Over with the old ladies. I dare not interrupt."

"Then let's not." He and Carmichael strolled into the card room side by side.

Miss Hillcrest was just sliding into a seat at a table of three other women. He stopped some distance behind her...and found the roundness of her rear on the seat momentarily distracting. Sylvia Hillcrest was a smallish woman, but nicely rounded in all the right places, he found. She wore long gloves and what skin he could see sported an occasional freckle. Were they everywhere?

He cleared his throat and hurried to ask Carmichael what he was doing the next day. He listened but kept one eye on proceedings. The game was going well. Everyone but Lady Norrington seemed to be in high spirits.

A footman approached the table and offered champagne to the ladies. He noted Miss Hillcrest accepted, but he quickly realized she wasn't drinking, favoring keeping her wits about her and on the game.

Watching someone else play on his behalf was frustrating business, yet he dare not move any closer.

Miss Hillcrest finally seemed to win a hand, and the ladies cheered for her success. As she dealt out the next hand, he became anxious. Would she really do as she'd promised?

He probably should have offered to compensate her for the favor she was doing him tonight, to ensure she kept his secret. But what could a cheeky woman without a fortune want from a marquess who asked her to do him a small favor? Introductions? She seemed to know everyone he did already. She had the Duke and, particularly, the Duchess of Exeter's ear already, too. Money? If she wanted more, she could always win a fortune at cards without any trouble anytime she liked.

No, money and the prestige of his approval would not be fitting reimbursement for such a woman.

Of course, he'd have to wait and see if she was as successful as she claimed. The night was young yet.

He moved slowly about the room until he stood surrounded by women and the players' husbands in the game. Miss Hillcrest ignored him. Her focus was solely for her cards and her opponents for the rest of the next hour. She won and lost. He grew more and more impressed by her skill as her winnings piled up around her.

Lady Norrington stuck to her side like glue, remaining at the table with Sylvia even when others had moved on and been replaced by new players. Sylvia made her losing streaks look utterly authentic, and her wins were graciously done. As she'd claimed the other night, she only took money from those most able to afford the loss.

Lady Norrington's luck was mostly bad, except when Sylvia Hillcrest made a mistake that benefited her. Miss Hillcrest lost enough to Lady Norrington that their hostess smiled proudly at her remarkable reversal of fortune. She eventually quit the card room, taking a great deal more money with her than she'd sat down with.

Alexander watched her go with a satisfied smile. No doubt she was headed for her personal safe, wherever that might be.

And he found himself a little in awe of the spinster.

It was only fair and right that Miss Hillcrest be offered a reward for her efforts tonight. But what to give her?

When it was time for the evening to end, he ended up in line behind the Carmichaels and Miss Hillcrest as he followed them out into the night and their waiting carriages. He overheard her promise to call on their hostess the very next day.

He nodded to Lord Norrington. "Excellent evening."

Norrington offered him a curt nod in return and turned to the next departing guest insultingly quickly. As Norrington snaked an arm out to touch his wife, Alexander sighed in exasperation. For goodness sake, the man's wife wasn't so desirable that he'd try to seduce her on the way out the door. Lady Norrington thanked him for coming, but was pulled toward her overprotective husband so all he could do was murmur a good evening and leave.

Norrington was being ridiculous. If Alexander was the slightest bit interested in the man's wife, he might only have to snap his fingers. That was, if Lady Norrington was interested in him in return. She wasn't. She loved her foolish husband above all others. Anyone with eyes should see she'd never be tempted to stray.

Alexander was actually much more interested in a certain lady with a flare for playing games, who also possessed a nicely rounded bottom.

By his reckoning, Miss Hillcrest had parted with one quarter of what he'd given her. When she might divest the rest of his charity troubled him only a little, but he was confident that one way or another, she wouldn't let him down. He wasn't sure why he'd placed his faith in her so easily, but he trusted her. And not just because mutual friends spoke so highly of her at every turn.

He'd had ample time to observe her behavior from a safe distance; perhaps that was why he was suddenly willing to take a deeper interest. She seemed like someone he could consider an ally, or even a close friend one day, if she'd been born a man. Friendships with women were too complicated to bother with.

Her face appeared at the window of her carriage and, before she drove off, he threw a smile her way. Yes, he considered her to be a potential asset to his business affairs. All in all, it had been a satisfying evening and successful start to their new partnership. Conducting the rest would take careful execution, but Alexander was very good at tying up loose ends.

He entered his carriage and smiled to himself as he was driven off. There was to be a masked ball in his home with his closest friends soon, but he'd failed to invite or even think of adding Miss Hillcrest to the guest list. He was thinking of doing so now...and perhaps not just for games conducted in the card room.

Sylvia Hillcrest had caught his eye. He sensed they might have a great deal in common, but only time would tell if that was the case or not.

If he could put Sylvia and Lady Norrington together again in his own card room, there was no telling how much money could change hands. Everyone would be masked and the play would be high stakes at every table. No one might notice Miss Hillcrest didn't really belong among them if she looked the part and kept her identity hidden all night long.

Yes. There would be ample opportunity for Miss Hillcrest's special talents to shine when she was under his roof. He could clearly see how the evening would unfold.

And later that night, perhaps, he'd discover how bold she might really be.

He pursed his lips, weighing his chances of seducing a spinster against the risk of escaping the affair again. Pursuit of unwed women for pleasure was a tricky matter. Caution was called for to avoid the parson's noose from choking a man of his freedom permanently.

But he was tempted indeed.

First, however, Norrington must be saved from his own stupidity.

Chapter Four

$\mathcal{I}$n any friendship, there were moments when a lady ought to know when to make herself scarce. That time was almost exactly five and forty minutes after she'd arrived at the home of her good friend Lenore, Lady Carmichael. The woman was simply besotted with her husband, and it showed. Sylvia set aside the pattern book she'd been leafing through and smiled. "I should be on my way."

"Oh, don't go yet," Lenore cried out.

"I must," Sylvia told her with a grin. "You've been peeking at the door for the past ten minutes, hoping you might see him standing there."

Lenore blushed and played with the fabric samples spread over her lap. "I don't mean to be rude to you. I do still need your help."

"I know, but your attention is far away. That's why I'm taking myself off now. I hate to see you suffer without him," she teased, and had a good laugh when Lenore blushed bright red. "I do love that you love each other so well, so often."

The pair were always touching and slipping away. As soon as she was gone, no doubt the pair would be straight back up to bed, where Lenore had confessed they spent a great deal of time. Sylvia could readily believe that. The trip to and from the Duke of Exeter's estate with them during the winter had been long, with frequent unnecessary stops overnight at small, cozy inns. It might have been very awkward if Sylvia had possessed any prudish tendencies whatsoever. The fact that Lord Carmichael was forever chasing his wife all over the house still for a bit of attention, Sylvia took as a very good sign. Her sweet friend was sure to have a happy and long marriage.

Sylvia stood and kissed Lenore's cheek. "I'll see myself out."

"Oh, I'm sorry," Lenore promised.

"I'm not. Go and get him," she urged, and then slipped out the door.

The butler appeared instantly. "Shall I call up a carriage, miss?"

"Thank you. I'd appreciate that."

"I'll find what's become of your maid, too."

"Thank you for that."

He handed over her hat and gloves and Sylvia paused before the mirror, making sure she looked her best. Not that she expected to stumble upon anyone she wanted to impress, but one never knew what handsome man might lurk just around the next corner.

Lord Carmichael poked his head out of his study doorway. "Are you going so soon, Miss Hillcrest?"

She caught sight of his grin and wagged a finger at him. "Try not to look so relieved at my going."

He grinned. "You know I enjoy your company."

"But you prefer your wife's more," she suggested.

Carmichael shrugged helplessly. "You know me so well."

She glanced outside but the carriage had still not arrived.

"Wharton took his defeat very graciously the other night," Carmichael confided as he came up to stand beside her and looked out, too.

"I'm pleased he could stand the loss, but please don't expect me to put on a show for all your friends."

"Surprises do Wharton good." Carmichael laughed. "Keeps his mind sharp."

"You make him sound as if his life is deficient of challenges," she murmured.

"Well, he conquered society more or less a decade ago when

he first took the title. He's easily bored," Carmichael admitted.

"A wife would keep him on his toes," she mused.

Carmichael burst out laughing. "That's what I keep telling him, but he won't take my advice. He should listen to both of us."

"Like everyone else—like you, too—he'll most likely marry when taking a wife becomes something he cannot live without," she warned. "Ah, here is your carriage. Thank you so much for making it available to me again."

"My pleasure." He bowed. "Until next time."

"Until next week," she promised him, just as her maid came running up from the servants' quarters below. "Ah, good."

"Sorry to be late, Miss Hillcrest."

"You're not late," Sylvia promised as they hurried outside together.

A groom helped them into the large open carriage, and even though the sky held a threat of rain, she smiled happily.

The carriage traveled slowly from Mayfair, angling toward her home. When they reached Berkley Square, and she saw the wide-open space, she had a sudden yearning to get out and walk the rest of the way home.

She stopped the carriage and bid the coachman a good day. Together, she and the maid skipped across the busy road for the quiet of a leisurely park stroll.

The woman she'd met the other day was there again, sitting by herself and watching everyone who passed her by.

Introduced or not, Sylvia approached the old woman with complete confidence that she was doing the right thing. "Good morning, my lady."

The old woman raised one brow as she held Sylvia's stare steadily. "So, you've come back, have you?"

Sylvia nodded, studying the woman closely and then waiving her maid back. The lady was very well dressed again in an embroidered muslin gown and crisply styled spencer in the same stunning hue of sky blue. Sylvia, in plum, was not the woman people would notice today. Sylvia's stranger held herself stiffly, as if she'd been warned never to relax her posture all her life. She didn't look to have been crying today though, and that was good. "I actually walk the square every day. It's a pleasure to see you taking the air again, too."

The old woman glanced around slowly. "You don't come from one of the nearby residences."

"No," Sylvia admitted, wondering if that would make a difference. Her home was more modest than those around her now. The families here were wealthier and more important, or at least they thought they were. "I share a home with my two cousins on Albemarle Street, not far away. I come here for the exercise and to take in the sights. I have an interest in understanding people and what makes them happy."

"Then you had better sit down, I suppose," the woman advised. "Though understanding what makes others happy surely is the work of a lifetime."

"I agree," Sylvia murmured as she settled at the old woman's side and folded her hands in her lap. "Do you like to watch other people, too?"

"If the view is pleasant." The woman shifted a little and a flicker of a grimace appeared on her face for a moment. "I wonder if you can spot a particularly obvious hen trying to attract an old, featherless cock?"

Intrigued by the description, Sylvia lifted her gaze slowly and easily noticed a young woman sneaking peeks at a pair of older, bald gentlemen sitting not far away. The woman was making it fairly obvious that she was definitely interested in catching the eye of one, or both. The lady adjusted her posture, thrusting out her bosom farther. Everyone should have noticed her with behavior like that. But the men seemed much more interested in their own conversation than what happened around them.

"Men are so often oblivious to what women do unless they are standing in front of them, aren't they? Who do you think she is?"

The older woman squinted. "Most likely a new widow come up to Town in search of a better match than her last."

"Why do you say that?"

"The state of her clothes and possessions—all new, I suspect—mark her as a woman trying hard to impress. The maid lurking behind her is clean but decidedly shabby. The woman has the funds to spend on herself but not the most important servant a lady could ever need." The woman shrugged. "And new to Town because she's been sitting there as long as I have been here, and has talked to no one of any consequence."

"I see," Sylvia replied, then looked at the woman curiously. "Have you had a pleasant morning speaking to your friends in the square today?"

The older woman threw a cross glance Sylvia's way. "I am a stranger here, too."

Sylvia had been coming to walk in this square long enough to spot the faces of any newcomers, and had assumed that was the case with this woman. "You have not always leased a home in this square before?"

The lady shook her head. "Needs must this year."

"Ah," Sylvia murmured and decided not to press for more information just yet. Perhaps this woman had fallen on hard times, too. Sylvia wished the woman all the luck in the world in improving her situation. She wished she could help. Sylvia inclined her head toward the young woman sitting alone. "Do you think she's in love with one of them?"

"Unlikely," the older woman said and narrowed her eyes a little. "Women of that age seek men for purely mercenary reasons."

Since the woman seemed to be of a similar age to Sylvia, she did not comment about the other woman's motives. Women had lots of reasons for making a match at any age. Security was the most frequent.

Sylvia glanced up at the sky. There were a few more clouds above their heads than when she'd first set out, but heavy now, and depriving them of precious sunshine. Rain would most likely fall before she headed home again. "Lovely day, isn't it?"

"If you think so, I daresay it must be to you," the older woman replied, her tone heavy with sarcasm.

Oh, she was a tough old hen, this one. Probably why Sylvia had sought her out for a second conversation without them being introduced yet. The old woman spoke her mind instead of pretending to be agreeable all the time, as so many in society tended to do. Sylvia liked not knowing how the stranger would respond.

The old woman turned to her suddenly. "You mentioned you have cousins. Where are your parents? Brothers and sisters?"

Gone. "My mother died when I was young and my father a few years ago. I had a brother once."

"Once?"

"He died, early in the war."

"My condolences," the lady murmured.

"Thank you. It was a long time ago." Sylvia was at a loss for what to call the woman. She felt the lady deserved the utmost respect, but did not want to assume she had a title in case Sylvia addressed her incorrectly. "Forgive me if this is too bold, but who are you?"

The woman looked away. "You may call me Lizzy, if you must have a name," she finally decided.

Sylvia raised a brow. "Is that your name?"

The woman glanced at Sylvia sharply, eyes narrowed, and then sighed. "My late husband once called me that. Before he took a mistress and we were young still."

Men with money to spare took mistresses, and more frequently if they were from the best families in society. That this lady had mentioned it to a stranger suggested she felt the existence of mistresses quite commonplace.

"I'm sorry about the mistress," Sylvia offered.

"All great men take at least one in their lives, or so he told me when I confronted him." Her expression grew strained. "My son took one before he even bothered to take a wife."

Sylvia had spent enough time in society to not be surprised or offended by the conversation about men having mistresses. "Then I am sorry for his wife, as well," she murmured.

"I would be, too, if he ever took the time to tie the knot. My son is dragging his feet in that arena, much to my continued annoyance."

Sylvia laughed softly. She had heard so many mothers complain that their sons had not married...or chosen poorly when they did. "I am well versed in the reluctance of gentlemen to put themselves out to propose marriage."

The woman seemed to mull over her remark for a long moment. "If you've no brother and only female relations, how could you understand the difficulties of a mother waiting for the next generation to be born?"

Sylvia bit her lip, and then decided to share the truth up front. Hopefully the lady would not condemn Sylvia for taking on a paying occupation to support herself and her cousins. Many turned up their noses, at least at first. "My cousins and I run the Hillcrest Academy. We are well versed in every excuse used to avoid the parson's noose."

"And what does this Hillcrest Academy do, exactly?"

Sylvia smiled. "We provide support, guidance and encouragement for gentlemen as they seek the hand of the woman they want to marry. The reasons and excuses vary. We educate them in how to be pleasing, smooth any rough manners, and help them understand what a woman most wants to hear."

The old woman blinked several times. "How extraordinary. Are your services much in demand?"

"Yes, indeed. Very much lately." Sylvia didn't like to boast but their little business had been the best thing she'd ever done for herself, and her cousins, too. "Our clients come to us often for a number of weeks to practice courtship rituals before they try them out on the women they've set their hearts on."

"I should send my son to you," the woman mused.

"I am certain we could help him or anyone find the right bride."

The old lady nodded. "I shall keep you in mind the next time I am granted a moment of his precious time." The woman looked up as the sun appeared, bathing them in a little bit of warmth. "At last."

"Now it is a glorious day." Sylvia sighed. "Though I do miss the long country walks and views I used to enjoy when I was young."

"You've not always lived in London?"

"We hail from Marlow, in Berkshire."

The woman looked her up and down again. "You've done very well for yourself since coming here, then. Quite stylish. Not at all overblown or pretentious."

"Thank you," Sylvia said, inclining her head politely. "I've been very lucky. Our enterprise supplies all we require to live on in modest comfort."

The old woman laughed suddenly. "Whereas I could never make my pin money last until the next quarter day whenever I was in London. When I was much younger, a new bride, I used to order a new wardrobe every season."

"I'm partial to sweet treats myself." She pointed across the square. "There is a charming little shop over there filled with the most decadent indulgences a woman could want. I highly recommend sending out a servant to bring you back a selection of everything to try."

The lady did not immediately dispute that she had servants to send out on errands, or the funds to buy one of everything in the shop, especially not if she'd once ordered a new wardrobe every season.

"You seem very bold for a spinster your age." The old woman nodded. "I approve of that."

"Then we are destined to be firm friends, I should think," Sylvia declared. Perhaps she was being too forward, but she felt very comfortable with Lizzy, whoever she really might be, and would like to see more of her.

The church bells began to ring out across London, and that meant it was time Sylvia returned home. They had a client coming the next time the bells tolled, and she had to change and prepare for the meeting. "Is it too bold to ask what your plans are for today, Lizzy?"

"Yes, it is," she warned, but then Lizzy shrugged. "More of the same, I suppose. Perhaps I will go and see my son. Perhaps not."

"Has he not come to see you?"

"I haven't told him I'm in London yet." The lady grimaced. "He tends to pull a face whenever he sees me."

"Well, if you were my mother and came to see me," Sylvia murmured, "I might not allow you to leave again."

That seemed to tickle the woman's fancy. "What a charming young woman you are. Your mother would be proud of you for making a stranger feel better."

"I always hoped so, but I remember very little about her. My father felt her loss most keenly and would never speak of her for any great length or detail. What he did tell me, I'm afraid has faded from my memory over time. All I recall now is a vague remembrance of her brushing my hair."

"It's always wise to remember your mother's best moments rather than the disappointments she'd prefer forgotten."

"I think so, too. They say she had a lovely singing voice. My father did, too."

"Mine always smelled of flowers, roses in particular."

Sylvia lifted her wrist to her nose and inhaled the residue of the perfume she'd swiped over her wrist earlier that morning. "I wear essence of roses, too."

"A charming scent. I prefer none but the soap my housekeeper concocts for me each spring. You know, some say I am perverse for bathing so often, but it just feels better. I've never caught a chill once."

"There can be great dangers if a body becomes too cold or damp for too long." Sylvia nodded. So the lady had servants who made the best soap. The best household soap was always expensive and made in the country. The recipe was often passed down for many generations of housekeepers. This woman was of the quality, certainly. It was surprising that someone of Lizzy's obviously higher station in life even wanted to speak to a nobody like Sylvia. Curiosity burned in her about why she remained in the square. "If you are not from Town, do you come from the country?"

"Cannot a woman come from both?"

Another non-answer. "Of course."

A tiny smile appeared on Lizzy's lips, and Sylvia knew she was being deliberately vague. That was why they were still conversing without a proper introduction. Sylvia considered the lady sitting at her side to be very clever. Lizzy had skillfully interrogated Sylvia about so many aspects of her life without her even realizing it until this moment.

But Lizzy herself had hardly shared more than a morsel of her own life, throwing out vague hints at a comfortable life without qualifying any. Lizzy didn't want to be known or understood, and Sylvia had no choice but to accept that, at least for now. "Thank you for the pleasant conversation today."

"You're going?"

"I'm afraid I must." She smiled warmly. "I hope you do see your son soon, and I hope your son is overjoyed to be with you again, Lizzy."

"Overjoyed might not be what he thinks when he sees me, but what can a mother do?" Lizzy inclined her head. "Do have a pleasant day, my dear."

"Sylvia," she murmured, offering her name since the older lady hadn't yet asked for it. "I do hope our paths cross again tomorrow." Perhaps tomorrow they could be introduced properly, and she'd find out the name of that terrible son of hers, too. The man should be taken to task for ignoring such a fine and lonely old woman.

Lizzy inclined her head. "We shall see what tomorrow brings."

Sylvia waved goodbye and, with her maid in tow again, headed for home at a brisk pace.

Chapter Five

"Remove that vase and store it in my study," he told the footman hovering at his elbow in his drawing room as it was being stripped of anything he truly valued.

The lady he'd tasked to host his event, Lady Chapman, the widow of an old friend, clucked her tongue. "Really, Wharton. How am I supposed to show off your superior taste when you are determined to hide almost everything of significance in your private chambers?"

"The guests are coming to drink, not stare at a vase of cut flowers. Do I want someone mistaking it for a chamber pot late in the evening? No, I do not, and neither do the servants who'd have to empty it tomorrow, I'm sure."

Lady Chapman sucked in a breath. "If only you'd let me invite a different crowd..."

"It wouldn't be a Wharton House party without my closest friends."

This wasn't the first party he'd arranged, but the first time Lady Chapman had acted as hostess for him. She seemed to have trouble understanding she was merely a figurehead. He'd thought she was ready for the honor of hosting his ball, but he was starting to have doubts. Past hostesses, mostly friends' wives, had never questioned his decisions so much before.

Having Lady Chapman constantly try to impose her will over his choices was wearying him already. He also hoped she was ready for what came after the first sensible hour had passed. The time when the drink had erased everyone's inhibitions and the fun truly began was always the highlight of the evening. Lady Chapman would be in for the shock of her life otherwise.

A party in the Marquess of Wharton's London home meant wine, women, and the occasional bawdy song sung badly by the end of it. Guests had been known to make themselves at home on the furniture. The dining table seemed a favored place for collapse. Drinking to excess was expected, and gambling, too. He'd a pair of large rooms set aside for dancing and gambling. Lady Chapman had tried to reserve one chamber for the quieter activity of taking supper instead, but he'd overruled her.

Food and drink would be constantly available in the large front hall from ten until everyone went home after dawn.

There would be musicians and singers, too, but for every guest there would be none of the restrictions imposed upon those attending a proper society gathering.

And of course, any amorous tendencies were catered for upstairs, with guest rooms set aside, and any indiscretions on the lower floor would be overlooked tonight by anyone who wanted an invitation to next year's party.

Lady Chapman drew closer, and her hand slipped onto his sleeve. "I'm looking forward to meeting your friends."

Alexander stepped away from her to pick up a rag lying on the floor that a harried servant must have dropped by mistake.

Lady Chapman snapped her fingers at the butler. "You there."

Alexander gritted his teeth at the way the woman snapped out an order to his oldest servant as if he were a dog. "His name is Lewiston," he reminded her, as if he'd not already told her six times so far.

"Yes, Mr. Lewiston," she said, turning to the fellow. "Haven't I made it clear that everything must be perfect for the marquess' party? Take this filthy thing back to whoever lost it."

"Yes, my lady." Lewiston glanced at Alexander and winced. "Forgive me, my lord. It won't happen again."

"It's not important." Alexander dropped the cloth into his puffing butler's hand and studied his red face. That wasn't mortification discoloring his cheeks. The man looked ready to swoon.

He nodded to the bastion of his household. "When was the last time you sat down?"

"I'm on my way to consult with the housekeeper now," the fellow advised.

"Make it a very long conversation, Lewiston. I don't want you back upstairs for the next hour at least."

The man smiled in gratitude. "Very good, my lord."

Lady Chapman sighed as the butler quickly scampered from sight down the servants' staircase. "We'll never get everything done in time if you coddle them all the time."

"Caring is not coddling." Lady Chapman wasn't doing any of the work. "My staff have done this before, and I have every confidence in them."

Lady Chapman had been harrying them unnecessarily hard. But everything would be done on time without her sharp words for his staff, he was sure.

Alexander glanced her way again. Yes, he might have made a mistake asking Lady Chapman to act as hostess so soon, but how could he have known this side of her personality before? Whenever he'd met her during her short marriage, she'd seemed utterly unruffled and the perfect hostess. "As for introductions, I'm afraid it is a masquerade," he reminded her unnecessarily. "No one can be introduced to anyone tonight. Names and identities will be hidden."

"Oh, yes of course. I have my costume. I shall be wearing a turban and veil across my face." She nibbled her bottom lip. "How will I recognize you?"

He looked at her in surprise. "Why would you need to? Once the party starts, there's nothing more we'll need to discuss."

Her gaze locked on his. "I assumed we could keep each other company."

He stilled and looked anywhere but at Lady Chapman for a moment. Did she think acting as his hostess was a precursor to something more between them? He'd definitely asked the wrong woman to host the party if she thought of him that way. She was a friend's widow, and he wanted to encourage her to have a little fun. Clearly, she had mistaken the nature of his request to mean something more personal could happen between them.

As a bachelor with a fondness for throwing parties, he unfortunately couldn't host them himself. Propriety dictated he must have a lady act as hostess. Lady Chapman was a fine woman, a widow, and very witty at times, but he had no interest in her beyond her organizational abilities. Next year, he'd host his own party and damn the dissenters.

He made himself chuckle softly. "You don't need me to act as your escort tonight."

Alexander had plans for the evening that did not involve Lady Chapman anywhere near him.

The woman remained at his side, but her hands were twisting nervously at her waist.

He smiled gently to her. "You should enjoy the fruits of your labors fully."

He moved to the end of the room, noting the absence of his mother's portrait from the wall. Good. He couldn't have any real fun under Mother's reproving gaze. He owed her a very long letter soon, too, but it would have to wait until tomorrow.

"The wall looks so bare without Lady Wharton hanging there."

"Just for tonight." Alexander absolutely didn't want to discuss his mother today. "Don't let me detain you."

He moved away from Lady Chapman.

Lady Chapman had known his family for some time and was a favorite of Mother's. He didn't hold that against her. Mother had a wealth of experience and many women had sought her counsel. He'd heard Lady Chapman had turned to Mother often in the past year since she'd been widowed. Alexander and her late husband had played together as boys, since the Chapman country estate was just three mile as the crow flies from his.

When Lady Chapman had returned to town, Alexander had called upon her at home and found her in surprising good spirits for a new widow. He'd impulsively told her of his party and she'd been keen for an invitation. He just hadn't realized that her interest had more to do with him than the party.

But Lady Chapman ought to finally let her hair down—with someone else—and if she chose to take her first lover from her bevy of admirers in attendance tonight, he wished her well. He knew a few good men who had their eye on her, actually, and not just for a singular romp, either. He imagined her remarried before the year was out.

Lady Chapman was suddenly at his side again, waving a sheet of paper under his nose. "We have a late acceptance."

"Who?"

Eyes alight, she happily turned the paper for him to read.

Alexander was relieved. The Norringtons were coming after all. Even though Norrington didn't quite like or trust Alexander anymore, apparently the fool could not pass up an opportunity for high-stakes gambling in a desperate bid to cover his mounting debts. "Excellent. That's everyone I expected."

They shuffled back to allow the large and delicate Persian rug to be rolled up and carted away for storage. Lady Chapman sighed as it disappeared from the room. "I've always loved that rug."

"Mother is much too fond of it to let it be trampled by dozens of uncaring feet." He glanced up at the chandeliers, and then scowled. They all seemed to boast new wax candles in them. "Bring those down and remove half those candles."

"But why? Surely you could bear the cost of a few candles," she chided quietly.

"Bright light would expose all manner of misdeeds conducted in this room, of course," he told her.

"Oh," she whispered. "Should I expect to be imposed upon?"

He grinned. "I certainly hope so."

The maids and footmen worked quickly together, and he gave them a nod of approval when the job was done. "If you have added all new candles in the card room, too, reduce the number there, as well. Only by a quarter, though. My guests still need to see their cards to play at their best."

One of them threw a defiant glare at Lady Chapman's back, and then masked it quickly when he noticed Alexander watching him. Had his servants tried to protest the additional candles to Lady Chapman before Alexander had spoken up? "Is there a problem?"

"No, my lord," they said quickly, eyes lowering again.

No, the problem seemed to be Lady Chapman. "Well, off you go."

He sighed. Yes, next year he'd make do without a hostess and host his own party. Society rules be damned.

"Is there anything else I've done that you want changed now?" Lady Chapman asked in a decidedly prickly tone he didn't care for.

"I don't know," he answered, crossing his arms over his chest. "Have all the guest bedrooms been made ready for use?"

"By whom?"

He shrugged. "By anyone who doesn't want to make love under the staircase."

She colored, cheeks flaming, and glanced around nervously. "I thought you spoke in jest about that?"

"Not even a little. I don't know about you, but I'd rather not stumble upon lovers lurking in the shadows myself."

Lady Chapman colored a brighter red and her hand rose to her lips. She looked up at him with huge eyes. "Should your bedchamber be prepared, too?"

"It's already prepared."

The bedding had been changed, a fire would be burning in the hearth to keep his lover warm later, and his favorite wine would be sitting beside a pair of crystal goblets.

At least, he assumed Miss Hillcrest enjoyed wine. He was sure he'd seen a glass of the stuff in her hand at some dinner over the winter. As for the rest, only time would tell if she'd really agree to meet him for a tryst later in the evening.

He looked about him and nodded, satisfied now. Everything was ready for when the first guests arrived, despite Lady Chapman's groundless fears that there was still too much to do. She would leave soon, to change for the party, and return at eight o'clock in costume to greet the first guests through the door with him. Once that was done, he didn't really care what she did next with her evening, so long as it wasn't following him about.

Alexander intended to enjoy himself thoroughly tonight. He had plans. He was always making plans. "Excuse me. I will see you later."

Next, Alexander had a meeting with his banker, then important business with another investor that really couldn't wait another day.

And he still had to make arrangements for his special guest's invitation to be delivered and transport arranged for her, as well.

He collected his papers, the invitation, and strolled out to the mews, where his grooms worked tirelessly to keep his horses and carriages in perfect condition.

The coachman burst to his feet upon seeing him. "We did not hear you were wanting the carriage today, my lord?"

"I hadn't summoned one yet."

The fellow snapped his fingers at the stable hands. "Ready his lordship's best carriage."

"The plain one instead," Alexander called, and the men scrambled in the other direction. The one without the family crest on the door would suit his errands perfectly well today. "I'd like my journey today to be done discreetly," he confided to the coachman as he sat himself down on the rough bench beside the fellow.

"Of course, my lord."

Alexander crossed one leg over the other and spread his papers out on his knee, making a last-minute review. There never was an end to the matters that required his attention. So much to do and still more tomorrow. He sighed and looked up.

"Is everything all right, my lord?"

"Fine. Fine." He smiled. "It's simply good to get out of the house."

"Very good."

He waited patiently for the carriage to be brought out, casting an occasional glance at the business of putting the horses in place. He quite enjoyed the company of his grooms, admiring their lack of polish and gruff ways with each other, and the fact that they had so few concerns. They rarely complained, which was a far cry from the House of Lords when the debates turned rowdy. Out here, the stable master was king of all he surveyed and he never let the others forget their place.

There was a pecking order in all walks of life.

As a marquess, Alexander was somewhere near the top, with his fingers in as many pies as possible. He'd made it his business to know everything about everyone he dealt with in his world. He did not like surprises.

The coachman returned, cap in hand. "Where shall we take you today, my lord?"

"The first is not far. I want an invitation delivered." He handed over the address he'd scrawled on a scrap of parchment, and the sealed invitation to his party addressed to Sylvia Hillcrest. Because it was a masquerade, only those carrying an official invitation would be admitted at the door. "Commit the address to your memory. You will be returning to collect my guest and will take her home again safely after the party concludes."

He winked. "Right you are. We'll keep your ladybird safe for you."

"She's not that," Alexander said quickly, cutting off any potential gossip. "We have a business arrangement. That is all."

"Of course, my lord," the fellow agreed, but he was trying not to grin, and it was obvious he didn't really believe Alexander.

He ignored the fellow's impertinence lest his protests add fuel to the fire. "After that invitation is delivered, you will take me on to Madam Bradshaw's."

The man nodded slowly, fingering the scrap of paper with Sylvia's address on it with a growing frown. "When are we to return for you?"

"You should remain nearby." He had no time for Bradshaw's usual pleasures today. "My business there should only take a few minutes. After that, I will want to go to my club, and then you can return home. I will make my own way back before dark."

"Very good, my lord."

The coachman set his cap firmly on his head as the carriage was brought up. He inspected the carriage, making a few minor adjustment before announcing everything was in order.

The trip to Albemarle Street took little time, and he remained in the shadows of the carriage as a footman successfully delivered Sylvia Hillcrest's invitation to his party.

Alexander hoped she would come out to play with him.

He was looking forward to seeing her pit her skill against the best society could offer. He had a feeling she would wipe the floor with them.

The carriage got underway—but suddenly he sat up straight when he noticed a gentleman start up the Hillcrest Academy's front stairs. If he was not mistaken, that was Lord Sullivan calling on them. Just how many lessons did one man need to make a second marriage?

Alexander shook his head. Nonsense, all of it. Making a good match required a man to find a woman with similar interests, loyalty and good sense, and a steady temperament that allowed a man free rein to conduct his business in peace. If a man wanted a wife, he had to make a plan and carry it out. Nothing should get in his way of achieving his goal.

Chapter Six

"Eugenia, can you see if the carriage has arrived," Sylvia called, rushing to make herself ready to go out in time. The last-minute invitation to tonight's party was unexpected but a night not to be missed.

She'd heard of Lord Wharton's event last year and was very curious to see for herself what went on there. Unfortunately, a series of late appointments had her now rushing when she needed to be calm and make sure she'd make the right impression. It was absolutely essential that no one recognize her tonight. There would be gambling, and excess, and she intended to enjoy herself thoroughly.

The event was rumored to be the most spectacular private function of the season. She was truly astonished to have received an invite, but she wasn't about to look a gift horse in the mouth. Tonight she could dance, flirt and gamble behind the safety of her mask, and not worry who might notice her lack of decorum…or a prolonged winning streak.

"There's a carriage standing outside now, but I don't believe it is the one you ordered. It looks far too grand to have come from your usual stables."

Sylvia rushed to peer out her window to see for herself the very black coach and matched pair of gleaming horses standing before her home. There were four smartly dressed grooms waiting before her home in the dark. "That's certainly not meant for me," she acknowledged. "I wonder who could be inside?"

A knock rang through the house, and Sylvia jumped.

"Perhaps it is Mr. Berringer, come to sweep you away on his arm at last," Eugenia teased.

"Oh, don't be foolish," she chided her cousin. "That young man is destined to become a duke."

"That doesn't mean he couldn't be smitten by your charms. You are, after all, the loveliest of us."

"No, Aurora has always had that distinction," she insisted.

"We are all beautiful in our own way, but I suppose it could only be Aurora who catches someone's eye."

"She'll make the most beautiful bride."

"Probably the most shocked, too," Eugenia said with a laugh.

Their cousin was the most likely to make a match out of all of them because she was younger. Eugenia and Sylvia had secretly decided to lend a portion of their inheritances to dower their cousin, should the right man come along and fall helplessly in love with the girl. They would not allow a lack of fortune stand in Aurora's path to true love.

A maid came to the doorway. "There is a message for you, Miss Sylvia."

"For me?" Sylvia rushed to take it and held it up to the light of her candle to read.

Get in the carriage. W.

How rude! She read the note again, frowning.

Was the carriage outside really for her? Sylvia moved to the window and peered out. There wasn't a crest painted on the door that she could discern to lend some idea where it had come from, nor did the grooms wear any livery she recognized. Obviously, someone very wealthy owned that carriage, though. Wealthy and bossy, and a man, too, judging by the strong penmanship in the note.

The only person she knew who fit that description was perhaps Lord Wharton. The party was at his home tonight, and she had his money still.

Perhaps he wanted it back from her before the party. She bit her lip, hoping he hadn't changed his mind about her gambling for him. She'd been so very excited about the prospect of nearly unlimited games tonight.

"Who is the note from, Sylvia?"

Sylvia tucked the note away before Eugenia glimpsed the handwriting. "Oh, it's from a friend who worries about my traveling arrangements. They sent their own carriage to collect me."

"That was very thoughtful," Eugenia said with an unconcerned smile. "Do remember to convey your appreciation. The roads in London are full of scoundrels and thieves on the best of nights."

Sylvia breathed a sigh of relief that Eugenia didn't ask who'd sent it. If the carriage had been sent by Lord Wharton, as she strongly suspected it had, it was imperative her cousins never learn of their arrangement. They would tease her mercilessly and suggest she had not one, but now two suitors vying for her favor. How wrong they were.

"I don't think anyone would be interested in stealing from someone like me, but I will be sure to convey my appreciation for their consideration."

Sylvia hadn't told her cousins about her most recent conversations with Wharton, or the money she carried hidden in her reticule from him. They would never approve of her gambling with someone else's money. But it had felt good to try to help him solve Lady Norrington's financial woes. For the first time in a long time, she'd done something involving a gentleman without expecting a marriage as the end result.

"You shouldn't keep the carriage waiting," Eugenia said, dragging Sylvia from her thoughts about the evening to come.

"I suppose not. Could you pass me my mask?"

Once she had it, she made her way to the front door, silk skirts swishing about her legs, and saw the waiting carriage standing beyond. It seemed a dream to have such an elegant carriage waiting at her front door and a pair of grooms standing at attention beside it.

She paused on the pavement, looked up at the first tall man, and asked in a soft voice, "Who do you work for?"

"Lord Wharton, miss," he whispered back. "He said you'd be suspicious and sent these. He said you'd understand." The fellow dug in his pocket and produced a stack of playing cards for Sylvia. "I'm John Morrow, head coachman of his lordship's stables in London, if that helps your nerves."

"I'm not at all nervous, sir, but any sane woman in my situation would question who sent this beautiful carriage for her," she chided. "Shall we be on our way?"

"Very good, miss." The man snapped his fingers, and another groom came forward to fold out the step and open the door. "Your carriage awaits."

She couldn't help but grin at the fellow. He seemed determined to show her every courtesy possible.

She entered the candlelit interior and lowered herself to the plush red velvet cushions. Sylvia sighed deeply in the pleasure of her luxurious surroundings as the carriage door clicked shut behind her. A lady could get used to such indulgences if given a chance, but of course, Sylvia would never take the boon for granted. This must be the compensation Wharton had decided she should have for her efforts in helping him with his friends. She set his deck of cards on the seat beside her.

Since she was alone, Sylvia wriggled back against the squabs, slipped off her slippers and settled her stocking-clad feet lightly upon the opposite velvet bench. Luxury indeed. As she flicked the little tassels on the window curtains idly, she almost felt like a princess going to a grand ball.

They turned toward Berkley Square—but then suddenly came to a complete halt in the middle of the road. Sylvia scrambled to get her slippers back on, and not a moment too soon. Her door was wrenched open and a large man was suddenly inside the carriage beside her.

"How dare you?" she cried out in shock.

But when she caught a glimpse of Lord Wharton's grinning face as he quickly doused the interior lamps, throwing them into complete darkness, she was relieved.

"I knew you'd be the type to want to arrive early," he teased.

Sylvia considered if she could hit his shoulder with her fan for that remark and get away with it or not. Most likely not. She clutched her fan tightly. "You scared me half to death, my lord. What are you doing in my carriage?"

"This is *my* carriage," he announced with a shrug.

Obviously. "Have you no care for a lady's reputation?"

"I'll only need a moment of your time." He tapped the roof, and the carriage got underway again.

A shiver raced over her skin as he became still. The illusion of security and comfort was gone now, replaced by a creeping suspicion about what the marquess could want her for in the dark. She had been foolish to think the carriage was for her comfort alone. A reward for helping him. That hadn't been the case at all. "What do you want with me?"

"Do you have my funds with you?"

Sylvia nodded quickly. "I do."

"Good. My men are going to protect you from thieves on your way to my home."

Now she knew the *why* of the carriage. Many an unwary hack driver had been waylaid by thieves in the dead of night—and a lady traveling alone might unwittingly put herself in peril because she hadn't her own servants to protect her.

However, Sylvia was not certain why the marquess thought *his* escort necessary, too. She was not carrying so much in funds that she needed his presence to fend off any would-be thieves.

Who was going to protect her—and her reputation—from the marquess?

"Thank you, but your presence is hardly necessary, and quite possibly damaging to my reputation if we are seen together alone. Did you even think of that?"

"Of course I did, Miss Hillcrest. I have considered every aspect of our association quite carefully. Now, we need to have a little chat." He leaned closer, and the scent of his spicy cologne filled her nostrils with a desire to be the sort of woman he found impossible to resist. She folded her hands in her lap to fight the urge to lay her hands upon him. "I want to know how your visit with Lady Norrington went today," he said in a low murmur.

Although she shivered at the intimate tone of his voice, she quickly narrowed her eyes on him. "Are you spying on me?"

"Of course not," he said indignantly. "I happened to be passing Lady Norrington's home earlier today and saw you enter her townhouse. What happened?"

Sylvia sighed. What a fool she was indeed to think he might have been interested in more than his own schemes. "I managed to stuff a handful of coins under a cushion today," she said proudly.

He seemed to choke. "Did you not think that would look suspicious? What if a servant finds them and keeps them instead?"

Sylvia smiled. "Oh, Lady Norrington found them all right, and she didn't suspect me at all. She discovered the funds while I was still there, but she was very careful not to let on about it. The housekeeper asked for a quick word with her, and as soon as she stepped out of the room, I had the job done. I put them under her chair pillow. Quite simple, really."

"Well," he said, sitting back. "Nicely done."

She squinted at him in the dark. "Why couldn't you have done the same when you called on her?"

"I don't visit her at home anymore." He winced. "Was there any hint of their situation changing?"

"How do you mean?"

"Furniture sold and items missing."

"I have never visited Lady Norrington at home before the ball, so I couldn't say for sure if anything was missing. Everything seemed as it should be, though. The right amount of good furniture and paintings on the walls."

Lord Wharton nodded and didn't say more for a while. Sylvia tried to study him in the dark carriage as he stared out the window at the passing view. Every now and then the moon illuminated his handsome features. He was at ease in the dark with her, more so than she was with him right now. He was the sort of man to make a woman breathless just by being near.

Sylvia fidgeted with her mask, wondering if she should already have fitted it to her face in case they were seen together. She had a reputation to protect, after all, not that Lord Wharton seemed the least bit interested in her that way. She had to remember they were in league together, not potential lovers. "If Lord Norrington doesn't trust you, why are you so keen to help them?"

His eyes turned her way. "That's none of your concern."

"Don't I deserve the truth for helping you?"

He crossed his arms over his chest, a defensive gesture if ever she'd seen one. He might trust her to carry his money under his watchful eye, but explaining himself, his real motives, to a woman might be more than he was capable of. So many lords were like that, she'd found.

His lips twisted. "You deserve something for your trouble, but I've yet to decide what I want to give."

"The comfort of the carriage is more than enough," she assured him. "Anything of greater value would have to be refused."

He studied her, and his smile returned. His glance flickered over her gown and back to study her face. "What else besides cards do you do well, Miss Hillcrest? You seem the kind of woman with other secret talents a gentleman might be interested in."

Ah, so they were back to flirting again. She had wondered if she'd imagined it the other night. "A lady never tells," she said primly, but then fluttered her lashes in an exaggerated fashion.

He grinned. "Neither do I, no matter how bold the lady might choose to be."

Sylvia had to admit she enjoyed the occasional flirtation. There was no harm in it with Wharton. He would never be a client of the Hillcrest Academy. He was much too self-assured to need any help courting a wife.

But might Wharton be something else to her? Something a little scandalous, perhaps? His eyes and smile hinted at wicked thoughts.

A little thrill of excitement rushed though her when Wharton held her stare overlong. He moved his foot, and then his lower leg was pressing softly against hers.

He *was* flirting with her, and it was working, too. She could feel her body react to him…and she liked it. She put her hands flat on her thighs, and then slipped one across to settle lightly over his knee.

His breath hissed out. "Bold, indeed."

Sylvia withdrew her hand. Eventually, he moved his leg away, but a smile played over his lips still. "You interest me."

Sylvia had to admit Wharton interested her, too. She had a weakness for confident men, and Wharton was certainly that. She'd had many months of discreetly observing him in the shadow of mutual acquaintances to know his character lacked for little to recommend it but a dose of humility now and then.

However, Sylvia was well aware she could not make a fool of herself over him.

If she was the marrying kind, he'd be quite the catch. The top of anyone's list. Luckily for him, she was not desperate to wed like so many women seemed to be. But a little flirting with a bachelor was always fun and caused no harm if the man respected her.

She smiled. "In what way might a lady be considered *too* bold, my lord?"

His lips quirked but she soon realized he wouldn't say what he was thinking out loud. He'd thrown out a lure and she'd taken the bait. All that was left was for him to reel her in. She wet her lips, anticipating being scandalous with him in the dark.

He lifted a hand and thumped the roof of the carriage. They came to a stop on another dark, empty street. "This carriage is yours for the entire evening, Miss Hillcrest," he said. "My men will take you home, too, whenever you wish to leave my party. I do hope you thoroughly enjoy yourself tonight. Perhaps we might see more of each other later, too."

An image of the marquess leaning over her, bare chested, flashed through her mind.

Her indrawn breath of excitement must have been loud, because the marquess laughed softly. "I was thinking that same thing about you, too."

When his hand stretched out and settled on her knee, Sylvia considered swooning. His fingers were so very warm through her thin evening gown. He moved his fingers a little, adjusting the fabric over her knees, then dipped between. Sylvia closed her eyes, waiting, anticipating...

A blast of cooler air swirled across her face and she opened her eyes.

Wharton was gone from the carriage. He'd left her in complete darkness with her overactive imagination running rampant and her desires truly out of control.

"Oh, that wasn't very nice of him," she grumbled under her breath as the carriage got under way again for the party.

Chapter Seven

Alexander slipped along the dark alley, hood of his cloak pulled far over his brow to hide his identity, and darted into the mews behind his home. The scents of the stables and horses housed there overpowered him briefly but he rushed on, eager for the evening to come. He had a spring in his step as he pushed open the door to the kitchens.

Sylvia Hillcrest interested him even more after their intimate little chat in his dark carriage.

She was not the shy spinster she appeared to be at first glance.

She was something far better.

He rubbed his hands together and took the servants' stairs up to his private chambers two at a time. His valet was waiting beside a full copper tub of steaming-hot water. His costume for tonight had already been laid out. "Shave first, then bath."

He dropped into a dressing chair and tipped up his chin.

The valet bustled around behind him, creating a lather with Alexander's favorite shaving soap. "Lady Chapman arrived half an hour ago and asked for you."

"Is there a problem?"

"Not that I heard of, my lord."

"She can wait," he decided. A cloth went around his throat and Alexander made himself relax. He didn't want the man to cut him just because he clenched his jaw at the wrong time. He closed his eyes as the valet went to work, and when his beard was scraped away, he stripped.

"I'll be back in a moment with your evening meal," the valet promised.

"Thank you."

Alexander stepped into the high-sided copper tub and immersed himself to scrub away any offending body odors, and scrubbed his head, too. Once clean, he stood and let the water drip from his body. The slight draft from an open window created a delicious thrill over his skin, like the touch of a skilled lover.

He couldn't wait to be alone with Sylvia Hillcrest later tonight and hopefully discover more of her secrets—like how she tasted, how she moaned when he pleasured her sex with his fingers and mouth.

Thoughts of bedding Sylvia aroused him, but…first things first. *Norrington.*

His arousal subsided as he reached for a length of cloth to dry himself.

There was a rapid knock on his door but before he could answer, a masked woman slipped into his chamber.

He recognized the gown. It had been described to him earlier. *Lady Chapman.* "Bloody hell!" he cried out, rushing to cover himself with whatever fell to hand. "What the devil do you think you are doing by coming to my chambers?"

"I couldn't wait to see you!"

Alexander cursed under his breath and started throwing on clothes. "What can I do for you this evening, Lady Chapman? Is there a problem with the party?"

"No," she murmured, and then sighed. "I just thought… I wanted to see you. See if you needed any help with your costume."

Alexander sighed. Lady Chapman was quite determined to throw herself at him. He wished he had been firmer with her earlier. "When I asked if you'd act as my hostess, that is all I ever intended for you to do."

"But everyone knows…"

"Knows what?"

"That being your hostess is just for appearances' sake."

Alexander shook his head. "If I want a woman in that way, I say so. She'd know before anything happened between us what I intended to do with her. I am sorry to disappoint you, but nothing will *ever* happen between us. You'll only ever be Chapman's widow in my eyes."

Lady Chapman seemed to reel at his announcement. "I could be more than that to you."

"Friendship is all I can offer. I will not replace Chapman in your bed."

"It wouldn't have been like that," she hissed, then turned on her heel and stormed through his bedchamber, slamming the door behind her.

Alexander moved to lock the door. He raked a hand through his damp hair, deeply annoyed that Lady Chapman had forced him to put her in her place.

He really had no time for this sort of thing.

Alexander finished dressing with no further interruptions save his valet returning with a plate of sandwiches. He devoured those quickly, tied a mask about his face, and then used the servants' stairs to join the party on the floor below discreetly.

There were a number of his friends lurking in the music room, glasses already in hand. He joined them, silently standing at the rear, and they didn't notice one more masked highwayman in their midst for some time. Scarsdale and Lord Foyle, an old school chum, were deep in whispered conversation. He recognized them instantly since they wore the same costume to every masquerade he'd ever attended.

A third man's identity eluded him until he asked a question. "Did you see that woman run off into the night?"

Alexander knew that voice very well. Norrington, and not in a costume Alexander had expected to see. He was impressed. Most of Norrington's head was covered in twisted silk, like a turban, and he had also somehow applied hair, a beard, to his lower face, when he usually was clean-shaven. He had a surprisingly dangerous look about him tonight. Not even his mother would recognize him.

"Couldn't miss her," Scarsdale admitted. "Nice pair of tits, too."

Foyle nodded. "Who do you think it was?"

Norrington smirked. "I've no idea, but she came down the staircase from the direction of his bedchamber."

Foyle chuckled. "Do you think she our host's new woman?"

"Could be," Scarsdale said, looking around. "None of my business unless I fancy the same woman."

"You'll have to find out," Norrington suggested, obviously hoping the other pair would, and then feed him juicy gossip about Alexander's life.

Strangely enough, if Norrington had asked the name of his mistress, Alexander would have instantly told him what it was. Still, he didn't care for Norrington snooping into his affairs...which was of course what Alexander always did with his friends. He was quite aware that made him a complete hypocrite, too.

Alexander leaned closer. "And they say *women* can't keep their noses out of everyone else's business."

Foyle jumped and cursed him.

Scarsdale threw a smile his way. "I knew you were there. You always use the servants' staircases during a party."

"That will be the last time ever I do then," he announced. "Norrington, what a pleasure to know you take an interest in my life still."

Norrington had stiffened up almost as soon as Alexander had spoken. "Still having no luck with the ladies, I see?" he sneered

"I have all the luck I'll ever need," he promised. He glanced about the room and then moved closer to his former friend. "Where is your wife?"

"Why do you want to know?"

"I should like to pay my respects," he murmured.

Norrington's expression soured. "She stayed home."

Alexander closed his eyes briefly. "Why?"

Norrington shrugged. "A sudden headache came upon her. You know how delicate women can be."

That didn't fit any description any woman he knew. But then, he wasn't married to one. "I'm sorry to hear that," he said, although what he *wanted* to say would be a lot louder and involve every curse he knew.

Lady Norrington was supposed to be in the card room so

Sylvia Hillcrest could find her, play against her, and lose to her. If she'd stayed home, his scheme to help Norrington was doomed.

Alexander would have to warn Sylvia that her services were not needed tonight, too.

"Excuse me," Norrington murmured, and then headed for the card room.

Foyle smiled quickly. "Marriage hasn't improved him."

Alexander wouldn't add to the gossip about the rift that had grown between him and Norrington. He slapped Foyle and Scarsdale on the shoulders. "Enjoy yourselves, gentlemen."

"And you."

Alexander moved on, checking the rooms and that all was in order. Of Lady Chapman, there was no sign. It must have been her leaving in a huff. She'd taken his rejection completely to heart and abandoned her duties as his hostess. He didn't approve, but he was glad she was gone.

He found his butler at the door, checking off invitations against a list. "Is everything in order?"

"Yes, my lord." The man leaned close to whisper, "Lady Chapman's left."

"Yes, I heard. Do you think you can manage without her?"

"Always, my lord."

Alexander picked up the list and ran his eye down the tally. Almost everyone invited had presented their invitations already. All but one.

"Good. Excellent." Alexander glanced at his pocket watch, cursing his tardy coachman. Where the devil was Sylvia? She should already be in his home. He hoped she didn't become too disappointed when he told her she wouldn't need to play cards with Lady Norrington tonight. He also hoped she wouldn't turn around and leave again before they had a chance to talk in private. He checked no one was nearby. "I might be unavailable for a time after midnight. Unless someone dies, I am not to be disturbed."

The fellow nodded quickly. "I'll make sure no one does."

Alexander smiled and then went to the card room. Like all others, Norrington kept up his disguise as he emptied his pockets onto a card table.

Alexander watched on, feeling helpless and concerned. Norrington hid it well but he was clearly desperate to win a fortune tonight. And with Lady Norrington gone, there wasn't much hope of a distraction. When Anna was around, Norrington wagered with a little more restraint.

As it stood now, the evening was turning out to be one unmitigated disaster after another.

Chapter Eight

The carriage deposited Sylvia at the Wharton House front steps at last, later than she should have arrived. A broken-down carriage on a dark street and a fight between two coachmen had delayed their journey considerably. She was very glad to be in Lord Wharton's home and not listening to the roughest of men fight with their bare fists right beside her coach window.

If she'd been in a hack, alone, she'd have been very afraid. But with Lord Wharton's grooms standing protectively around her, she'd felt immeasurably safer.

She swept into Lord Wharton's ballroom, eager to put the ugly event behind her and enjoy herself at last, full of anticipation for the evening. She took up a glass of champagne immediately just for something to hold.

The crowd was thin yet but she easily saw Lady Carmichael standing alone, mask dangling from her fingers across the room. Sylvia should have expected to see her, and Lord Carmichael, too, as Carmichael was Lord Wharton's good friend. However, she'd not shared her good fortune in receiving an invitation with their mutual friends yet. She might be wise to remain in disguise.

Unfortunately, the decision was taken from her when Lady Carmichael waved excitedly at her.

Sylvia rushed over and kissed her offered cheek. "How do you do tonight?"

"Very well. I didn't know you'd been invited to this event," Lenore whispered.

Her invitation had come from the owner of the house himself, though she wasn't going to tell anyone. "Where is your husband?"

"He darted off to fetch punch for us both. He should be back at any moment." Lady Carmichael looked Sylvia over. "You look beautiful. And very mysterious."

"So do you. Pregnancy becomes you," she whispered.

"I'm getting fat," she said with a laugh then swept her mask back into place. "Oh, I should have chosen a mask that tied in place like yours. I'm already tiring of holding it up before my face."

Sylvia had tried to talk Lenore out of the purchase but it had been so very pretty in the shop, the new countess simply had to have it for her own. Lenore wouldn't countenance purchasing a second one. She might now be a countess and wealthy, but at heart, she was still the frugal companion she'd always been.

"Well, this way, your husband can hide behind the mask with you while you kiss," Sylvia suggested, knowing that just might be very often tonight.

They smiled at each other, and then laughed out loud.

Then they watched others arrive together for a while, trying to figure out who might be beneath the masks and clever costumes. She did not see Lord Wharton anywhere, and that made her a little disappointed in the evening.

She had enjoyed their flirtation in the carriage. Perhaps too much.

Lord Carmichael returned, sporting two glasses, and appeared very surprised to see Sylvia standing beside his wife. But he forgot there was anything strange in her attendance after a moment or two and soon fell to teasing her. "No hiding with the wallflowers tonight. If you were invited to this party, you're one of us now. Besides, that gown you're wearing deserves to grace the dance floor at least a dozen times."

"Are you asking me to dance with you, my lord?" she asked, fluttering her fan and acting coy.

He laughed. "Indeed I am."

"I'm afraid I must decline," she told him sadly. "Tonight

surely must be a rare occasion when a husband might dance with a wife more than twice without the possibility of shocking anyone." She gestured to Lenore. "Wouldn't you rather spend the evening with only this beautiful woman in your arms?"

"You have a point," he conceded with a grin, slipping his arm around his wife's waist. "I would like nothing better, actually."

Sylvia understood passion very well. "Perhaps we might dance together at a different ball, my lord."

"Agreed." He exchanged a loving glance with Lady Carmichael. "You know, we were actually discussing you on the way here tonight. We think that you should attend more events with us, so you are seen by as many eligible gentlemen as possible this season. Surely one will become smitten by the end."

She laughed outright at the thought of someone falling in love with her now. "My dear friends, it is *I* who is often mistaken for a matchmaker, not you."

"Everyone needs a little help when it comes to love," Lady Carmichael said quietly, stealing a glance at her beloved husband. "Can you blame us for wanting to see you happily matched? After all, you did so much for us, and we cannot think of a better way to repay you than by making others notice you."

The strains of the first dance sounded. Sylvia shushed them quickly. "Go and dance and be happy together. That is all I want in return for the little help I gave you both."

"If you are sure?"

Sylvia waved them away. "I am perfectly capable of beating back my hoard of admirers without any help."

Carmichael paused, and then moved closer. "A word of warning. This is not the usual sort of gathering you might have experienced before in society. Be careful of rogues and scoundrels."

Sylvia was *hoping* for a little more excitement than what she was used to. "I'll be fine, my lord."

Carmichael clapped his hand on the side of Sylvia's arm companionably and then swept his wife away to the dance floor. Sylvia watched them from the sidelines for a few minutes and their happiness made her so pleased. They were good together; after a slightly rocky start, the pair was very much in love.

Sylvia wandered away, marveling at the beauty around her in

this home.

Wharton House was exquisitely decorated for the occasion. Pared down, she assumed, to the bare essentials to display his wealth and good taste. There were crystal chandeliers shining over her head and beautiful gilt-framed painting on every wall. The guests, anonymous too, looked utterly marvelous in their evening finery as they competed with the house for her attention. She explored the public rooms of Lord Wharton's home, drinking champagne and smiling as if she had always belonged in such a setting.

It was a very large home for a bachelor, though she had heard the marquess possessed a mother and several siblings. Where they were tonight was a mystery, and she wondered if she'd ever meet them. Would they be tricky like Wharton? She stopped before a portrait of the marquess himself. The painting did not do him justice. It had failed to convey the man's virile strength, and the flirtatious side of his nature, too.

She turned—and found the flesh-and-blood Lord Wharton standing directly in her path. He wore a mask but she'd recognize those strong thighs and smirking lips anywhere. Now *this* view was better than any she'd had so far tonight. He wore a mask as well as he wore everything. Above the mask, his hair hung rakishly over half his face, and he carried a glass of red wine, negligently dangling from his lovely long fingers. He evoked a sense of decadence and an invitation to sin, and perhaps he had every night she'd ever seen him in society.

But now, with him watching her so intensely, she felt it more. She felt it everywhere.

She nodded to him and started to move past, close, when he brushed his fingers against her thinly covered thigh. She shivered but continued out of the room.

Wharton fell into step at her side. "Thank heavens I found you. Were you dancing?"

"I've only just arrived, my lord, but the night is young yet," she admonished. She fluttered her fan to cool her face. Talking with Wharton so much was making her overheat. "Perhaps I shall dance later. If I am asked by the right partner, that is."

"Norrington is here, but his wife never came. A headache."

Sylvia crashed back to earth upon hearing that news. "Ah, so that is why you keep me company now."

"That is not the whole of it," he promised in a suggestive tone. "However, the one goal I had in mind for the early part of our evening is impossible to achieve now."

"Do you want me to leave?"

He shook his head. "Not at all. Feel free to gamble with my funds if you like. You can win us a fortune, instead."

"I will do my best to only increase them."

"I expect nothing less. Later, perhaps, you'll allow me to do my best for *you*."

Sylvia's thighs went up in flames at the thought of how he might begin. If not for the mask covering most of her face, everyone might know how his words excited her.

There was a commotion at the door, and Lord Wharton excused himself. Sylvia watched him go, enjoying the view as she applied her fan vigorously to cool herself. Lord Wharton was a deliciously built man—from every angle. Powerful and well put together. Those long legs propelled him quickly out of sight. A great many young lords could do themselves a favor by using Wharton as an example of how to dress and move.

She made another circuit of the dance floor, discovered her friends occupied with each other still, and decided to make her way to the card room, where she had an important job to do.

The activity there was already heating up. A number of tables had been set up and players were taking seats. Most of the tables were full but a few still had empty chairs. She already knew from talking with Lady Norrington the other day that her husband would be wearing a false beard with his costume. She found Lord Norrington easily in the card room crowd, and her tension increased as she saw him sitting down alone at a distant table.

Sylvia squared her shoulders. If she could not lose to Lady Norrington, there was always Lord Norrington to play against. Lord Wharton hadn't suggested that she couldn't approach him. She moved toward Norrington's table, determined to claim a place at his side.

Norrington acknowledged her with a nod, but it was clear to see he was eager for the game to come. He hardly looked anywhere but at the little pile of coins piled up beside his hand.

There were three empty seats at his table. Sylvia took one,

quickly placing Lord Wharton's money out on display. "You don't mind if I join you."

"Not at all." Norrington stared at her funds, hunger in his eyes but quickly masked.

She could sense his anticipation for her money. That would work to her advantage tonight. If he was so focused on the coins, he would not pay too much attention to the identity of the woman who was about to change his luck.

The chair opposite was claimed by an elderly gentleman, one Sylvia didn't recognize. But Norrington must have. She couldn't help but notice that his demeanor changed with the new arrival. He seemed no longer eager to play at this table, and started looking at the other tables with empty seats. But he was stuck here for the moment. He wouldn't dare leave until at least one hand had been played, perhaps two.

Was this older man a far better player than Norrington?

Given that the most accomplished players learned to disguise their skills to fool their opponents in one way or another, Sylvia had to assume the older man was the greatest threat to her game.

Sylvia took a deep breath as play commenced. She fought to win the first hand. Lost the second because she wanted to, and round and round it went. Soon, she and the older man were evenly balanced combatants. Usually Sylvia relied on people assuming she'd won by chance. But the way her winnings were piling up around her tonight meant her skill at cards would be obvious to a blind man.

Lord Norrington was looking quite downcast now. He had a pitifully small pile of coins hidden under his tapping fingers. He played with them endlessly, and Sylvia wished he'd stop.

The older man opposite was an intense sort. He viewed her and Norrington through narrowed eyes. Whenever they lingered on Sylvia too long, she tapped her finger, too, as if discomforted by his scrutiny when she was anything but.

There were many ways to throw off an opponent rather than staring. False signals worked well for a round or two.

The older man's gaze switched to Norrington. "How's that lovely wife of yours tonight?"

"She's very well."

So they knew each other. Sylvia's interest was piqued,

especially since Norrington had just lied about his wife's health. Not that he had to be truthful if he didn't want to be.

"Is she here tonight? I should like to pay my respects."

"It is a masked ball," Norrington murmured. "You'll see her, if she lets you."

"Wharton will discover her first," the old man said lazily as he dealt the next hand. "He sees through all our disguises, especially those of pretty women he favors."

Their fourth, until now silent, agreed. "He does like a challenge. I thought he'd be playing but I wonder where he has got to tonight? Did he leave his own party to meet his lover like he did last year?"

Norrington's coins scattered across the table. Sylvia gently nudged a stray coin back toward Lord Norrington's clenched fist.

The older man was trying to put Norrington off his game by throwing suspicion on his wife, and Norrington had foolishly taken the bait. Now his attention would be split from his desperation to win the game to confirming Lord Wharton's whereabouts. And his bad play would likely only get worse.

Sylvia picked up her cards quickly. She had to lose this round before Norrington had no more money left to win with. If he left the table now, she might never get a second chance.

The cards she was given were appalling, but she made her play as if she had a fighting chance.

Norrington, she noted, only had one eye on his cards. He kept scanning the crowd. Sylvia had no idea where the marquess had got to either, but she did not imagine he would be far away. He was too worried about Norrington to abandon the man at his own event. She hoped to see him in the room soon because she had to remind Norrington that it was his turn. When Sylvia faced her real opponents, the pair were exchanging knowing smiles—and betting high.

A cautious player would fold. Sylvia couldn't.

Sylvia made a bold play, discarded and picked up another pair of cards and bet heavily.

To her astonishment, she found herself with a surprisingly good hand. Very nearly the best possible.

If Norrington was going to lose, then she would win and find another way to get Wharton's money into his coffers. She would not let this pair, obviously acquaintances of Norrington's, take a penny more through ungentlemanly tactics.

"Call," the old man drawled.

There was, by her estimation, six thousand pounds on the table. It should have gone to Norrington, but she'd win it instead. Sylvia nodded. It wasn't an ideal outcome but what else could she do?

The old man opposite laid down his cards, a low hand that wouldn't win against hers.

Their fourth revealed his hand next, wearing an insufferable grin as many onlookers whistled and cheered.

"Well played," the old man announced, as if the game were over already.

Sylvia was quite looking forward to making the pair lose those false smiles.

She spread out her cards, smiling serenely as she trumped them both.

The old man choked. "What the devil?"

"It looks like my luck has returned," she murmured softly and clapped her hands together. "How exciting. It's my lucky night after all."

"I say," Lord Norrington muttered to himself. "Oh, I say."

Sylvia turned to him, concerned that he might be upset that she'd won the hand that could have been his.

However, Lord Norrington was trying not to smile.

He suddenly laid down his cards and grinned. "I believe this is *my* hand, my lady, gentlemen, and I'm truly the luckiest one tonight."

Sylvia tried not to show she was thrilled for Norrington as he dragged his winnings across the table and started stacking everything into tidy little piles. She made a quick tally of his winnings and wanted to hoot with happiness. Norrington had won several thousand pounds more than Sylvia had hoped to lose to him.

Celebrations were short lived as the older gentleman quickly started to deal out cards for a new round, determined to win his money back.

Sylvia held up a hand. "Gentlemen, I am afraid I must leave you now."

"Too rich for your blood, madam?"

"Not at all. But I have promised to dance with a handsome stranger." She hadn't really, but it was as good an excuse as any to leave the card room right now. They couldn't dispute her claim unless they followed her to the ballroom and tried to meet her imaginary dance partner. Men like these were addicted to the game. They wouldn't follow her. She'd made a little money for herself and was satisfied. Sylvia also had no further need to lose any more money in gambling tonight, so she was free to leave at any time.

When she rose, Lord Norrington rose as well, and drew near. He held out his hand, searching her gaze. "Thank you for an enjoyable game, madam."

"And to you, too." She took a step away, but then turned back. "Are you not forgetting something, my lord?"

His brow creased.

She could not leave Norrington at the mercy of better players with his pockets replenished. "I thought you'd be off to find your wife to share the news of your good fortune?"

Norrington hesitated, clearly torn. She could see him debate within himself whether or not to keep playing in the hopes of winning further funds.

Sylvia so hoped he wouldn't stay. A poor gambler ought to know to quit while he's finally ahead.

"Maybe your wife is being entertained by Wharton," someone suggested somewhere behind Norrington.

Lord Norrington stiffened and turned to the table. "If you gentlemen will excuse me, I have a promise to keep," he said, and then, money secured in his coat pockets, he fled the card room.

The old man's jaw clenched and he made a joke about Norrington running off to find his mummy.

Sylvia seethed at their bad grace, but made herself saunter from the card room. She was quite satisfied with her success on one hand, but now disappointed on the other. She'd more or less fulfilled her promise to Lord Wharton, and the excitement and thrill was fading fast. Would she be just another dull wallflower to him after this? Wharton would likely have no further need to seek her out again.

There was a short corridor between her and the ballroom, and to her surprise, she found Wharton lounging against one wall there.

He was engaged in a loud conversation with a group of gentlemen, blocking the way.

She moved toward them, but none seemed to notice her presence at first, probably because she was a full head shorter than them all. She had to clear her throat loudly to garner their attention. "Do move aside, my lords, so I might pass by."

The gentlemen all apologized and clustered together on one side.

All but Wharton.

He remained an immovable obstacle in her path until she cleared her throat again. Wharton straightened and put his back to his friends, casting an admiring glance over Sylvia before moving closer. She shivered at the heat in his eyes behind his mask. A slow smile grew over his features. The man was flirting again—just by smiling at her.

There remained a sliver of space around him, and when she was level with him, he whispered for her ears alone, "Meet me in my chambers at the top of the stairs in five minutes."

Her step faltered but she kept her chin high as she passed him by, as if he'd said nothing untoward, as she would have done with any unwanted attention from a scoundrel. But her skin tingled with excitement over his invitation.

Whatever Lord Wharton wanted with her would undoubtedly be ruinous for her reputation. Did she dare meet him? Did she dare not? It might just be the last time she was alone with him.

Chapter Nine

$\mathscr{A}$lexander stood in the center of his bedchamber, fearing he'd be let down tonight. By his calculation, it was nearly thirty minutes since he'd spoken to Sylvia Hillcrest and invited her to join him upstairs. She had not appeared yet. Admittedly, she'd not said that she would, but she hadn't said no, either.

He was fairly certain he'd conveyed the urgency of his request well enough. He'd said five minutes, but perhaps she had decided the risk to her reputation was too great.

He was disappointed by that.

He'd thought he and Sylvia Hillcrest had understood each other. They had things to discuss. First and foremost in importance was her loss to Lord Norrington at the card table. He wanted to congratulate her. Thank her for a job well done. She had exceeded even his expectations. Norrington had immediately left the ball after leaving the card room, pockets full and hopefully gone off to take care of his suffering wife.

The second—and by no means less important, now—was to convey his wish to improve their acquaintance in private. Tonight. Here. But adherence to decorum and propriety must have, as usual, spoiled any chance of frank conversation concerning desire with a woman he found attractive. He was not usually so impulsive when he pursued a woman for pleasure.

Negotiations with his last mistress had taken a whole month before he'd taken her to bed. But with Sylvia, he'd only just discovered their mutual interest. Perhaps he'd been too bold himself where Sylvia was concerned.

Or she mustn't want what he could offer, and of course, without coming up, had no way to tell him.

She wasn't coming.

He glanced around the room and sighed. The warm fire burned brightly for her, the wine and pair of glasses were ready to drink from, and there was also a pretty bunch of flowers by the bed to brighten the room. He'd turned back the bed linens himself, anticipating seeing Sylvia Hillcrest lying there, naked upon the sheets as he made love to her.

He tugged down his waistcoat. "Enough," he muttered to himself. He'd made a mistake. There were in fact other pleasures he might indulge in tonight.

Disappointed more than he expected to be, he snatched up his mask on his way to the door and wrenched it open, ready to rejoin the party.

But Sylvia Hillcrest was standing just outside his doorway. She let out a startled gasp at seeing him, a sound that seemed far too loud despite the din from the guests below.

Alexander's spirits lightened immeasurably at the sight of her. He caught up her hand and pulled her into the room, then closed the door and locked it for good measure.

He turned and leaned back against his door. Pretty Sylvia in her unusually revealing evening gown was in his bedchamber, possibly all his for the night.

He smiled and, since he still held her hand, pulled her closer. She didn't resist. He brought her gloved fingers to his lips and pressed a kiss there. "I can't begin to thank you. How did you manage it so effortlessly?"

A frown formed on her face. "What?"

"How did you make Norrington win that last hand?"

"He won fairly," she protested with a sudden soft laugh. "I was so focused on besting that horrible old man opposite me that I missed the signs Norrington held a good hand himself. No one was more surprised than I, or perhaps Norrington himself."

"Well, I'll be damned." He kissed her hand a second time.

"That horrible old man is miserly Lord Pulling, a man Norrington owes a large debt to. But he won instead. Lord Pulling has been trying to force Norrington to sell a valuable piece of his property in exchange for the debt, which he now won't have to agree to. What makes *you* dislike Lord Pulling?"

"It was the way he mentioned Norrington's wife. From that moment on, I knew he was no friend to either of us."

"What did he say?"

"He and the other fellow teased Norrington that his wife might be with you. Inferring a rendezvous was taking place while he gambled. I sensed Norrington wasn't concentrating on the game properly after the mention of that."

Alexander shook his head in denial. "I was in the card room, watching you in combat with two of the *ton's* most accomplished players. The other fellow is Lord Holcombe, and he's no one's friend. Pulling and Holcombe make a formidable team when they want someone to stay in their debt."

"I'm glad I could stop them."

"As am I." He twined his fingers with hers a little tighter. "I was afraid you were not coming."

"I was afraid you wouldn't still be here." She looked at him shyly. "You were on the point of leaving, weren't you?"

He inclined his head. "I would have walked very slowly back down to the party, hoping to run into you along the way." He smiled too. "Did you find your handsome stranger to dance with?"

"Oh, you *were* in the card room, and close, too, to have heard my lie," she said with a laugh. "There never was anyone. I just said that so I could leave the card room since my work was done. I ran into the Carmichaels again, and it took some time to extricate myself, unfortunately." She looked up, held his gaze. "I was hoping you might still be waiting here."

"I'm glad you came. Now about that other matter." He brought her hand to his lips again, turned it over, and pressed a kiss to her wrist, right where the button held the glove together. "You interest me. Very much."

"You interest me, too," she admitted, and a soft sigh left her lips.

His senses soared high with the news. "What should we do about that?"

He'd already made arrangements for the servants to be in charge of the event now. They would not disturb them in this room unless the mansion was burning down around their ears, or someone died. He wondered if Sylvia would stay with him alone for a while tonight, and what she might permit him.

Alexander would never push a woman to be intimate. It was always her choice, and in this case, he was almost certain the lady nearly in his arms had some experience of men and pleasure. However, she had a reputation to protect. She was no light-skirt or paid mistress. If they were found alone together, her reputation would be irreparably harmed. He would not marry anyone to fix their reputation for them.

"Perhaps you should kiss me and find out," she whispered as she removed her mask and let it fall to the floor beside them.

"You read my mind." He found the button on her glove, undid it, and parted the fabric with his thumbs to reveal more of her skin. He pressed his lips there softly, and while he did, inched down her glove from her upper arm. He kissed his way up her arm slowly, reveling in her soft gasps and moans. The delicate skin above her elbow was so soft and inviting that he took his time moving farther up.

Eventually he reached her softly rounded shoulder, and her delicate collarbone.

Miss Hillcrest shivered and wriggled closer. He was kissing the base of her throat when her arms rose, hands sliding up his body to embrace him. "That was lovely."

"There's more to come," he promised, wanting nothing more than to kiss her all night long and hear her sigh. "May I continue?"

"Yes," she agreed breathlessly.

He bent again, paused to inhale the intoxicating scent of roses on her skin, and then set his lips to her throat in a harder kiss. A shudder racked her body, and then another as he continued to pepper her skin with a thousand kisses. Gently, he nipped at the column of her throat, too, and she jerked and gasped in pleasure.

Alexander loved to kiss, and responsive women were a joy to bed.

He lifted his lips a little and blew across her neck. Sylvia shivered again, and then her fingers teased into his hair, and across to his own ear. Her touch was light as she traced the edge. Alexander shivered. He pressed his lips to her brow, and offered little pecks that made her sigh again and again. He put an arm around her waist, tugged her harder against him, and finally moved them away from the door.

There was a large bed behind them, and he moved near it, almost dancing Sylvia across the room in his haste and excitement. It had been a while for him. He'd not found the time or inclination to replace his last mistress with another over the winter months. Now he felt quite impatient to have a woman, *this* woman particularly, gasping beneath him.

Her arms wound around his body then slid down his back. She lowered her hands and gripped his buttocks hard enough to make him grin.

He'd been correct. This was no virginal spinster being led astray for the first time, but a woman good at keeping secrets. One intent on enjoying a midnight tryst with him.

Alexander tipped Sylvia backward and rained soft kisses down the front of her throat and onto her very pale chest.

When he brought her back up, Alexander claimed her lips at last.

Their first proper kiss was soft and sweet and made him harder than he ever expected to be so soon in the evening.

Aware that he was more eager for a woman than usual, he found the fastenings of her gown and started to undo the tiny buttons. "I've no desire to crush your gown any further. It would be noticed later. I'll redress you, I swear."

"You've done this before," she teased even as she tried to help him undress her.

"Once or twice." Alexander concentrated on the last buttons lower down.

"Is that why you hold this party every year? To seduce someone new?"

"To seduce *you*, if you want to be," he admitted.

"I do." Sylvia stepped out of her gown, wearing nothing but stays, stockings and her thin chemise. The satin slippers she discarded herself, and then she lifted her chin. Proud. Almost defiant. Anticipating his reaction. There was a fiery look in her eyes that he recognized all too easily, and felt, too.

He admired her curves, hungered for them, and told her so very directly. "I want to pleasure your body all night long."

Admitting his need and admiration for her body seemed to please her immensely. "Show me?"

Alexander swooped to pick her up and sat her on the edge of the bed. Framing her face with his hands, he stole a deep kiss that could have gone on forever.

However, Alexander wanted to be closer, so he broke the kiss, placed his hands on both her knees, and pushed them wide apart. Sylvia's moan filled the room, and he quickly silenced her mouth with more kisses, sweeping his tongue inside to dance with hers.

Sylvia wasn't an idle bed partner. He was aware of her warm little hands as they boldly explored his body while they shared yet more drugging kisses. Alexander felt the fastenings of his breeches give way and she brushed over his bare belly, under his shirt. He sucked in a breath, momentarily startled, but quickly got ahold of his breeches and eased them lower over his hips.

He was pleased Sylvia was eager for him, and when she touched his cock, he almost roared with the pleasure it. There was nothing like a bold woman in his bed to stoke the fire in him.

He let her touch him for a little while, since she seemed to know what she was about, but then he urged her to lie back on the mattress to make her release him. Miss Hillcrest's breasts interested him. The gown she'd arrived in had offered only a tantalizing glimpse of her hidden charms. He wanted to weigh them in his hands, thumb her nipples, and then feast. They looked just right for his hands. Heavy and full, and so very soft.

Alexander drew back to finish removing his lower garments and shoes, then tossed his coat away, too. He kept the waistcoat on so he could tuck his shirt up and out of the way. Then he turned all his attention back to the lady panting with lust on his bed.

Slowly, he crawled over her. Sylvia lost to passion was a thrilling sight, and she was quick to take him in hand again, languidly stroking him back to fullness without his urging. She was rather good, he found. She'd grasp the base firmly then pull, slide her hand up to the tip, then start over again until he was panting hard.

Alexander teased her chemise and stay straps from her

shoulders to reveal her breasts, and he openly admired them. Miss Hillcrest sported a lovely pair. He put his hands on them, and then leaned down to lavish them with attention.

Sylvia wound her legs tightly around his hips and clung to him, encouraged him. The sensitive head of his cock scraped against her chemise, and Alexander hastened to lift it up so nothing came between them.

He touched her curls, earning another moan, stifled this time by the back of her hand. Yes, Sylvia knew a thing or two about pleasure. She enjoyed giving and receiving, but Alexander enjoyed giving more.

He wet the tips of his fingers and slipped them between her legs, between her folds to toy with her expertly. The delightful woman gasped loudly, lapping up all his attention. He pleasured her breasts, too, with his mouth, and soon she had slipped her fingers into his hair, scratching her nails across his scalp.

She pulled at him, drawing him closer. Creating a lovely friction and urgency between them he couldn't possibly resist for long.

Alexander found her entrance and teased a finger into her depths. Sylvia's legs fell completely open, and she lifted her hips, encouraging him to explore her fully. He was more than happy to oblige her desires.

He moved down, watched his finger disappear inside her with ease, and then he added another, testing her limits. The woman writhed, in the grip of utter ecstasy. He added a third finger but that made her hiss, and then she ground down onto his hand in complete abandon—apparently loving his invasion.

He kissed her sex, finding her wet against his tongue. He loved her with his mouth and tongue and fingers until her hips started to buck in an urgent rhythm.

He eased away from her and removed his fingers from her wet sheath.

Sylvia was gasping softly as he hovered over her. "Are you all right, my dear?" he asked with a teasing smile. Who would have thought such a woman could make such lovely wanton sounds?

"Yes, but why did you stop?"

He kissed the tip of her nose. "Paused, so I may enjoy that expression of bliss on your face."

"I want to enjoy you," she whispered. She glanced down his body, and then both her hands were on his cock again, stroking him, bringing him great pleasure so quickly, his head fairly spun. He rocked his hips into her hot little hands, driving his cock harder, faster, until she mimicked him.

Alexander closed his eyes, savoring his new lover's touch. When her fingers wandered lower, brushed over his balls, he let out a groan and looked down on her. "That feels very good, too."

She grinned and kept it up, circling his balls and tugging on his sack until he feared he would be unable to hold back his seed another moment longer. He had to sink his cock into this wonderful woman *now*.

He shifted to bring her under him, aligned their body's for the closest of contact, and then slowly started to enter her. Sylvia's eyes were huge on him at first then fluttered closed as he possessed her. He went slowly, taking his time, savoring their joining until he was lodged deep inside her. Despite her experience, Sylvia felt damn tight, but oh so wonderful around him.

He started to move, leisurely at first, and when Sylvia started to pull at him, urging him down to lie heavily upon her, he gave himself over to their lovemaking entirely.

He found her tiny hand and held it high over her head. He kissed her lips when she sought his, and she gripped him tightly against her. He didn't know how long he loved her, but Sylvia peaked first, muffling her joy against his lips.

He held her face gently when she finally subsided, still twitching around him, and gave her a long, deep kiss. When he pulled back, he held her gaze and lost himself again to the pleasures of her willing body. As he felt the familiar thrill racing over him, he managed to draw back in time to pump his seed into his hand. He balanced on his knees, gasping and shaking above her, hand full of his own release and his head spinning like a top.

"My waistcoat pocket, if you wouldn't mind," he gasped.

Sylvia fumbled at his chest and produced his handkerchief. When the handkerchief proved insufficient for the task, Alexander had no choice but to climb off the bed before he was ready and use the wash basin. Once done there, he stumbled back to the bed and collapsed beside his lover, who still lay flat more or less as he'd left her.

But Alexander felt very good, and he put his hand over Miss Hillcrest's quim affectionately. "What a wonder you've turned out to be."

She flexed her hips up into his hand, and Alexander laughed softly and turned to look down on her again.

For some women, once was enough, and a man must wait an eternity until they could be aroused again. There was a glint in Sylvia's eyes that suggested she was far from sated still.

He teased her sex lightly with the tips of his fingers, watching for confirmation of his suspicions. Sylvia didn't move her hips away or suggest he stop as he grew bolder, dipping between those soft, warm, and very wet lower lips. She took her bottom lip between her teeth and watched him.

"Shall I kiss you again?"

Her hips rose immediately, pushing his fingers nearly into her quim.

"Well, that was certainly the answer I was hoping for." Alexander grinned, pleased to have discovered a woman of extraordinary hungers lurked under the prim disguise of a proper spinster.

He went to his knees beside the bed, using his shoulders to burrow between her legs, and jerked her hips toward the edge of the mattress. He kissed her warm, damp quim eagerly…and stayed there until she cried out one more time.

Chapter Ten

Sylvia had a secret. A delicious secret that kept her warm and excited as she walked along Bond Street on a sunny Tuesday afternoon. She'd taken a lover. And not just any lover, but a man whose only priority seemed to be delivering immense satisfaction.

When the Marquess of Wharton had made love to her, it had been the most glorious encounter of her entire life. One she was sure could never be surpassed.

She brushed her gloved fingers over her hip, yearning to feel his touch there again. That delicious man had loved kissing her, too. Anywhere and everywhere. She shivered, remembering his insatiable appetite for her body.

After making love the first time, he'd pleasured her with his mouth and fingers, and then they'd begun all over again. Their second lovemaking had been slow and entirely wordless. She'd been gently turned onto her knees with the marquess kneeling close behind. His hands and lips had been wondrously arousing, but it had been his cock she'd really wanted to feel inside her a second time. She'd wiggled her hips into him, and that was all the invitation he'd needed to give her the tupping of her life.

She had felt a little tender down there, right afterward, but any discomfort had been brief and welcome. It had been a good soreness she already missed.

Yes, the Marquess of Wharton had made her feel utterly desirable, and he'd been flatteringly reluctant for the night to end, too. But end it had to. After redressing her carefully as the sky had begun to lighten outside, the marquess had whispered promises of discretion and revealed an eagerness to meet in private again one day. He had not pressed her for an actual time or place and had left the decision in her hands. He'd sent her away in his unmarked carriage with one last tender kiss, stolen in the shadows of his home.

Sylvia was truly tempted to meet him again in private, but she did worry how a second meeting might be managed without discovery. Wharton couldn't again host another masquerade just to invite Sylvia into his home and his bed. She also had a lot to lose if she was discovered in his arms. No matter how pleasurable their encounter, she had her reputation, and that of her family to protect. And then, too, how likely was it that they might come together and recreate that perfect night again?

"What do you think, Sylvia?"

Sylvia blinked and glanced around guiltily. "About what?"

"Goodness, you really are woolgathering a lot today," Aurora complained.

"I have a lot on my mind."

"Such as? Oh, I suppose you are worrying about our new service. I promise, the introduction will go well today," Aurora insisted. "If Miss Quartermane and Lord Sullivan hit it off, what's the harm in doing a little real matchmaking. She's exactly the kind of wife he's been asking for."

Sylvia did not agree, but she'd been outvoted two to one in the decision to introduce one of their oldest clients to the friend of a new friend. They were to make the suggestion to him later tomorrow and see if he cared for the introduction.

"I am not at all easy with this change in the services we will offer our clients. Advice and instruction is one thing, but pushing men and women together for the purpose of matrimony is always fraught with problems. We should have waited for the pair to have met at a society ball, and then encouraged and supported his decision if and when he expressed any interest in her."

"What could be better? Miss Quartermane comes from a respectable family and has pots of money for a dowry, and Lord

Sullivan needs someone keen to wed him. I coached Miss Quartermane myself on what to say so she'll turn his head when they meet."

Sylvia stared at her cousin, a sinking feeling in her heart. "You don't think very highly of Lord Sullivan, do you?"

Aurora put her hands on her hips. "A man like that shouldn't need anyone to find him a wife. He's handsome, rich, and titled. He's procrastinating for no good reason."

Sylvia was starting to think Aurora wasn't cut out to give unbiased advice. She was often too impatient with others, Lord Sullivan especially. "He really did love his late wife and fears the perils of childbirth for his next."

"For goodness sake, every single woman who sleeps with a man understands the perils they might face in childbirth later. It's not as if he has to push the babe out himself."

"Aurora, really! That was unforgivably crude. You know he's being pressured by his family to choose quickly. He does *not* need our impatience as well. I think he was, and will make again, a wonderful husband. Would you want him to do as his family wished and marry a woman he felt absolutely nothing for?"

She shook her head slowly. "He's overthinking the matter. If he's meant to marry for love again, he will know it the moment they meet."

"Not everyone feels as you do, cousin, about falling in love at first sight. Sometimes love can take a while to become apparent."

Aurora held up her hand. "Please don't cite our good friends the Carmichaels as an example again."

"I will indeed." She sighed. "They knew each other for so long that they nearly missed the moment when they fell in love. And look at them now. So happy together."

Aurora linked arms with her. "My dear cousin, you are still such a romantic."

"It is hard to remain a romantic in our line of work," she noted. "It's sometimes a struggle to remain optimistic and to be patient with those who are slow to see what's right under their noses."

"Which must be why you're always woolgathering, imagining yourself being in love with one of our clients," Aurora teased.

"You're the same, and it's not just over the clients, either.

Some gentlemen in society are very worthy of a little woolgathering over," Sylvia noted, casting a glance down the busy street. Handsome gentlemen were everywhere around her today, and Sylvia really was feeling decidedly lusty, so she indulged her fantasies about the men she saw nearest her. A pretty face did not always deliver a skilled lover. She was pleasantly surprised that Lord Wharton was both.

She found herself hoping to see him on Bond Street today. "We don't really know that much about Miss Quartermane other than what your friend told you," Sylvia confided. "Why, I've never even seen her at a *ton* event in the past year."

"They had a death in the family, a close relative, and have only just returned to society. She was very much about the year before we all came to live together in London, I hear."

Sylvia couldn't shake the feeling Miss Quartermane—and Aurora's new friend, Lady Douglass—were being deceptive in some way. Any enquiries she'd made so far had been fruitless, though. "I would have preferred to know more about the young woman before Lord Sullivan meets her."

"Well, today is the day, and then Lord Sullivan is no longer our problem to solve." Aurora shrugged. "I'm sure you'll see I'm right."

"I just wish I could see him one more time before they meet," she murmured.

But instead, she spotted a confident young man she'd met during her winter holiday striding along the pavement.

Mr. Thaddeus Berringer was a tall streak of desirable masculinity to some women, even before you took into consideration that he would inherit a duchy. Untitled until he did inherit, though, the young man had seemed uncertain of his own appeal, especially when surrounded by the members of the Duke of Exeter's inner circle. Some young men with similar prospects might have strutted about, but not Mr. Berringer. She'd discovered him to be quite thoughtful and kind and genuinely fond of his older cousin—the man from whom he'd inherit the duchy.

Mr. Berringer noticed them and waved. He quickened his strides until he was towering over them on the footpath. "Miss Sylvia Hillcrest, now this is serendipity indeed. Good morning to you."

Sylvia smiled up at him with genuine fondness. "Mr. Berringer. What an unexpected pleasure for me, too."

"Would you believe her grace intended to send me to your door later today with a note she would write while I was out at this very moment?"

"No. Really?" Sylvia said, grinning. "I had no idea the duke and duchess had returned to London already."

"They are inseparable, and when Sinclair—I mean his grace—needed to be in London, she wouldn't hear of staying behind. We arrived very late last night, actually. The duchess mentioned to me that she hoped you might visit her soon if you are free."

"Of course she can," Aurora cut in quickly, her smile inviting as she looked up at Thaddeus Berringer.

"Oh, I'm sorry. Mr. Berringer, may I introduce my cousin, Miss Aurora Hillcrest to you?"

He bowed and smiled. "Indeed you may, because I have many a lengthy conversation I wish to have with her about her mysterious cousin Sylvia. How do you do?"

"Very well, thank you."

"Tell me, Miss Aurora, is your cousin always so dreadful at saying good things about herself?"

Aurora eyes sparkled with mirth, and she moved to stand by his side. "My cousin has always been the retiring sort."

Mr. Berringer smiled warmly at Sylvia for so long that her face started to heat with an uncomfortable blush. "One day, I vow to find out all her secrets," he warned.

Sylvia had always found other people's lives much more interesting than her own. "There are none to be discovered."

"That cannot be true." He gestured to the footpath ahead. "Might I walk along with you?"

"It would be a pleasure."

Mr. Berringer offered his arms to both her and Aurora, but it was Aurora who was quickest to claim one. "And what of you, Mr. Berringer? Do you have a great many secrets a lady can learn?"

"Like your cousin, I won't say."

Sylvia laughed softly. "Are you happy to be in London again, sir?"

Berringer waggled his hand. "My cousin prefers to know where I am, and I prefer to know he's keeping out of trouble."

"Usually it's the other way round with older relatives," Aurora whispered with an arched look in Sylvia's direction.

"Please don't tell him," Mr. Berringer begged. "I have my cousin just as I want him, finally."

"And how is that?"

"Happy," Mr. Berringer said quickly with a sincere smile. "He deserves every good thing in life after being alone for so long."

Sylvia smiled too, having seen firsthand the obvious affection the duke had for his duchess. In a private setting, the pair were most comfortable, and many times Sylvia had felt a little envious. However, the pair had waited a long time to be together, and she didn't begrudge them their happiness. "Indeed, they both do."

They paused at a shop window. Aurora had an appointment here today, and they would have to part company now with Mr. Berringer before they could go inside. "I'm afraid we're going inside this establishment, sir."

Mr. Berringer studied the signage and then grimaced. A dressmaker's shop was not a place to take a gentleman unless he was related, or perhaps a husband. "How sad that we must part so soon, but I do have the consolation of needing to call upon an acquaintance who lives not far from here."

"I'm glad to hear you'll be well entertained without us."

"Well, but not better," he swore.

"I'm sure that is not true. Thank you for the pleasant walk, sir," Sylvia said politely. "It was very good to see you again, and do convey to the duchess my hope of seeing her soon, too."

"I certainly will," he promised. "Until we meet again."

He offered a jaunty wave and walked off alone, away from the busy shops and down a side street.

Aurora heaved a heavy sigh when he was away. "Good gracious, you said he was handsome but you neglected to say just how devastating that smile of his could be at close quarters."

Sylvia nodded, watching Mr. Berringer until he disappeared from view. What a pity she felt not a hint of sexual longing when he was around. He was excellent company, and funny, but that was all. "He was all the ladies could talk about during the winter. Exeter's heir turned many a head."

"He certainly turned mine," Aurora said with a laugh, as she pressed her hands to her cheeks. "But I think I've little chance of turning *his* head."

"Why do you say that?"

"All he could do is smile at *you*. I think you have an ardent admirer, my dear."

Sylvia blushed. "Gracious, no."

"Don't discount him out of hand," Aurora warned. "Young men have stamina older women like us can appreciate."

Sylvia stared after Mr. Berringer in concern. Surely the young man could not really fancy *her*. She'd never even flirted with him. "No. No, you are mistaken," she said decisively, and then turned for the door.

They entered the little shop, finding the proprietress still occupied. They waited, Aurora tapping her foot with impatience until she was summoned. Sylvia, on the other hand, poured over the fashion plates, finding many gowns she dreamed of wearing. She'd love nothing more than to have a new evening gown, but she was only here to keep Aurora company today before going home empty-handed.

After an hour, Aurora's business was done and Sylvia was free to do as she pleased. She accompanied Aurora home but still felt too restless to remain there. Collecting her maid, she ventured out for a walk in Berkley Square again.

Sylvia didn't immediately spot her new friend in the park and, feeling disappointed, strolled toward her favorite sweet shop. The crowd there was thin, and she purchased three small pastries to share with her cousins later.

As she stepped away from the shop and started handing the wrapped package to her maid, her shoulder was bumped and her purchases went flying into the busy roadway. The package unwrapped on impact, and her lovely pastries came to decorate horse manure, and then a carriage wheel finished them off.

Heartbroken, Sylvia looked around for someone to blame. A well-dressed man was watching her closely.

"Bad luck," he said.

"Did you see who bumped me, sir?"

"Oh, I'm afraid not," he apologized. "Let me purchase replacements," he offered, turning toward the shop.

"No, thank you," she quickly told him. She was more than capable of paying for her own indulgences, though now pastries had lost their appeal. "It's my own fault for not paying attention."

"Well, if not a sweet treat, I'd be happy to offer any other service you could name," he said slowly, holding her gaze. "Perhaps you'd grant me the privilege of seeing you home so we could discuss it."

Sylvia observed the man through narrowed eyes, saw a speculative gleam in his, and shook her head firmly. "You're very kind, but I need no help today."

She gestured to her maid to quickly follow her away from the man. She crossed into Berkley Square for her regular exercise, hoping that he was gone from the area before she and the maid walked home.

She spotted Lizzy seated upon her usual bench seat, but today she had a pair of young women with her.

Sylvia nodded politely to them but intended to pass by.

"Are you not speaking with me today?"

She stopped and turned to face Lizzy. "I did not wish to intrude."

Lizzy glanced to the young women. "Take a look to see what is keeping young Mr. Marshall. He should have returned by now. Go no farther than the edge of the square, and take my maid with you."

The young women were up on their feet and off faster than she could blink.

Lizzy smiled. "My daughters. I'd introduce you when they returned, but..."

"You're not yet done with being mysterious," Sylvia finished for her.

"Precisely," Lizzy agreed. "Do sit down. Your cheeks are a little pink today. Why is that?"

"An accident."

The lady inhaled sharply. "Were you hurt?"

"No, I was jostled, and the pastries I purchased to share with my cousins fell into the road."

"What a pity. I have to say, I am enjoying the pastry shop you recommended. Mr. Marshall, one of my daughter's suitors, has gone to purchase something new for us today."

At the edge of the square, Lizzy's daughters were talking to the man who had offered to walk Sylvia home just a few minutes ago.

He held out his arms to the pair and, head high, chest thrust out, began the short journey to meet them. Sylvia saw his eyes widen with recognition at the sight of her, and then he quickly veiled it. "Well met again?"

"Sir," she said, inclining her head stiffly. What a rogue. He'd offered to escort her home when he was expected to return promptly to Lizzy and the daughter he was supposed to be courting.

"Nigel found all sorts of things for our afternoon tea," one of the young women gushed, pointing back to the maid, who carried an expensively sized wicker basket.

"You may return to the house now. The pair of you, off you go," Lizzy ordered. Her daughters hastened to go, with many a glance over their shoulders for Mr. Marshall.

Lizzy narrowed her eyes on the rogue. "And you, sir, may take your leave, too."

As any good gentleman should, he immediately agreed to take himself away. "Until tomorrow. Ladies," he said, and then glanced at Sylvia. "I hope we meet again very soon."

In a matter of minutes, Sylvia and Lizzy were entirely alone. Sylvia held her tongue as long as she could. "You sent them away so they wouldn't reveal your identity."

"They've given me another headache, and I'm much too tired to hear more about their suitors today."

"I'm sorry to hear that," Sylvia promised, casting an eye over the woman discretely. Another costly gown but in deep green. There was definitely tiredness in her eyes and a slight stooping of her posture. "How old are your daughters?"

"Old enough to be married. I know I should be more excited about them making a match this season, but today I am just not in the mood to think about the future."

"Is that young man a contender for their hand in marriage?"

"Jocelyn seems to like him best of all the others."

Sylvia bit her tongue rather than issue a warning. She was nearly certain that man had bumped her arm as a way to start a conversation with her, and she was very sure he'd have jumped at the chance to know her intimately, too.

"You have an opinion of him," Lizzy mused. "And judging from your silence, it's not favorable."

"I'm sorry, my mind wandered just then to another gentleman."

"Oh? Is he a better catch?"

"I wouldn't know," Sylvia said quickly.

"For your sake, I hope he's clever. Men are, in general, fools. My sons included," Lizzy warned. "Are you going to tell me where you've been today? I thought to see you here this morning."

"I'd promised to accompany my cousin to the dressmakers. I've only just returned."

Lizzy glanced sideways. "Tell me, do you always were such dull and unflattering dresses? Is it a costume you wear to hide behind or do you lack fashion sense entirely?"

Sylvia choked on a laugh. "It's a ploy. I've no choice but to hide from my legion of admirers behind my ugly dresses."

Lizzy began to chuckle. "When I have the time, I must take you shopping with me. You need someone to take your wardrobe in hand. You'll never catch yourself a husband if you hide your charms."

Sylvia could have been offended but instead she was amused. What did it matter if what she wore wasn't the height of fashion? She wasn't in need of a husband. "What I wear is perfectly suitable for my life."

"Then you need a different life," Lizzy suggested with a tight smile. "Now look over there and tell me what you see different today."

Sylvia spotted the woman they'd noticed the other day had come to the park again. She was sitting on a bench, just as coy and pretty as before, but today she had a man by her side. "She caught his attention."

"So it seems, and I believe the odds are in her favor for making a match, too."

"I'm so happy for her." Sylvia grinned and sat back to secretly observe the budding romance unfold with her new friend.

Chapter Eleven

Alexander was definitely feeling an itch he couldn't scratch. He didn't like it one bit, either. He tossed the day's mail aside, little caring that half the envelopes slid off the slick desktop and onto the carpeted floor.

Why hadn't she written him yet to arrange another meeting?

Sylvia Hillcrest had become a problem.

Alexander had expected to hear from her the day after their tryst had taken place. He had certainly satisfied the woman beyond a shadow of a doubt. And she had him, too.

However, the glow of that pleasurable meeting hadn't lasted beyond a day for him. He craved a woman again, and only Miss Hillcrest seemed to interest him at the moment. Despite spending an hour or two at Madam Bradshaw's House of Pleasure last night, he'd gone away without indulging in more than a few drinks. He found himself looking for Sylvia everywhere, too, and now he was on the verge of doing something unheard of.

He was considering a risky romantic pursuit of a most outwardly proper woman in the hope of something decidedly wicked.

He'd made discreet inquiries at luncheon today when he'd been at his club with their mutual friend. Lord Carmichael was full of praise for the woman and had spoken at length of the business enterprise Sylvia was engaged in with her two female cousins. They were doing quite well for themselves, apparently. Gentlemen in want of a wife called on the trio constantly.

Alexander wasn't in need of a wife, but he did want to see Sylvia again. He couldn't wait for random chance to put the woman within arm's reach. He would have to design a plan to ensure he could fulfill his desires discreetly.

With that aim in mind, he gathered up his new invitations and studied the hostesses' names. There were several who might do him the favor of extending an invitation to the Hillcrests, but not without a good reason. His sexual satisfaction probably wasn't a good enough excuse.

Aside from showing up at her door unannounced, and being mistaken for a client, he could only hope to see her at dinner with the Carmichaels sometime in the future. They had invited Miss Hillcrest there several times to partner him at dinner to make up the numbers. It couldn't hurt to see if he could engineer an invitation to dine with them at short notice, and her, too.

He rang the bell.

A servant appeared a few minutes later. "Yes, my lord."

"Would you send a man round to Lord Carmichael's residence asking what his dinner plans are for this evening?"

"Is that all, my lord?"

"Yes, but have him wait for an answer."

The matter of his evening almost decided, Alexander settled behind his desk. He accepted and declined invitations to parties, and then picked up the paper to read while he waited on a response from Carmichael.

He was totally engrossed until he heard a female throat being cleared.

Miss Hillcrest had done that the other night behind his back, and he smiled, hoping his thoughts about her had summoned her to his home.

Unfortunately, the first words the lady uttered disproved that wish as a dangerous mistake on his part.

"How many times have I told you not to put your feet on the furniture?"

Alexander lowered the paper with a sinking feeling in the pit of his stomach and glanced at the doorway in dread.

At only five feet tall in heeled slippers, Alexander's mother, Lady Elizabeth, Marchioness of Wharton, overpowered the chamber just by stepping into it. "Mother, what are you doing in London?"

She smiled tightly. "Is that any way to greet your mother?"

Customary. At least for him. He got to his feet and slowly walked toward her. He bent to kiss her upturned papery cheek like the dutiful son she expected. "It's unlike you not to write and say you're coming to stay."

"I am not staying," she informed him.

He drew back in astonishment. "But you're already here."

She looked around her and huffed in disapproval at the lived-in state of the room they were in. Mother was of the opinion that the London residence should reveal nothing of the occupant's true interests. Alexander completely disagreed on that score and made no bones about it. This was his primary residence, and he would do as he liked within these walls.

Her gaze returned to him. "I've taken a lease for the season."

"What?"

She shrugged. "You've made it abundantly clear that our presence here is considered a nuisance, so I've made other arrangements."

Alexander wasn't sure whether to cheer or worry about this startling development. "Did you bring the children with you?"

Her gaze turned decidedly hostile at his question. "Your siblings are hardly children anymore."

Alexander had two sisters and one disgraceful brother. None had married, a sore point with Mother, and the reason he hardly ever went to the country. His siblings needed schooling in how to keep their opinions to themselves before they were allowed to sit down at one of his dinners. "They act like they still are," he complained, gesturing toward the chairs set around the fire.

Mother stayed on her feet. Immovable, as always. "One time they got into the wine at dinner, and you refuse to forgive them for it," she argued. "It was years ago."

He threw up his hands. "They were tipsy and argumentative in front of the prince regent!"

"Well, he's often drunk and slovenly in front of *us*," his mother grumbled in a low tone.

"Mother," he warned. Speaking ill against the prince regent was always a sore point with him. The man was of royal blood. He might be lacking in a little common sense at times, but he would be king one day. Getting on his bad side was not in the family's best interests. "What is it you want?"

She clasped her hands before her waist. "Can a mother not visit her eldest son?"

"I am *not* getting married this season." Alexander made that announcement every time he saw his mother, and still she tried to introduce women to him who were acceptable to her, but not one had been acceptable to *him*.

She shrugged. "I'm not interested in your love life anymore. I am here for your sisters' sakes."

Alexander sat down on the edge of his desk, exaggerating his shock. "Don't tell me *they* want husbands at last."

She shook her head hard enough that the ringlet curls at the back bounced wildly from side to side. "They've always wanted husbands, just not the fools you would have thrown them to. Since we are not staying under your roof, I demand that you leave us all alone to get on with it."

"I beg your pardon?" he said, glowering at the woman who'd given birth to him.

"Your sisters and I will go about society without your escort this season. You are not to interfere with any suitors your sisters attract."

He stood again. "I'm not about to let them marry just anyone who asks for their hand in marriage. Their dowries—"

"Their dowries are separate from your management, and none of your concern. Your father set the amount, not you, a long time ago. I want to see my daughters made happy, and with children of their own coming along soon after. I warn you to stay out of my way in this."

He narrowed his eyes on her. She was asking too much. "Are you capable of staying out of *my* life?"

"We move in the same circles, my son."

"You know what I'm referring to. I will not be introduced to another daughter of an old friend of yours and forced to dance with them this season."

His mother winced. "Has it really been such an imposition to be polite and dance with a few young women?"

"Yes, it has."

Mother suddenly swayed a little on her feet, and although he moved to catch her elbow, she wouldn't let him touch her. She hugged her arms under her breasts and pressed her lips together.

"Please, won't you sit down? I don't want to argue with you."

"Nor I, you." She sighed and then sat down, stiffly, in a chair before the desk. "I cannot stay long. I promised your sister that we would attend the Marshall Ball."

"Which sister?"

"Amelia."

Alexander sat back down behind his desk. "I wasn't aware she knew the Marshalls."

"Your sister met their son a few months ago, and is quite keen to continue their acquaintance in Town."

Alexander rubbed his hand over his jaw, a little unprepared to discuss his sister and potential husbands. "So, Marshall's son has been courting her? Why didn't you tell me?"

"Why haven't you come home to visit them?" she asked in a cutting tone.

Alexander wisely didn't respond to that one with an honest answer. "He's a little young to marry yet, isn't he?"

"He's been pleasant company," Mama promised.

That didn't make anyone good enough in his opinion. He had a list of potential candidates hidden away somewhere but he couldn't consult it in front of Mother. Given her mood, she might just tear it up and burn it in the fire behind her. "What of Jocelyn? I suppose she's standing sadly on the sidelines longing for a suitor of her own."

Mother's smile was smug. "Not at all. Your younger sister has become quite popular, with a number of her own admirers, too."

He could hardly believe he was hearing this, but he wouldn't contradict Mother until he'd had a chance to judge the matter for himself. "If only Father were here to scare away the unworthy rogues instead of leaving me to do it."

"I have to do the best for them now." She shook her head angrily. "The girls barely remember your father. They looked to you once upon a time."

Alexander shifted uncomfortably. "I'll talk to them, and the importance of making the right match."

"Will you? When?"

"Soon," he promised soothingly. But not this week. He had a full schedule that he might have cleared if Mother had told him of her plans to come to London in advance. But she had not, so he'd make plans to see them in the next week or so.

"You always forget your promises to them. They are not little girls anymore. They are young women, and they deserve a proper season."

"I do not forget them." He considered his chances of just escorting one sister about and dismissed it as hopeless. They would complain, and loudly, too, if they were separated. It was both or none. And he was not capable of keeping his nose out of any plans to marry off his sisters. "Fine, I'll try to escort both of them to a few events I've already agreed to attend and hope for the best."

"You'll try? Please don't strain yourself to accommodate your family when there are such important decisions to be made. I am quite capable of helping my daughters find good men without your belated meddling mucking things up for them. Please, do go on with your own life of ease."

He stared, and Mother stared, but Alexander looked down first. He consulted his open appointment book discreetly—shifting and rearranging his appointments in his head. There was nothing so urgent in his schedule that he couldn't delay it so he could, in fact, spend a few evenings with his sisters, and his mother, too. "I can escort you all tonight."

"One night? Oh, thank you," Mama said, sarcasm dripped off her words in waves. "Don't bother throwing any more crumbs our way. You're much too busy. I can manage our lives without any help from you. No matter how wearying your sisters can be, you've made it clear I am on my own with them, and all of us are unwanted around here."

"You are not unwanted." He gritted his teeth and chose his next words with care. Perhaps he *had* abandoned his responsibilities at home and heaped them all on his mother. No wonder she'd grown surly over the years about his absence. She was clearly at the end of her tether, and in need of immediate relief. "I'll have their rooms prepared and the servants ready to receive them within the hour. Would their presence here for a week be long enough to begin with?"

Mother thrust out her hand suddenly. "Yes."

They shook hands, but Alexander was taken aback by how speedily they'd settled the matter. Any time Mother was too biddable, he immediately looked for signs of deception. He had a feeling he'd just been tricked into something he would regret later. He also hoped she wasn't about to foist an unmarried friend of theirs at him and expect him to be interested.

Mother stood. "Now that is settled, I will bid you good day."

Alexander stood, too. "Where are you going?"

"Home, for a good long rest. I think I deserve it." She clutched the back of a chair, swaying a little bit again. "I'm sure you don't need me checking up on how you're all getting along, so I won't bother."

He cocked his head to the side. Was he really free of her interference for a whole week? It was too good to believe he might be left alone to shepherd his sisters toward the right men. There had to be a catch. "Where are you staying?"

She frowned. "Why do you need to know that?"

"To send the carriage to collect my sisters."

"Pfft," his mother snorted. "I'll send them to you by dinnertime so you don't forget they exist again."

He crossed his arms over his chest and glowered at her. "The location, Mama."

"You're always telling me how smart you are. Find us yourself," she suggested, and then turned on her heel. "Remember your promise to keep them for a week."

"Yes, Mother, as long as you remember to stay out of my affairs, too," he called to her back.

She did not trade another volley of words with him as she marched to the front door. This had once been her home, before Alexander had inherited the title. They had struggled with command of it for a few years after he'd inherited, until she'd finally retreated to the country and the family estate, along with all his siblings.

Alexander had left her entirely to her own devices in running their country estate, and she did it very well, too. As he'd known she would. Profits were steady and the land steward was full of praise for her decisions.

But having Mother and his siblings in London was not in his best interests right now. Despite her promise, he would bet he'd see her before the week was over. He could only hope that his sisters' marriage plans would keep her occupied enough after that to never stick her nose in his business this season.

He moved to the front of the house, saw his mother enter her carriage without a wave of goodbye, though he was sure she saw him standing at the window watching her.

"Excuse me, my lord. Message from Lord Carmichael," a servant informed him.

Alexander held out his hand for it as he watched the coachman prepare to get under way. He read the note quickly. The Carmichaels had plans to go out.

Disappointed by the news he wouldn't see Sylvia, he crushed the note as mother drove away.

He waited all of a minute before deciding to follow Mother to this new home she'd leased, wherever it might be.

Chapter Twelve

"It's very quiet here tonight," Sylvia murmured, glancing toward the doorway, where beyond not a sound could be heard. "Are your daughters out at an entertainment tonight?"

"They've gone to stay with the marquess for a few days to give my ears a rest," Lizzy told her candidly.

Lizzy did not speak of her connections often, and only then in the vaguest of terms, and yes, Sylvia had considered that the woman might be a member of the aristocracy. But a connection to a marquess was unexpected. "Which marquess?"

"Wharton, of course."

Wharton?

There was only one Wharton that she knew of in society.

Sylvia pressed her hand to her stomach as it fluttered. "Is the Marquess of Wharton your son?"

"Yes. Have you heard of him?"

Sylvia's cheeks grew warm. Heard of him, touched all of him, even tasted him, too. Not that she would mention that fact to his mother.

Sylvia began to tremble. What had she done by coming here? She swallowed hard. She couldn't admit to not knowing him at all. They had mutual friends. "Yes, we've met, spoken, on several occasions, my lady." And she was desperate to leave it at that.

"He can be quite cold to unmarried women. I hope you were not offended by his indifference."

Sylvia wanted to slide under the table to hide her flaming cheeks. Wharton hadn't been indifferent to her at all. "You never mentioned you had a connection to such an important family. If I had known of your proper title, I would have—"

Lady Wharton raised one brow, and Sylvia clamped her lips shut quickly. "If you had known my title, you would have behaved very differently, I expect. Everyone does."

In Sylvia's case, if she had known of the connection, she might have at least considered the potential implications of becoming friends with her lover's mother. The woman was far above her on the social ladder, and would be offended to dine with a woman who sought pleasure out of wedlock. If she found out Sylvia had spent a scandalous night in Wharton's bed... Sylvia shuddered at how she might react. One wrong word, too, from Lady Wharton could destroy her tenuous position in society.

Sylvia would have to tread carefully to save them both the awkwardness and slowly withdraw her friendship by degrees, so Lady Wharton never learned the truth. "If I had known who you were, I would have offered a deep curtsy when we first met," she suggested.

Sylvia would not have walked away from a lady in distress, though. She had been concerned enough to approach the stranger, titled or not, and offer what aid she could. Not that someone of Sylvia's lower status had much to offer a member of the upper ten thousand. They were not the same in society's eyes, or her own.

Sylvia lowered her gaze, mortified by her presumption to think herself this woman's near equal. "You must find my ignorance amusing."

The lady sighed. "Sometimes it's a pleasant pastime pretending to be a nobody again."

Sylvia wasn't sure how to respond to that, or if she should encourage further confessions. She glanced around the room surreptitiously, but saw nothing of significance to mark the lady as a wealthy and powerful member of society. The furnishings around them were nothing at all like those found in Lord Wharton's exquisite Cavendish Square home.

And there was no battalion of servants lurking to wait on the lady hand and foot, either. How was she supposed to have known who she was? Lady Wharton had been alone in Berkley Square the day they'd met, sad and withdrawn. Sylvia's sensibilities had been stirred to approach her again and again.

From the beginning of their acquaintance, Sylvia had attempted to draw out the older woman, thinking her in need of a friendly ear and, like Sylvia, eager for the companionship of a sensible woman. But that was before she knew who she was and, more importantly, who she was mother to. "I'm sure it is, my lady," she murmured, lowering her eyes respectfully.

Lady Wharton clucked her tongue. "None of that now. I'm Lizzy."

"Forgive me, my lady, but it would not be correct or proper for me to address you with no consideration for your position in society."

"Who would know tonight?"

Sylvia gulped. "Your son would not approve."

Lizzy threw her hand up. "My son is well distracted by his own concerns most of the time. I'm sure he hasn't given what I do a single thought in many years."

"That's terrible."

"That is the way of sons. They forget they mean the world to us when they come of age."

"I would have thought he'd be kinder."

"You and me both," she said sourly.

Sylvia quickly took a sip of water, praying her hand remained steady as she calculated how quickly she might take her leave without giving herself away.

Sylvia was still reeling as Lizzy, Lady Wharton, spoke of her eldest son by his title, marquess, in the most candid fashion. "Of course, like any son, he refuses to oblige his mother and marry, too." Lady Wharton took a sip of her wine, and then another. "It's anyone's guess where my eldest might be tonight. I'm sure he's set his servants to watch over his sisters so he can slip off to parts decidedly unsavory. I know the company he keeps is unsuitable."

"I'm sure he hasn't abandoned his sisters so quickly."

"He's just like his father before we met and married. His head is easily turned by a pretty face or a scandalous party, but he'll never find a proper wife that way. My eldest is far too puffed up and self-important to pay his family the attention they deserve. But they will need him very much, soon, I'm afraid."

How strange that Wharton could seem one way to Sylvia and another entirely to his mother. She might argue the good he's done for others recently, but what point would that serve? It would only reinforce Lady Wharton's belief that he cared about everyone but her. And the longer they talked, the greater the danger of revealing more than she should. "I only have my cousins now, and I've always enjoyed their company immensely."

"It is different when you are a mother, and without your husband. You alone worry about your children's futures. You want them around but, even so, you do long for the day they are safely off your hands and settled with their own lives. I fear I will have to entrust that task to Wharton."

Sylvia chuckled softly, imagining Lord Wharton appearing even on the sidelines of the marriage mart. What a stir he would cause! "So do you intend to make the most of your family's absence from your life and kick up your heels?"

"Perhaps." Lady Wharton pushed her plate away, and a servant suddenly slipped into the room to take it.

"That was a wonderful dinner, my lady." Sylvia could have eaten more perhaps but with Lady Wharton finished, she ought to finish, too.

"I'm glad you enjoyed it. Shall we repair to the drawing room for tea?"

"Gladly," she promised, but rose with her stomach in knots. What if Wharton did come and call on his mother tonight? If he found Sylvia here, what would he do or say?

They made their way from the dining room to the drawing room and another servant shut the doors behind them silently. Tea had already been set on the low table ahead of their arrival. "Shall I pour, my lady?"

"Yes, just for yourself."

Sylvia thought that a little odd at first until she saw the marchioness head for the decanters of spirit lined up on a heavy sideboard. The lady seemed to enjoy spirits and had consumed quite a number of tiny glasses during the dinner she hadn't really eaten. "So what will you do without your family to stop you?"

"A great deal they will not approve of."

"Oh?"

Lady Wharton turned from the sideboard with another glass of spirits in hand. She cradled the small crystal sherry glass against her chest, and then drank it all, her mind obviously elsewhere.

Sylvia sipped her tea, perched on a chair, waiting for Lady Wharton to finish whatever inner consideration she was engaged in. After the tea was drunk, Sylvia would find a way to leave Lady Wharton sooner than she'd originally planned.

She set her teacup back in the saucer and Lady Wharton startled. "What did you say?"

"You were about to tell me of your plans while your daughters were away from you."

The lady blinked. "Was I?"

Sylvia swallowed. By rights, she shouldn't pry, however, there was something about the lady's demeanor that troubled her, and had troubled her from the start of their acquaintance. "No, but I must admit to great curiosity. There is something on your mind that worries you. I can feel it."

"Then you are more observant than those who've known me all their lives," Lady Wharton told her, and then inclined her head.

Sylvia set her teacup and saucer on the table. "What's wrong?"

"I will tell you, but only if you give your solemn vow to keep that knowledge to yourself until I release you."

Lady Wharton returned to the sideboard and refilled her glass as Sylvia considered the request carefully. What Lady Wharton did was truly none of her business, and yet something prodded her to agree to her terms. Sylvia knew the value of keeping secrets in a competitive society such as the *ton*. "I will not tell a soul, I swear."

"On your mother's grave?"

She nodded but then dread washed over her. What was she about to learn?

Lady Wharton moved to sit at Sylvia's side. She raised her free hand to her right breast and rested her fingers there a moment. "There is an unnatural growth, here."

"Oh, my," Sylvia gasped. "Are you sure?"

The woman nodded decisively. "I have consulted with several doctors and they all agree it is increasing in size." Lizzy took a long sip, and then her attention settled on the far side of the room. Her face, finally, relaxed enough to reveal the awful terror she must be feeling. It was only a brief glimpse, and then it was deftly hidden by a wry smile.

No wonder the marchioness had hardly eaten a bite at dinner. She must be so afraid, so in fear for her life that she had no appetite at all.

Sylvia took Lizzy's glass and set it aside. Then, presuming a great deal on the woman's tolerance, she took up both Lady Wharton's hands in hers and tried to warm the chill from her fingers. "What can be done?"

"They say my best hope is removal."

"Surgery?" Sylvia flinched away from the notion. "That would be very dangerous."

Lady Wharton patted Sylvia's hand, and upon release, picked up her glass again, only to find it empty. "Yes, it will be, I expect."

How could she sound so calm? "What does Lord Wharton say?"

"I have not told him."

Sylvia gaped. "Why not?"

Lady Wharton's chin lifted but her lips trembled. "Because he is much too busy to talk to his mother."

Sylvia shook her head. "He must be informed."

"No." A furious expression crossed her face. "I have tried to speak with my son alone for the past year, and he has avoided me. Now, it is much too late to influence my decision to go ahead. He will not be informed until afterward."

"But your daughters will surely tell him."

"They, too, ignore their mother in their own way. My daughters prattle on about having suitors, and pretty new dresses, and never notice my pain. If I told them now, they would not be a comfort to me. They will try their best to stop me, or delay me, so their lives are not inconvenienced."

Sylvia's emotions reeled again. How cruel to have a family ignore you so completely you'd confess your worries to a stranger you met just a week ago. "Are you not afraid?"

Lady Wharton stood suddenly. "I am terrified."

She went to the sideboard and, upon consideration of the decanters, returned carrying one with her…and a much larger glass. She sat them on the table before them and her hand shook as she poured herself a fresh glass.

"You must tell them. You cannot endure something like this alone."

"I will," Lady Wharton insisted.

Sylvia considered the matter. "I'll go to the marquess myself tonight, I know where he lives. I can tell him what you intend to do and bring him here to comfort you."

The woman glanced at her coldly. "Will you now? Do you always forget your promises when they become inconvenient? You promised to keep my secret. Was I wrong to place my faith in you?"

Sylvia gulped. "But Wharton will be furious if he is not informed. With me, too. Not that I matter to him, of course."

"I will not give him the opportunity to stop me or decide who is to doctor me at this late stage. Every day I delay brings the risk of failure and certain death closer. Everything is arranged for tomorrow morning."

"Tomorrow morning!"

"It must be done."

Sylvia studied the woman, the determined set of her jaw as the bleakness of her stare returned. "How long have you known you would do this now?"

"A few weeks. I made arrangements to have the surgery performed in London, here in this house, so I could have the best physicians attend me." The woman looked at her sourly. "Did you believe I'd let just anyone cut into me on a whim?"

"No. No, of course not." Sylvia took a breath. "I'm simply astonished by how unconcerned you sound."

"I assure you, I am not at all calm, but the spirits help tremendously," she said as she drained her glass.

Sylvia rushed to refill it.

"Thank you, my dear," Lady Wharton said as she leaned back. She put her hand beneath her breast a moment, a slight wince crossing her features briefly. "I will be under the care of ten experienced butchers and their underlings."

"Surgeons," Sylvia whispered in horror. It was not a given that a person could go under the surgeon's knife and expect to live to tell the tale later. There would be great risk and unimaginable pain for the patient. Lady Wharton would suffer, and suffer without support. That was a terrifying prospect to her, but Sylvia put her own distress aside in a bid to understand. "What exactly are they to do?"

"They will brandish their sharpest knives and cut off my afflicted breast."

Sylvia blanched. "All of it?"

"All of it. I hope they can." Lady Wharton sipped again. "The lump has increased in size very quickly. It hurts to wear stays already, and my arm gives me great difficulty at times, which is why I no longer dance or enjoy the carriage. Too much jostling about is painful. I've no other choice but to have the lump removed from my body."

"You could die," she whispered. Such surgeries had been done, she'd heard, but the risk was enormous. The chance of infection great afterward. The loss of blood would make recovery a difficult and lengthy process.

Lady Wharton should prepare her family. She should not try to go through this alone just because her children were selfish.

"Yes, but I'm dying regardless" the marchioness conceded. "I prefer to hope I can be saved and live to see my grandchildren grown."

Was that all she cared about? Seeing the next generation born had often been a topic of conversation between them. Sylvia hadn't been asked for her opinion about the surgery but, given a choice between early death and a chance of one much later, she too might take the same risk with her life.

She captured Lady Wharton's hand and squeezed. "If you will not call your family to keep vigil, I'll stay with you," she offered.

"I cannot allow that."

"You must have someone, and if not your family, then you have me." She quickly considered what might happen on the day of the surgery and afterward. Lady Wharton would not be in any fit state to make her wishes clear. "The surgeon's will need to speak to someone who is capable of making decisions on your behalf. You might not be able to talk to them. And your care afterward? Who will decide when to inform the marquess that you will be all right or not? You cannot leave a servant to convey that sort of news, especially if you were about to die. He—they would be devastated."

The marchioness considered her a long time and still shook her head. "It will be an ugly business. I cannot ask someone to see or hear what happens to me tomorrow morning. I expect I will scream very loudly."

Sylvia shuddered at the thought of what she'd volunteered herself for, but she wouldn't back down from her promise now. "You didn't ask me to stay. I offered," Sylvia reminded her friend. "I will be at your side tomorrow morning, and nothing you say to me now will change my mind."

The woman who Sylvia had befriended on a whim without knowing her connections burst into ugly tears there and then.

Sylvia soothed her, stroked her back, and when Lady Wharton turned away, they pretended the outburst had never happened.

Lady Wharton drank more spirits until her glass was empty again. "Thank you."

Sylvia glanced around the room, at the darkness of the entrance hall, and shivered. The emptiness of it now made her afraid for tomorrow, too. Lady Wharton shouldn't be alone the night before her surgery. She should have her family around her, but she was too proud to beg for their attention. Sylvia understood but she didn't like it.

She stood. "I need to write a letter."

Lizzy glared at her.

"To my cousins, Lizzy. I have to give them a reason why I will not return home tonight or they will worry. I know just what to say not to rouse suspicion, I promise. I will also need a few things sent over so I can stay with you until you are on the mend."

"Over there." Lady Wharton tossed her head toward a far desk, and sank back in the chair, nursing her drink.

Sylvia hurried to the writing desk and, finding paper and ink, quickly scrawled a note to say she had been invited to stay with her new friend for a few days. She made it sound like a holiday of sorts to cheer up the lady. She did not mention who Lizzy really was in her letter.

Sylvia didn't have time to explain everything so she left a great deal out. However, she had told them already that the lady she'd met in the park was melancholy. They would be pleased just to know Sylvia could help, and that she was doing a good deed. And since she was close by still, they wouldn't be the least bit concerned or think to pay a call. She'd write to them again in a few days.

Sylvia sent the letter off with a hastily summoned servant, and then returned to Lady Wharton's side to keep her company. The marchioness had poured yet another glass for herself, and had procured a second glass, too. "Indulge me?"

Sylvia took up her glass. "What is it?"

"Brandy."

She took a cautious sip. "Ooh, at least it is not as strong as gin. A few sips of that and I'm not fit for company."

"Gin is in that far left decanter. Remember where it is for after the surgery."

Would there be an after for Lady Wharton?

Sylvia shook off the terrible thought that there might not be and raised her glass high. "To victory over adversity."

"Victory." Lady Wharton smiled dreamily now. "If you don't mind, I would like to overindulge tonight so I don't have to think about tomorrow."

Sylvia drank deeply, feeling the burn of spirits slide down her throat. "Indeed we both will," she gasped out.

Lizzy studied her glass, and then lifted it again. "To the only brave woman I know in London."

Sylvia took a hasty sip before she burst into ugly tears, too.

Chapter Thirteen

Alexander put a finger in his ear to dim the sound of his sisters' squabbling over nothing again, and then gave up trying to be subtle. He put his hands on the breakfast table and rose slightly. "Enough! Silence the pair of you before I lock you in your rooms for the day."

Amelia and Jocelyn stared at him in shock.

But they were finally, blessedly silent, and that was all he wanted. "Eat your breakfast."

He sat again, tugging down his waistcoat, and resumed eating. The news sheet was open at his side as it always was. He preferred to read at least a quarter of it before he left the breakfast table and began the real work of managing his vast interests.

The silence lasted all of two minutes. Silverware tapped on a breakfast plate. "Mama never yells at us," Amelia accused. Amelia was the eldest of the pair, and quite prone to pouting about the injustices she believed she suffered in life.

"Our mother is too much of a lady to yell at anyone," he replied.

"Except that one time in Bristol when you nearly walked into the path of that carriage," Jocelyn teased.

Jocelyn was very good at pointing out everyone's flaws. For that reason, she was an absolute disaster around other people.

He'd had to carefully choose from a limited number of social engagements so Jocelyn didn't risk offending everyone in London in one season.

"I did no such thing," Amelia exclaimed, her voice rising to a shrill tone that really stabbed into the mind. "It swerved toward me."

"I certainly saw it coming," Jocelyn claimed. "I would never have been struck, but you were done for that day."

"Quiet," he warned.

His sisters never stopped squabbling. In the short time of having them under his roof, a total of three days now, he'd come to remember all the reasons why he didn't spend much time in the country with them. Competitive and often petty-minded, they'd not uttered a sensible or civil word in days. He was already regretting bringing them here to stay and wishing he could send them back to his mother.

But he'd made a promise to watch over the silly twits for a few days more still, and he always kept his word. Besides, if he did send them back to Mama too soon, he'd just be giving her additional proof of his so-called disinterest in his family. He was a busy man, but he had perhaps slacked off a bit in spending time with this pair. For good reason, mind—he was saving his own sanity.

Making a good marriage for them quickly, as mother wanted, was no easy task but it was growing in appeal daily. His sisters were a full decade and more younger than him and, to his mind, almost too young to have their wings clipped in wedlock. Yet it was often all they talked about with any great enthusiasm. Perhaps marriage would lend them maturity they currently lacked. But not just to anyone. Alexander had standards. He would not allow them to go off with the first man who asked. They had to be good men, from good families, with steady temperaments and limitless patience to deserve a place in his family.

Surprisingly, Mother's choices had won him over from the first meeting. Lord Barnaby Miller and Sir Fredrick Mosely were leading the pack at the moment. Still, it wasn't wise to rush into any decision too soon.

Alexander was supposed to escort the girls to a luncheon later today, and then go on to a dinner before a ball tonight. It was another busy but tedious day ahead for him, watching over this pair.

"What are you reading?" Amelia asked.

"*The Times.*" He glanced at his sister with hope. Perhaps a sensible conversation was possible still with Amelia, if not Jocelyn. "Do you want it when I'm done?"

"Oh, no. I might get dirty ink on my fingers and clothes." Amelia appeared horrified by that prospect. "Mama says a lady must always keep her hands and gloves clean and tidy."

Amelia was the most interested in her appearance of the pair. She had always been responsible for the highest portion of the dressmakers' bills. Jocelyn favored practical gowns over something new or daring.

"I'm sure she's right," he murmured, hope disappearing. The pair had been given the best tutors, governesses, and nursemaids money could buy. Yet neither one had an interest in reading anything but the notes they slipped to each other. He turned the page. "Eat your breakfast."

"Mama says you're a great reader."

"It is a requirement of being a marquess," he murmured, turning another page, and then he glanced at his sisters. He didn't really know them well. "I have a great interest in other people, too, and their opinions."

"Mama said you don't care to hear ours, though."

He sighed. "That is not true, but I do like a quiet breakfast. I often read while eating."

"Mama says that's not good for your digestion," Amelia warned.

"No, it's hurrying right after eating that is bad for you." Jocelyn regarded him through narrowed eyes. "Reading at the breakfast table is just plain rude."

Alexander sighed and put his paper aside. Obviously he'd never continue his usual routine while this pair was under his roof. Only four more days until he was free again.

He studied his sisters' grinning faces across the table and reminded himself that he did love them every now and then. He'd been the first to hold them and was sure he'd never dropped them on their heads. He'd taught Amelia how to play hide and seek. Then later, he'd shown Jocelyn all of Amelia's best hiding places. He conceded he might have had something to do with their competitive natures. "Right. Now you have my full attention."

They looked at him expectantly. "What shall we talk about, brother?"

"We could talk about Bristol," he said, sitting back in his chair and stretching out his long legs. "How did I never learn you were there? And *when* were you?"

The girls shuffled their chairs closer to Alexander's along the table until they were very nearly on top of him. "That's close enough," he warned. They were much too old to sit on his knees like they'd done as infants.

"Oh, I think it was this time last year," Amelia suggested.

"No, it was later," the other swore. "Not in summer, but the weather was cool. Remember we kept running through the fallen leaves and our governess got that terrible pain in her side. And she left us right before winter had set in."

"It was just us and Mama at home for Christmas. You didn't come," Amelia said, and then pouted.

He winced. He'd had a lovely Christmas with friends last year for a change. "Whom did you stay with in Bristol?"

"With no one," Jocelyn said in great excitement.

"Mama didn't visit anyone we knew before," Amelia explained. "We even got to pretend to be someone else, too."

Alexander blinked. "I beg your pardon."

"She was Mrs. Lennox, and we were her daughters, Amelia and Jocelyn. I'm glad she let us keep our own given names."

"Why would she not use her married name?"

"She said it was a secret. We *were* supposed to visit Aunt Hermione in Bath, but Mama changed her mind and we went to Bristol instead."

Had Alexander known any of this? He didn't think so, which was unusual. "I guess Mother's letter explaining all this must never have reached me."

"I suppose. We had so much fun, Alex! Mama said we had to pretend to be of the lower classes."

"But not too low. She wouldn't allow us to curse like a sailor could," Jocelyn added. "She said you'd be cross about that."

"I would have been." Alexander rubbed his neck. Having his sisters sitting on either side of him and taking turns competing for his attention was exhausting. He wriggled his shoulders to ease the ache and pushed his chair back another few inches from them. "So where did you stay?"

"At a hotel," Amelia blinked. "Do you know they let anyone rent rooms if they have enough money?"

"Yes, it's not unusual." Alexander wasn't liking what he was hearing today at all. Mother was supposed to inform him when she was traveling away from the estate, or changed her plans while traveling. "What did you do there?"

"We took long walks and slept late and went to bed early."

"Mother was the only one who kept Town hours," Jocelyn noted. "She absolutely wouldn't allow us to stay up late. We wanted to keep her company."

"And she talked to so many low people, too. Strangers."

Alexander bit his tongue. His sisters had lived a sheltered life in the countryside and often spoke without thought at times. But he was sure Mother would not have consorted with anyone truly unworthy. Her origins had been quite humble before her marriage, after all. She was more than aware of the need to maintain a spotless reputation for the sake of her daughters' futures. More so than him, perhaps, Mother was always concerned with appearances.

But he was still a bit puzzled by his sisters' recollections of their holiday, and Mother not using her title in Bristol. "Where was our brother?"

"Gone off about his own business." Jocelyn colored a little. "Mama said we were better off not asking or thinking about what he does with his time."

Mother could be very wise at times. If their brother was up to his usual tricks, and their sisters found out, they would tell simply everyone about what he'd been up to. Especially the low places and low friends he might choose to consort with. The pair couldn't keep a secret if their lives depended on it, which was why he preferred them in the country so they did not unwittingly interfere with his interests in London.

God help their poor future husbands if they tried to keep any secrets.

"Or yours, either," Amelia said shyly. "We were absolutely not to pester you for an introduction to any female acquaintances of yours."

"Why's that?"

"In case they were light-skirts." Jocelyn frowned. "What's a light-skirt?"

Amelia giggled into her hand as Alexander choked.

"Any woman Mama doesn't approve of, silly." Amelia told her sister with a superior air. "I'm sure our brother doesn't want to talk about them," Amelia smirked, her eyes alight with mischief.

Alexander studied Amelia through narrowed eyes. She might not be as smart as he would like, but she clearly knew about light-skirts already somehow.

A footman appeared in the doorway, and Alexander almost cheered with relief at the sight of any other member of his own sex. "What is it, John?"

"Flowers have arrived for Miss Amelia, my lord."

Amelia bounced in her seat and squealed with happiness.

"Bring them in," Alexander urged. He'd welcome any distraction at this point.

Amelia danced about until a modest bunch of Hyacinths arrived in the room, and then she gushed over them excessively. There was a note from the sender, and of course it was read out loud immediately. "I had so hoped Barnaby would remember my favorite flower."

"That's *Lord* Barnaby, Amelia," Alexander warned. Amelia had too quickly adopted her young suitor's given name in all conversations.

"Oh, he doesn't mind," she promised. "I'll have to call on Mama and tell her about the pretty bouquet he sent me," she gushed.

"No, you will not." Alexander was in no mood to ferry his sisters back and forth between here and Mama's rented Berkley Square townhouse. "There will not be enough time today."

"Oh," Amelia moaned. "I'll write her a note instead then. Is there flowers for my sister too, John?"

"No, my lady," the footman murmured with an apologetic wince.

Jocelyn appeared crestfallen at the news.

"But that's not fair," Amelia cried in protest.

Alexander quickly waved the servant away. "I'm sure your suitors have not forgotten you, Jocelyn."

Jocelyn's lower lip quivered and she nodded, lifting her chin bravely.

Managing two sisters and their suitors, and their wildly spinning moods, was bloody challenging. Mama certainly deserved this peaceful week without all this nonsense. "Save up all your news for when you return to Mother's household in a few days."

"We have so much to tell her," Amelia gushed. "I hope she'll let us stay up late to finish it all."

"If she's not tired again," Jocelyn added, still sounding a bit low.

"She just needs another holiday," Amelia declared, pouring herself another cup of tea. "I know. Let us convince her to visit Brighton after the season is over."

"We tried that before already," Jocelyn warned, refusing another cup from her sister.

"That's right. She said she'd be too tired to take holidays after this season." Amelia offered him the teapot. "Alexander?"

Could no one remember he didn't like tea? "No, thank you." Forgetful creatures or not, Alexander liked his sisters. He liked that if he were patient enough, they'd tell him anything he wanted to know. "If Mama was so tired, why did she come up to London then?"

The pair shrugged. "I've no idea," Amelia promised. "One day she just decided she'd had enough of the countryside, and now here we both are with you."

Jocelyn sighed and leaned forward, resting her chin on her hand. "I wonder where Mama's gone?"

Alexander absently corrected her table manners by knocking her arm out from under her chin. "You should know better than that, Jocelyn," he chided. "And what do you mean, gone?"

Jocelyn sat back, hands folding neatly on her lap now, and heaved another sigh. "I sent my maid to fetch a ribbon Amelia was sure she'd left in the library there, but the girl was sent away. Very rudely, too. That ribbon was very much needed yesterday."

"Mother never said she was going out of Town," Alexander

mused aloud. But maybe Mother was hiding from her children the way he'd found *he* wanted to do in the last few days. He still had a few hours' worth of work to do before he escorted his sisters anywhere, and he was stuck here talking nonsense.

John reappeared at the door, bearing a large bunch of hothouse roses before him and a grin. "These have come just now for Lady Jocelyn, my lord."

Jocelyn didn't wait for them to be delivered to her. She was on her feet and round the breakfast table in two shakes of a lamb's tail.

"Oh, my, just look at the exquisite color!" she cried. "Exactly the shade of my gown the night we met."

Amelia joined her, but kept a distance. "They're pretty, but they are roses."

Then she sneezed. And sneezed again.

"Oh, dear. I'll keep them in my room," Jocelyn promised, rushing off to admire her flowers in private.

"Every single time," Amelia complained under her breath as she sneezed again and again.

Alex rose quickly and handed her his larger handkerchief. "Perhaps you'd better retire to your room, too, until the spell passes," Alexander suggested, patting her back. He knew it wouldn't help the girl, but it was all he could do at a time like this.

She nodded quickly and, after collecting her own bunch, departed the room in a rush, leaving Alexander entirely alone at last with his paper and what remained of breakfast before he really must tackle his work.

Sylvia wiped her brow with the back of her hand, weary to the bone. She'd never been more tired or afraid for another person in her life. She turned and set her back against the bedchamber wall and tried to hold back her tears. Lady Wharton's surgery—more like butchery—had been performed three days ago, and the lady was showing no sign of improvement. Quite the opposite, in fact.

The physicians, now only a pair, consulted with each other in whispered tones and made sounds that were not reassuring. Sylvia was terrified the marchioness might never recover.

She eyed the door, considering if it was time to break her promise and inform the marquess.

She swore to never again make rash promises when someone was putting their life in danger. Even if there had been a glimmer of hope the first day.

Given how often the remaining physicians wore constant frowns now, and frequently checked Lady Wharton's wrist and brow every hour to see if her fever was abating and pulse improved, it probably hadn't.

Lady Wharton lay pale and largely unresponsive, save for her breathing, which at times seemed very loud or almost undetectable.

She was going to die.

Sylvia clenched her teeth together as her eyes prickled with tears yet again. She should have told Lord Wharton what his mother had intended before the surgery had even begun.

She angrily swiped away the tear that slipped down her cheek and went to rinse out the warm cloth she'd been clinging to. She dipped it in cool water, wrung out a little and refolded it loosely, ready to begin again. Keeping vigil over a dying woman was the only thing she could do now to ease her conscience, and that didn't feel even close to enough.

She crossed the room back to the bed. The physicians had shuffled out into the hall and watched on with sad expressions. Lady Wharton's eyes fluttered as the cloth was placed on her brow, and then she became still. So horribly still.

After her earlier tortured screams, the silence was unnerving.

No matter what Sylvia said or did, the woman did not respond to her questions.

After the operation, after the horrible ordeal that Lady Wharton had screamed through, she'd barely made a sound. The strongest memory Sylvia had of the operation was when the physician had paused, nearly deciding to stop altogether before they had removed the growth. The marchioness' eyes had flashed open, and she'd ordered them to finish what they'd started.

Lady Wharton was the strongest woman she'd ever known or ever would. Sylvia couldn't bear the thought that her pain might be for nothing. She leaned down to whisper in her ear, "Lizzy, please don't go away. I'll never forgive myself if you don't get better."

She pressed a kiss to the back of the lady's clammy hand and eased down in a chair set close beside the bed. Sylvia hadn't slept in days, and she wouldn't until this ended, one way or the other.

She pulled a blanket up to her chest, not for warmth but for comfort, not that it helped very much.

One of the physicians came to stand behind Sylvia. "She's not doing as well as I would like."

"Then help her," Sylvia bit out savagely. She looked up at the man quickly and winced. "I apologize for that outburst, Mr. Prendegast. I don't hold any grudge against you for her current condition. I know how tirelessly you worked. But…"

The man nodded. "It is very hard to watch a friend suffer and feel helpless to do anything about it."

"Yes, it is hard to bear when I could have, should have, informed her family."

"She made us all swear that promise," he murmured. "Though it went against the grain, my colleagues and I agreed to her demands. Unfortunately, all we can do now is wait and hope."

"That is hard to do a second time."

Prendegast walked round the bed and picked up Lady Wharton's hand gently. "I take it you've sat with a loved one about to die before?"

Sylvia steadied her emotions when they threatened to overwhelm her utterly. Not even these men really believed there was more than a glimmer of hope.

She pulled herself together savagely, determined to see this through. "My father fell down a set of stairs a few years ago. He broke a leg, and they say a rib or two. He never fully recovered and died soon after."

"I'm sorry for your loss." The man winced. "It is a hard thing to watch a parent expire."

"It happens all the time," Sylvia noted, but not like this. She couldn't accept anything less than a full recovery. Lady Wharton had promised she'd recover, and Sylvia would hold her to that. "She just needs time."

"I hope you're right. You should get some sleep soon, Miss Hillcrest. There isn't anything we can do but wait."

Sylvia shook her head. "I promised to stay with her, and I will."

Keeping vigil, applying cool compresses to Lady Wharton's brow, dribbling a little water into her mouth every hour, and challenging her to wake up was all Sylvia could do to keep her own spirits up. Sylvia had kept the same vigil for her father. She had wanted her father to die in the end, but not Lady Wharton. There was still a chance she could recover. She was strong—strong-minded, too—and had wanted to survive this. Father hadn't.

Lizzy had to live to see those grandchildren she so desperately wanted come into the world.

When the physician slipped away, Sylvia adjusted her chair and took hold of Lady Wharton's hand again. Perhaps she'd close her eyes for just a moment. If the lady roused at all, Sylvia would feel the change and wake to see to her every need.

Chapter Fourteen

"What do you mean, she's not receiving? Why?" Alexander demanded.

Mother's butler lowered his gaze respectably. "I regret that is all I am allowed to say, my lord."

"Where is she?"

"Lady Wharton is not at home, my lord."

"Damn that woman. She's gone and left me with her children and absconded to enjoy herself somewhere else." Alexander turned around for the door but then shook his head.

No, Mother would never have left her daughters to make a match with just his help alone. She'd want to plan their weddings, as she'd always threatened to do with his. "No. I do not believe a word of it. She's hiding from me."

The man stared at him, but offered up no other hints to her whereabouts except for a slight coloring of his cheeks. He was lying. Most likely the butler was under orders to say nothing of her whereabouts, even to him. Alexander turned for the stairs. "She's probably sulking in her room. I'll find her myself."

"My lord, you cannot go up there!" the butler protested. "I promised."

"Try and stop me," he urged, taking the stairs two at a time in his haste. It was high time he took his mother in hand and stopped all the nonsense he'd allowed to go on for too long. She should never have taken a lease on this house. She should have written to him about her desire to come to London. He would have made all the necessary arrangements. They should be escorting his sisters about society and vetting their suitors together, not him alone.

Alexander had not been upstairs in this house before, but the master suite was most likely in the front of the townhouse overlooking Berkley Square. He headed there first.

A pair of oak doors were shut against him, and he grasped the handles to throw the pair wide, then looked around eagerly.

But Alexander was confronted by the sight of a middle-aged gentleman rolling down his sleeves beside a curtained bed.

Alexander staggered back a few steps. "Who the hell are you?"

"Quiet!" the man cried, rushing toward him, one hand raised. "Keep your voice down, sir."

Alexander was not about to comply with that request. "I'll talk as loud as I like, and you will explain yourself, sir. This is my mother's bedchamber and it's the middle of the day. Have you no honor?"

Another middle-aged fellow was suddenly standing beside the first, arms full of bloody rags, and looking frankly terrified of Alexander. "My lord."

The pair were complete strangers to him, but at least one had the wits to know he was speaking to a peer. Alexander directed his attention to that man only. "Where the hell is my mother?"

Silence reigned until a frail female voice called out, "Let him pass."

The doctor's immediately stepped aside.

Alexander walked around the bed—and then swore out loud.

The frail woman he'd heard speak was his own Sylvia Hillcrest, and his mother was...

He stared at her shrunken form in the bed, and his breath caught. Swaddled by bandages and propped up on the bed, Mother lie deathly still. He glanced sideways at the man holding the bloody rags. "What has happened?"

The first physician rushed to his side and began to whisper, "The surgery was a complete success, but recovery has been slow. Very slow indeed."

Alexander blinked at him. "What surgery?"

The doctors explained, and after the first rush of words seeped into his brain, Alexander had to fumble for a bedpost to support himself. He was appalled. "Did you not think to inform me?"

"It was the marchioness' express wish that you not be informed until we were certain she would die or live," the second man announced. "We remain hopeful, my lord."

For the first time in his adult life, he didn't know what to do—and he didn't like it. "Leave me," he ordered, and the pair, after a brief consultation, scurried from the room together.

"They must return to care for the wound," Sylvia informed him, wringing a piece of cloth between her reddened fingers. She stood, crossed to the basin, and wet the fabric from a jug. "She has a fever and has not spoken since the surgery took place."

"Why are you here?"

"I'm very worried about her."

"You're worried about her?" he bit out savagely. "Do you think that I would not be?"

Sylvia lifted her gaze to the window, and the view of Berkley Square. "I tried to persuade her to take you into her confidence, but she refused to consider it. Made me promise not to tell anyone her business."

"You should have known better than to make any promise's like that!"

Sylvia shrugged and returned to the bedside. She lay a cool cloth over Mama's brow and sat down in the chair by the bed. Her head turned a little toward him. "You might find it easy to deny your mother, but I'm not so cold-hearted as you must be. She knew the risk was great, and that she'd struggle to survive it. It was the only way for her to live a long life, and she made me promise not to tell anyone—especially you."

"You should have sent for me immediately."

A flicker of contempt touched her expression. "She was adamant that you were not to be told. She did not want anyone to see her like this, especially you. If I broke that one promise, should I be willing to break the one I made to you, too?"

"That's different."

"It is exactly the same to me." Sylvia turned over the damp cloth on his mother's brow and leaned close to her ear. "Open your eyes, my lady. He's finally come to see you, if you haven't heard him shouting at everyone yet. You don't want to miss him while he's here."

Alexander studied his mother's features but saw no sign of a response to Sylvia's request. Sylvia sat back...and he was astonished to see her wipe tears from her face. "I had hoped your presence might bring her round finally. Half the square must have heard you yelling by now."

Alexander set his jaw and glared. This woman presumed too much to speak to him in such a way. Didn't she appreciate the gravity of her reckless disregard for good sense? She had conspired with Mother to keep him in ignorance, and blamed *him*. He'd known she wasn't like other women, but this was beyond the pale. "What is it you want from me?"

She seemed taken aback. "Nothing at all. But you should start acting like her son and give a damn about her welfare before she's gone."

He ground his teeth. "I would have if she'd informed me of her intentions."

Her expression hardened. "She tried for a year to speak to you alone about this, but you were always too busy for private conversation. She gave up trying to reach you and made this decision on her own. Surely you must have sensed her distress? I only found out the night before the operation because I dared to pry into her long silences."

Alexander would not be berated by the woman who'd lifted her skirts to him. "And that is another thing. How dare you ingratiate yourself with my mother just to get close to me again?"

"Do you really think so little of me? I suppose you must." She shrugged again. "I became friends with her before I knew she was your mother."

"Then you should have withdrawn that friendship."

She shook her head. "I could not sever our friendship the night before her surgery. Not even for you. Your mother was terrified. Besides, it's not as if what you and I shared was more than a fling."

"It certainly isn't now."

She smiled tiredly, and then lifted a watery gaze to his. "I cannot understand how you don't want to be around the woman who gave birth to you. She is so brave, witty, and so very lonely, too. You should love her."

"Of course I love my mother."

"Prove it. Give her what she wants before she dies."

He bristled at her demand. He didn't know what confidences Mother had shared about her life, and his, but there was one topic Mother simply would not be quiet about—*him* making a match. "I'll not be blackmailed to marry you."

"I don't want to marry you!" she claimed. "All your mother wants is for you to *see* her. To be part of your life. Open your ears and stop being in such a hurry about everything. Women like to know they have your attention, and would it hurt you to display affection? You're lucky to have her."

Alexander was not accustomed to being dressed down by anyone, least of all a woman who'd lifted her skirts for him once. "How dare you. Get out. Leave."

"No." Sylvia lifted the cloth from Mother's brow and stood. "I promised Lizzy I would stay until she was on the mend, and I will not break my word. Not now."

The use of his mother's nickname, and Sylvia turning her back on him, made him see red. He would *not* be ignored. Sylvia had gone too far and needed to be taught her place. Defiance must be quashed immediately. She would learn he was a man not to be trifled with. "If you won't leave of your own accord, I'll do it for you."

He captured Sylvia and easily lifted her into his arms. He held her tight against his chest...but then his feet refused to obey. Dull, tired green eyes turned up to his, luscious pink lips trembled, and he fought—with some difficulty—the urge to kiss her.

Giving into passion, in any form, was not the way he'd assert his authority with her.

He hardened his heart, threw his chin up high, away from the temptation of her mouth, and pivoted to face the door. As he headed there with her nestled snug and warm against his chest, she started up a weak protest by kicking her shapely legs. "Wharton, what are you doing?"

"Asserting my rights," he promised, trying not to look down as he firmed his grip. The woman's curves still appealed to him, and even though he'd had her once already, he was still tempted. He fought her appeal for all he was worth.

"Someone will see us together. Put me down!"

He shook his head. He wouldn't relent. He was too annoyed with Sylvia, too worried about his mother to care about anyone seeing him like this. To say he was upset was an understatement.

It didn't matter that Sylvia had been on the mark about his failures with his family. That didn't mean he had to like hearing it from her.

The best solution was to put a distance between them as quickly as possible. He continued with his original destination in mind and carried her to the head of the staircase.

"Where are you taking me?"

"I'm putting you out for the night."

Silence reined, long and awkward. Alexander risked a peek at Sylvia's face and saw mulishness written all over it.

"I am offended by that remark," she nearly growled at him. "I am not a cat."

"But you do have claws," he noted, thinking of how pleasant it had been when her nails scraped over his bare back when they'd made love.

More words came out of her mouth then, but Alexander closed his ears to her and concentrated on not tripping down the stairs and killing them both. Sylvia might have been a quiet and polite woman once. Now, though, she squawked and complained all the way to the front hall without pause.

He would be seeing to his mother's recovery personally now with no help—interference—from her.

Mama's butler materialized before him in the hall, startled and gaping, and Alexander ordered the front door opened.

"My lord, really," he cried. "Is that any way to treat a lady?"

It was how he was going to treat this one, for the time being at least, whether she liked it or not. He was pleased when the butler finally did as he was ordered, but Sylvia redoubled her struggles in front of their audience as soon as she saw the world outside. She was a slippery little morsel. A woman he'd like to tame if he had the time.

"Put me down, you great beast of a man!"

He did. On the townhouses front steps.

The moment Sylvia seemed steady on her feet and met his gaze, he shut the door in her face.

Fists pounded on the wood. "Wharton, no! Let me in. Let. Me. In!"

"Not a chance." He looked around with satisfaction, feeling he'd won a significant battle.

The butler backed away, eyes wide with fright.

Alexander jabbed a finger in his direction. "Never let it be said that I'm not in charge here. Do not let that woman through that door again or I will throw everyone else out, too."

The butler gulped. "Yes, my lord."

Alexander rushed back up the stairs. The physicians were milling in the hall, so he urged them back into Mother's bedchamber and demanded a retelling of the operation, and everything that had happened up until that very moment.

According to them, Sylvia had first appeared at Mother's side on the morning of the surgery, three days ago. She'd taken no part in Mama's earlier consultations. The physician's had tried to dissuade her from staying but Mama had wanted her to remain, so she had.

"My lord, your mother is a very ill woman."

His mother lay barely breathing upon her bed. Her chest was so thickly bandaged, her bosom seemed twice the expected size to him. And Alexander was completely unnerved by the way she lay so deathly still. "Why isn't she awake?"

"The surgery was very hard on her," he explained. "She had fainted well before it was over, but now perhaps the shock of it…the pain she suffered has proven too much for her mind."

Alexander swallowed the lump forming in his throat before he attempted to speak. "Will she really recover? The truth, if you please."

"We don't know, my lord. We hope."

He nodded slowly, reeling still but grateful for their honesty and optimism.

The pair shuffled their feet like naughty children. "We were against the marchioness not telling you about her troubles."

He remembered, then, Sylvia's accusations of neglect. "When did she decide on this course of action?"

"We first discussed her concerns over a year ago."

A year? So Sylvia had been telling him the truth there, too. How had he missed the signs Mama was unwell?

He studied his mother…and then lowered his gaze, filled with shame.

Mother had tried countless times to get him alone, and he'd fobbed her off with excuses, promising to talk later. He'd not gone home for Christmas because he was sure she only wanted to discuss marriage and the succession. He'd ignored her. Neglected her.

He'd neglected one of his most important responsibilities.

If he'd not been so impatient with her, she might have been spared so much pain.

"We?"

"My lord, perhaps you would allow us to start at the beginning." Alexander nodded. "Your mother came to me after feeling a lump in her breast last season. She said she had pain when her maid laced up her undergarments too tight, and that her arm, too, seemed afflicted at times—tender and heavier than the other. The lump was examined as best could be managed with dignity then, and upon her return visit, it did seem to have increased in size in the half a year since the first discussion.

"I recommended your mother visit a brilliant man of medicine in Bristol last year for a second opinion. After a discreet meeting between them, he regretfully confirmed my fears. After consulting with my colleagues over the winter, and a further examination by other learned men of similar vocation, we all concluded that surgery to remove the lump might be her ladyship's only chance to avoid certain death."

Mother had spent a year fearing for her life, while he'd been enjoying his own.

It did not surprise him now that Mother had been pushed to make such a decision on her own. She couldn't have waited much longer for him to find time for her.

Alexander moved to the side of the bed and picked up his mother's limp hand. He couldn't remember the last time he'd actually held her hand, but her skin was hot to the touch today. As much as he might have tried to avoid her in the past, he didn't want to lose her. "Did you succeed?"

"Indeed, yes. Our colleagues were quite excited to view so

large a specimen," the first man enthused.

"How large? No, don't answer that." His stomach clenched with worry and revulsion.

The second fellow, obviously more attuned to delivering bad news with tact, shushed the first fellow. "We do understand the need for protecting the sensibilities of family members, but I must tell you that the extent of the growth was more than we anticipated, and made removal of the entire left breast absolutely necessary."

Alexander nearly gagged but held it in. "You could have killed her."

"Your mother was well aware of the risks involved, and she took her time in deciding to go through with it. She could not be dissuaded, and has provided letters absolving us of any wrongdoing, should she perish."

"How good of her," he said in tones dripping of sarcasm.

The second fellow threw a warning glance at his colleague before he spoke again. "The next weeks will be crucial. Lady Wharton needs rest and loving support if she is to find strength."

"For what?"

"To decide whether she wants to live or not," the second man announced. "We have heard of similar cases where the woman passed away shortly after the surgery concluded. But Lady Wharton is strong-minded, and perhaps her strength of character, her stubbornness, if you will forgive our use of the term, can help her endure."

The first man cleared his throat. "What has become of Miss Hillcrest?"

Sylvia was the least of their concerns. Right now, his mother needed them to put her care first. "She will not return."

"We are very sorry to hear that."

"If Miss Hillcrest is gone, we will need to engage a woman to act as nurse," the first man interjected in a worried tone.

"See to it." Alexander turned from them. "I will stay with Mother for now."

"Yes, my lord."

The pair moved toward the door, talking between themselves, and Alexander heard them clearly deliberating the likely cost and trouble of finding additional servants quickly.

"Perhaps a pair of women would be best now," one remarked. "At least one should remain by Lady Wharton's side at all times until she wakes."

"We certainly could not expect just one to remain awake when Miss Hillcrest could not always keep her eyes open, but the expense?"

"We've been compensated more than enough," the second fellow warned the first. "Leave the hiring to me."

The first fellow sighed. "Such a shame to lose her, though. Lady Wharton will be disappointed to wake and find her friend gone."

Alexander glanced at the door, annoyed the pair could not be quiet, still. Mother would hardly know of Sylvia's absence in her current state. And when she did—because Alexander couldn't imagine her not improving—he and Mother would discuss many things, including Sylvia and their unwise friendship.

When they finally moved out of earshot, Alexander dropped into the chair Sylvia had so recently vacated close to his mother's side and searched her face. "How many times have I warned you to be wary of pretty young women offering you friendship? You will come to know why Sylvia wormed her way into your heart soon enough, Mother. She's not the proper lady you thought she was. Those soft smiles and gentle touches of hers were artfully done to reel us both into her confidence. She deceived you, and betrayed me utterly. We're better off without her, aren't we?"

Mother said nothing to that, and Alexander leaned back in the chair to study every breath his mother took, hoping to glimpse some sign of a change for the better soon.

Chapter Fifteen

Sylvia twisted and stretched, suddenly waking in the dark. The last thing she remembered was Wharton, furious with her at the door of his mother's home.

Sylvia sat up quickly and looked around, discovering she was at home, in her bedchamber. "How did I get here?"

Aurora rose from a chair beside the bed. "You walked, or should I say stumbled and sobbed your way through the door."

"I did?" She looked around again. "How long have I slept?"

"Just a day."

Sylvia blanched. "It feels like only a moment has passed since…"

She looked at her cousin warily as she remembered more details of the previous day.

Aurora looked back at her steadily. "Yes, we already know what you were a party to. You've been keeping secrets from us again. I thought we promised each other to be honest."

"It wasn't like that," Sylvia swore. "I wanted to tell you everything, but she insisted on privacy."

"That's what Eugenia knew you'd say in your defense," Aurora complained. "We know a bit of what transpired, so how about you tell me all of it now before I decide if I should be cross with you, too."

"She…

"Lady Wharton. A wealthy marchioness, and our social superior."

Sylvia nodded. "After dinner that night, she revealed to me that she would be operated on the very next morning. She refused to tell her family anything about it. She was afraid and alone and too proud to ask for their support. I couldn't leave."

"Oh, Sylvia," Aurora chided. "That great big heart of yours is a magnet for lost causes."

"She needed a friend."

"She has a family." Aurora stood, leaned over the bed, and gave her a huge hug. "I hope that friendship means as much to her as it does you. Perhaps if she recovers, our reputations might have a chance to survive the damage your actions have caused," Aurora whispered.

Sylvia blinked. "What damage?"

Aurora sighed. "You were seen being thrown out of Lady Wharton's house by the marquess himself, her son. Word has spread like wildfire, and none of it good. Your hair was half falling down, grown crumpled, and you were yelling and screaming like a madwoman at the door you pounded on, too. You were in such a state that your condition was noticed by many members of the *ton* passing through Berkley Square at that hour, and your behavior has managed to offend every single one of them.

"There is speculation that you were attempting to seduce the marquess, which is why he threw you out and banished you from ever returning. Others mutter that they knew you were utterly unbalanced all along and might be a danger to society. And there are many other variations along those lines, I imagine, each one more implausible than the next."

"I hadn't slept in days! I'm not mad. I promise. I was overwhelmed with fear."

"That is what we easily deduced when you couldn't go three steps deeper into the house without crying that you had to go back. You've always hated to cry in front of us."

"I have been doing a lot of that since the operation took place." Sylvia winced. "I didn't expect to be thrown out. Lord Wharton had no right to manhandle me out the door like that, too. I wasn't myself, and neither was he, I imagine. He had a shock."

"You forgive him far too easily," Aurora said, and sat down beside her on the bed. "You should have warned us of what you were doing there. At least we would have known what to say when someone approached us for an alternative explanation that didn't cast you in the worst light."

"I made a promise not to."

"Keeping promises is a risky matter in society." Aurora reminded her, but then shook her head. "What is the one thing we warn all our clients about?"

"That gossip is always a wild exaggeration," Sylvia whispered.

"No, Sylvia. It is that everyone too easily believes the worst of women."

Sylvia nodded, utterly aghast at the certainty of that statement. "It will all blow over as soon as he calms down."

"I don't think so," Aurora said. "While Lord Wharton was never known to be a client of ours, his actions have put the devil into those who are, or might have been in the future. No one is really sure what transpired between you, and they don't want the truth anyway. But what they *do* know for a fact is that you angered an important man. Lord Wharton disapproved of you yesterday, and that means he disapproves of us all today. We have been on the receiving end of scathing criticism by letter this morning. Accusations that would curl your hair. No one can cross the Marquess of Wharton, apparently, and expect to survive in his society."

Sylvia clapped her hand over her face. "I was there for his mother. Only for her!"

"And the mother is so ill, said to be dying. She cannot set matters right until she's well again, even if she wanted to."

"I'm sure she will. Has there been any news of her?"

"The blinds are drawn. No one has come or gone from the house all morning. The servants cannot even be bribed to tell the truth. Everyone waits for the worst, I suspect." Aurora sighed again. "Sylvia, do you understand the depths of our disgrace? We have no clients, and likely might never have any again."

"I'll talk to the marquess. Explain. Beg his forgiveness." Sylvia scrambled out of bed and rushed to the mirror. Her hair was tangled and knotted, pushed up on one side from her sleep. She dragged a comb through the mess quickly, feeling that she must go back right away to confront the marquess and try to set things right again. "When she recovers, she will confirm my story."

"You will do no such thing! I forbid you falling to your knees before that heartless lout. I remember what you said about Lady Wharton's son before you must have known who she really was. I have no sympathy for the marquess. *None*. He's neglected his dying mother for years."

"He didn't know that."

Aurora turned Sylvia forcefully from the mirror and took the comb from her. "You've always had such great faith in those you befriend in the *ton*, but we could never really be one of them, could we? As soon as we put one toe out of line, they washed their hands of all of us without justification. You have been uninvited to *ton* events, and I, for one, am glad. I know we pushed you to make friends there."

"I can't abandon her now!" Sylvia cried. "What are we going to do?"

"I don't know, but Eugenia wishes to have a family meeting as soon as you have changed and eaten. We have no clients to see, so no rush at all," Aurora promised, starting on Sylvia's hair. When it was smooth and neat again, twisted into a bun, she put the comb away. "I'll send a maid to help you dress and bring you something to eat. Eugenia and I will be in the library, reading there for a change when you're ready to talk."

Sylvia caught her cousin's arm before she left. "I never meant for any of this to affect you."

"I know, but we can't pretend our lives haven't changed," Aurora said, wincing. "You were our presence in the *ton*, our flawless ambassador, and now you've been turned out. It was only a matter of time I suppose. I'm sorry."

"I am too."

Aurora slipped from the room as Sylvia fumed silently. She only had herself to blame. Society were sheep, and Wharton one of their most admired leaders. If he'd shown his disapproval of her anywhere but on the front step of his mother's house, she might have survived with only a slightly dinted reputation. But he'd used his superior strength to express his annoyance and had tossed her out like refuse.

Should she even blame him for acting as he had? She should

have told him. She would have but for that unthinking promise she'd made to his mother. She hadn't been the only one, though. Lady Wharton had made her physicians sign a letter promising not to send for the marquess while she still breathed, or they wouldn't be paid. Money always had a way of ensuring loyalty.

Sylvia hadn't needed to be bribed. The lady had a claim on her affections.

Sylvia gnawed her finger, wondering how she could possibly salvage the family business and restore their reputations. Unfortunately, every idea she came up with hinged on Lady Wharton's complete recovery, and Sylvia had no way to ensure that happened.

She put her head down on the bed and let out a muffled scream into her pillow. She should have never become friends with the mother of a marquess. He was too powerful, too stubborn. She might never win him round.

There was no point lying in bed, castigating herself, when there were decisions to be made for her family. She had the means to solve part of their problems, though the others didn't know it yet.

She got out of bed and summoned a maid. With her help, she dressed in a bright yellow muslin gown to cheer herself up, ate well when the promised tray of food arrived, and then squared her shoulders to face up to her responsibilities. This was her mess, and she'd do all she could to make things right for her cousins.

She fetched her old reticule from its hiding place and hurried downstairs, straight into the library.

Eugenia was behind the desk, fingers running over the ledger. Even from the doorway, Sylvia could tell the news would be bad. They kept an accounting of the business and their inherited fortunes in the same book. There never had been very much to go around.

"Good morning, cousin," Eugenia murmured. "I hope you are prepared to discuss the future."

"Indeed I am." Sylvia sat, holding her reticule tightly in her hands. "Where do we stand?"

Eugenia rested her elbows on the desk and her chin on her fingertips. "I see you are in no mood for small talk. Very well then. Since Aurora tells me she has already shared our predicament with you, I'll get straight to it. We have a few outstanding client fees to receive yet, and we are in good shape for the season, the summer, and into the autumn. But without new clients coming through our doors, I fear our income will fall short of our needs again when winter comes," she announced.

"No, it will not. Not this year."

Sylvia upended her old reticule on the desk.

Inside had been all her winnings from the games she'd played and won in the last nine months, the largest addition coming from attending Lord Wharton's little gathering recently.

Aurora bounced to her feet and gasped. "Where did all this come from?"

Eugenia glanced up, frowning severely. "You assured me you would limit your presence at the card tables."

"I had to fit in." Sylvia slid a few pound notes around. It wasn't a fortune, but it would all be needed. "I saved and saved everything I've won since last season, to make sure we wouldn't have to spend another winter apart again."

Aurora started piling it up and counting how much additional money they had now. Sylvia could have told them the tally, but counting the money themselves would make them understand and appreciate what she'd done for them. Counting her winnings always helped Sylvia when doubts about the future assailed her.

Aurora finished and sat back, staring at the piles. "This is a small fortune. Why did you not tell us sooner?"

"I was worried it might be used for the wrong purpose. You've always insisted I had to dress to fit in with higher society. New gown and hats, presents for new friends and such. I didn't want it wasted on them. So I saved up for a rainy day in secret, and I was right to in the end," she murmured. "There has ever been a chance that our venture would prove insufficient to our long-term support."

"Who did all this belong to?" Eugenia asked, clearly still disapproving.

"To a great many entitled members of society. Don't worry. I never ruined anyone. They hardly noticed the little losses, and that is to our advantage now."

Eugenia counted the money herself, too, and added that figure to her tally. She heaved a sigh and sat back. A small smile played over her lips. "You have saved us a great worry."

For one year perhaps, but not for all the years ahead of them. Sylvia was painfully aware that if she'd really been cast out, she'd no longer have the same access to society, with its incumbent opportunities to gamble. This might be her only and largest contribution to their household. In the future, they would still need a steady income unless they returned to the countryside and to their former quieter lives.

Aurora hurried round the table and hugged her tightly. "Thank you," she whispered.

Sylvia squeezed her back, glad for proof that one of her cousins appreciated her skill at cards. Eugenia wasn't fond of anyone who gambled, as a rule, which was understandable, since her only brother had been a wastrel and had died leaving her family penniless.

Gambling really was Sylvia's only true accomplishment. She couldn't sing, act, or play an instrument. She embroidered only passably well. But in a room thick with vice and frequent poor judgment, she could always hold her own.

Aurora started to pace the room. "Now the immediate future is settled, I think it is time we consider an alternative to matchmaking for others."

"We were never matchmakers," Sylvia protested.

"We were advisers," Eugenia declared, puffing out her chest. "We did well at that."

"But not well enough. And now London society is closed to us. Quite frankly, I don't think we can ask Sylvia to go back out there to charm idiots into liking us again. It could very well be an uphill and fruitless battle."

Eugenia nodded. "I am willing to listen to new ideas for what the future should hold for us. What did you have in mind?"

Aurora put her hands on the desk and studied them both. "We have been having fun helping others make matches for a year, and for what? A pittance in funds that will soon run out again. My suggestion is that we devote all our energies, and not inconsiderable talents, to finding a spouse for one of us."

Sylvia studied her cousin carefully. That was quite a reversal of opinion. "But you said you never imagined being married. You were quite vocal about it, too, before we even came to London."

"I have had some time to rethink my position on matrimony. I might have been wrong. We each still have our inheritances but that money won't last all our lives. As frugal as we have been, the funds won't last. So we need a husband. But since we are sensible women, we won't require an obscenely wealthy husband. We're not hunting a title or fortune but we do need just the right man. Someone willing to have us under his roof and accept us all. After all, two of us only need food in our bellies and a roof over our heads, though the husband must favor highly the one he weds. One sensible marriage is infinitely better than three terrible ones and separation. I've grown tired of being in a constant state of panic over what happens to us next."

Sylvia narrowed her eyes on her cousin. "How long have you been thinking about this?"

"Oh, not at all long."

"It shows." Sylvia sat forward in her chair. "That is the most unromantic thing that's ever come out of your mouth. I will not be involved in such an unfeeling scheme. I could never marry a man I did not love with all my heart, and I would expect no less from either one of you."

"But one of us must consider marriage as a means to our survival."

Sylvia pinched the bridge of her nose. "Oh, cousin. You can't really mean for one of us to marry so coldly."

"I would do it for all of us if I had to," Aurora promised, chin rising. "I think in the next few days, we must find out which of our clients still support us in some fashion, and then we should encourage them."

Sylvia gaped. "You want us to marry our clients?"

"Surely one of them should do? Or perhaps one of our past clients has an unmarried brother who's well off. I can't be without you again. You're all I have."

Sylvia exchanged a glance with Eugenia to judge what she thought of the idea. Eugenia appeared speechless, so Sylvia stood and moved close to Aurora and hugged her tightly. "I love you too," she whispered. "Did you pick out a husband for yourself already?"

"No, but," her gaze switched to Eugenia, "I thought with

Eugenia being the eldest, she should have first pick. She probably knows who would make a good husband already."

"I do not have a favorite, and I am not in the market for a husband," she said crisply.

Aurora took a deep breath, and then nodded. "Well, then there's nothing for it. We put the name of our favorite into a hat and choose among ourselves who will have him."

Sylvia shook her head, "I am not going to do any such a thing. You know how I feel about marriage. It's love or nothing for me, and not one of our current or former clients could claim my heart. I guess I'll stay a spinster forever then."

A man cleared his throat—and then all spun about to face the door.

Only Sylvia knew the man, and she gaped. "Mr. Prendegast?"

"Well, I have to say after hearing that, I'm not sure whether being already married is cause for celebration or regret, Miss Hillcrest." He shuffled awkwardly.

But Eugenia was suddenly standing in front of the man, hand extended in greeting. "My younger cousin has an extraordinary fondness for taking ideas to extremes. Pay her no mind. I assure you, none of us are seriously considering matrimony as a means to our salvation."

She smiled upon Mr. Prendegast, and the man stared back, seemingly mesmerized by Eugenia looking at him so directly. She settled her other hand over Prendegast's and stoked his skin like a lover of old.

Sylvia hid a smile as her cousin's actions deftly wrapped the unwitting man round her dainty fingers with just a few gentle touches. Eugenia had a talent for handling married men. She could charm them into doing anything she wanted without them even knowing it. Of course, it worked best on men who were unhappily married and ignored by their spouses.

Prendegast suddenly shook himself. "I'm very glad to hear such a scheme merely idle speculation."

"What else could it be?" Eugenia gently withdrew her hand. "How may we help you?" She spun about and took her customary position behind the desk.

The man blinked, coming out of his stupor at last. "Yes, well. I do hope you will forgive my unexpected arrival at this late hour."

He kept his attention on Eugenia, and Sylvia found it impossible to catch his eye. "What are you doing here? Is Lady Wharton all right? Is she awake at last? Is she—"

The man threw his hand up to halt the flow of Sylvia's words. "Lady Wharton's situation is unchanged, I'm afraid."

Sylvia nearly collapsed in relief. "Then what are you doing here? How did you find me?"

"I spoke to her maid, and she was kind enough to give me your directions." He frowned. "I came here hoping we might find a way around a particularly thorny problem I face."

Sylvia swallowed. "What problem?"

"In all my time caring for the dying, I've never met anyone with greater compassion than you. I believe you want to be at the marchioness' side still, and more importantly, she expected you to still be there now. Unfortunately, the marquess has forbidden anyone to allow you through the front door. But you are exactly the right woman to help care for the marchioness as the end draws near."

"He won't stop me trying to see her again."

The man grinned. "I was hoping you'd say that. I think, too, I have found a way around his restriction, but it is not at all an honest endeavor. But I've no choice. I've come today because I have a proposition for you, Miss Hillcrest. One that should meet both our desires to care for the marchioness. Unfortunately, there's bound to be additional risk to your reputation if you are discovered. I saw what happened. I believe the marquess' anger has brought ruin down upon your heads unfairly."

"A trifling matter easily resolved once the marchioness recovers," Eugenia assured Mr. Prendegast with a saucy smile.

The man's face reddened. "I'm sure of that, too. The lady was quite taken with her friend, which is why I feel confident she would approve of my desire to help you return as soon as possible. Today."

"I would like that, but..." Sylvia glanced at her cousins, seeking their permission. Sylvia's reputation was in tatters, the family business shut down. Her cousins were supported for now and the future was still up in the air. But Sylvia had given her word, and keeping her promise to Lady Wharton was important.

Eugenia sighed. "You have to go, if only for your own peace of mind."

She smiled at Mr. Prendegast. "What did you have in mind, sir?"

Chapter Sixteen

"I think that bonnet will make you look fat," Amelia whispered somewhat callously to their younger sister behind Alexander's back.

"It's better than yours," Jocelyn hissed. "It's so hideous it will drive all gentlemen of taste away."

Amelia choked. "Barnaby likes my choice very well. He even complimented me on the extraordinary colors yesterday when he came to call on you."

Jocelyn, who'd revealed her partiality for the young lord, laughed. "He was shading his eyes at the time."

"That's so mean," Amelia cried.

"You started it," Jocelyn muttered.

Alexander pinched the bridge of his nose as the bickering continued. Despite the best education possible, his sisters were often silly twits about certain things. They constantly bickered over nothing and, after only a few days of listening to them, he was contemplating arranging their murders.

Or hasty marriages that sent them as far away as possible.

He marveled that his mother had put up without complaint— or voiced too few. And the greater wonder still was that Mother had found any suitors for his sisters at all, given the way they talked to each other. But their callers seemed oblivious to their shallow minds and kept coming back.

Alexander turned around to face the pair. Amelia and Jocelyn were not cut out for the sickroom. He had already severely limited their time there, hoping to somehow instill concern and worry for their mother's welfare in them. A few days of near silence had been all the reprieve he'd been granted before they'd returned to form. "Keep it down."

"Yes, Alex," the pair murmured, eyes lowering in contrition.

Alexander hadn't been sure bringing them back to Mother's townhouse was a good idea, but they absolutely couldn't be left at his home alone without his supervision. Why, the day he'd found out about Mother's condition, he'd returned home briefly after being gone a few hours, and he'd discovered Amelia and one of her less-favored suitors enjoying a private tête à tête behind a partially closed drawing room door.

Amelia had seemed bewildered by his initial ire, but the young man was wiser and utterly guilty of trying to take advantage of his sister while he was out. The fellow had quickly fled Alexander's wrath, and Alexander didn't expect to hear of him calling on Amelia again anytime soon.

Or he'd better not.

Alexander had made his opinion of the man quite clear. Scoundrels could not court his sisters.

So there had been no option but to bring them home to Mother and seriously curtail all future interactions with suitors in the future unless he could be present. They hadn't liked him for carting them back to Berkley Square, but they claimed to understand the need to gather round Mother during this crisis.

Alexander had had time to decide who among their suitors was acceptable, surprisingly agreeing with Mother's original choices, and he had written them, informing them of their change of address and the unfortunate reason for the move. Both gentlemen had shown a gratifying concern for Mother's welfare and for the rest of the family.

He turned back to face Mother and sighed. She was not doing as well as he wanted, and he'd no idea what to do next to help her. The wound was said to be healing, with no sign of infection so far. That was the only good news he'd really had about her health.

"Do you think Mama would like us to sing to her?" Amelia asked in a low tone meant only for Jocelyn to answer.

"I don't think we should. Alex insists we be quiet now," Jocelyn reminded her.

"But Mama loves our singing," Amelia claimed a little too loudly.

"Shh," Jocelyn warned. "I'm not going to sing until Mama says she'd like to hear me herself. What if she has a bad head again?"

"Yes. She does often say she can feel a headache coming on in the mornings."

Alexander nearly laughed at that. Mother most likely had meant the pair was causing her headache to grow, only they didn't understand that. They never stopped talking until they were fast asleep, he suspected.

Alexander suddenly reviewed their last conversation, and realized to his shock that Jocelyn had finally found her voice after years of deferring to the older Amelia. Would wonders never cease? Perhaps there was hope that Jocelyn might turn out all right, after all. Alexander wholeheartedly approved of any newfound independence from her and hoped it continued. Sooner or later, his sisters' lives would be very different and lived very separately from their siblings, when they were brides.

Mother would probably miss them not being at home with her at least a little bit of the time, he supposed.

He turned the page of the book he'd tried to read all morning but soon lifted his head again to study the woman lying so still in the bed for the third day…or sixth from the day of the operation. Every year of her one and sixty years was showing on her familiar face this morning. He still couldn't imagine a world where he didn't have to answer to Mama for his shortcomings as she saw them.

He wished he could turn back the clock and have Mama recuperating at home at Wharton House where she belonged. But he'd been warned that Mother could not be moved under any circumstances for quite some time. So he was stuck here waiting on her to recover.

He'd had his valet pack up a few trunks of his clothing, clear his schedule, and had moved himself immediately into this tiny townhouse. A great number of his important documents from his study had come to this house as well because he could not, ever, neglect the estate or be idle for long periods of time.

He'd sent off men to try to find his brother, but didn't expect to see him back in London anytime soon. Toby would be almost as useless in the sickroom as Alexander was, and much too loud, too. But Alexander still wanted him close to hand should the worst come to pass and they lost Mother.

He glanced over his shoulder. His sisters were quiet again, working on their hideous bonnets by the window. They smiled as they compared their work, and it was as if the earlier disagreement had never happened.

They never held a grudge.

He stood up, stretched his back, and put his book aside by the door to take back to his room later.

Something also had to be done about Sylvia Hillcrest, and soon. He couldn't get the blasted woman out of his mind.

He kept remembering her defiant little face as she'd argued with him over Mother, kept hearing her moans of passion every time he closed his eyes for a few minutes' rest. How had someone he'd thought so unremarkable once become someone he couldn't seem to forget? He didn't quite know if he wanted to put her over his knee or put her on her own again.

Perhaps it was a little of both. And perhaps he was simply too tired to make sense of his feelings right now.

Alexander cocked his head when a knock sounded on the front door below, and he listened hard. He had arranged for an hour or so of peace for himself, and Mama, too, by default. Since yesterday he'd been inundated with letters from concerned acquaintances, offering support and hoping to hear good news. From that number, he'd called in a few favors in a bid to distract and amuse his sisters.

He waited impatiently for the butler to arrive to announce the first one—Lady Norrington and Lord Barnaby Miller were scheduled to take his oldest sister Amelia out driving for an hour.

The butler eased into the room to whisper the announcement a few moments later.

"May I please go?" Amelia begged, casting a worried glance toward their mother.

Alexander pretended to consider the matter then gave her a

nod. "Very well."

Amelia jumped up to kiss his cheek and then flew out the room, her hideous bonnet going with her. Jocelyn watched her go in silence, and then flounced into a chair—clearly disappointed to be left behind. However, Alexander hadn't forgotten Jocelyn. He was simply waiting for the next callers to be announced, Lord and Lady Carmichael, and Sir Fredrick Mosely.

When the Carmichaels came in their carriage, asking for Jocelyn's company, he suffered another enthusiastic kiss on the cheek.

He glanced at his pocket watch, disapproving of Sir Fredrick Mosely, who seemed to be running late to join them. But when Alexander strolled to the window, he was just in time to see Mosely rushing up the front stairs and knocking upon the door.

Alexander reveled in the silence of a nearly empty house. But eventually his sisters would return, and he would have to endure more of them for a good long while without help. He couldn't start sending them to bed at eight o'clock like they were still little children just to get some peace. Something had to be done about them, and soon. Mama had insisted Amelia and Jocelyn were ripe for marriage. Only now did he understand why she'd considered the matter of their marriages so urgent.

He wished he'd understood before she'd done all of this to herself.

"Well, that's them gone for a few hours, Mama. Let's enjoy the silence while it lasts. Mosely isn't so bad once you spend a little time with the fellow. He isn't brilliant or clever. But he's earned your approval, so that counts for a lot."

"It took you long enough to get rid of them," his mother whispered suddenly behind him. "I was starting to fear I'd have to suggest it myself."

"My God!" Alexander spun about to see Mother lift her fingers in a wave. Alexander's eyes stung with the first tears he'd considered shedding in two decades, and he rushed to her. "Mama! What took you so long?"

She stiffened. "Don't shout, boy. I'm in terrible pain here."

He caught her hand. She was warmer than she'd been before but not feverish anymore. "What can I do?"

"Water."

He found a glass, poured water into it, and carefully lifted her head enough that she could take a few sips. "More?"

"Wine next," she gasped. "Lots of wine, I think."

He already had a glass of his own, so he held that to her lips rather than leave her for a single moment. Mother drank it all and then lay back, gasping for breath.

Her breathing took some time to quiet and grow steady but her face became clouded by pain. He smoothed his fingers over her cheek very gently. "Mama, why wouldn't you tell me what you were doing?"

"You would have tried to stop me."

"Damn right. I would have succeeded, too."

"That's why I didn't tell you." Her eyes fluttered open again, and her gaze darted about the chamber. "Where's my girl?"

"I'm afraid Amelia and Jocelyn won't be back for an hour." He left her to refill his glass and returned to the bedside quickly.

Mother's eyes were narrowed on him. "I meant the other one. Fetch her to me."

Alexander was fairly sure Mother was referring to Sylvia Hillcrest. It seemed Sylvia's professed friendship with his mama was a fact, and apparently reciprocated. "You'll be better in no time. Here, drink this."

"Liar." She huffed but sipped some more wine before turning her head aside with a groan. He waited patiently for her to speak again. "I intend to suffer for as long as it takes. Now what have you done with my Sylvia? She promised to be here when I woke."

"I sent her away," he told her.

Mama's jaw worked, and then her eyes flashed with anger. "You had no right."

"I have every right." He tried to hold her hand but she pulled away. "I am the head of this family, and while you recover, I will decide who you see and who you will not."

Mother narrowed her eyes on him in a look that hinted that she resented him. "I know why you're doing this."

"You really don't." He would never allow Mother to find out the truth about Sylvia. If she even suspected Sylvia had been his lover, and using her, she would feel humiliated. He couldn't have that. "Now, you will lie there and do nothing so you get better. Do you want more wine to dull the pain you must be feeling?"

For a moment, he thought Mother would refuse in favor of continuing their argument. However, she wet her lips and her left hand gestured him closer. Alexander hid a grim smile as she guzzled the fresh glass, draining it before asking for another.

Once Mother was well on her way to being drunk from the wine and becoming drowsy again, he rang for a servant and gave them instructions for the evening. If Mother was awake and in pain, she'd need food and every comfort money could buy. His sisters could spend a few minutes with Mother when they returned but they would be spending the night in their own rooms.

He returned to sit beside the bed, and Mother's sleepy stare returned to his. "Have I ever told you how much you remind me of your father?"

"I look a great deal like him," he said as he took a sip of wine himself. He didn't care that she was about to point out all his flaws and failures. He was just relieved to have his mother back to speak of them. He'd never ignore her again. "You've told me that many a time."

"Not just that. I was talking about how his preoccupation with everything but family made him grow so cold and distant. It's hard to live through that a second time with you. But I suppose it's a relief, too, that no woman has set her heart on marrying you. You'd only break it. If she loved you, she'd be waiting in vain to claim any of your time, like I did with your father. I learned too late that his heart could never warm to me again."

He choked back a protest. He was not an exact copy of his father. He might have studied at his knee, but Alexander directed his own life and learned from the mistakes of others, and his own. Alexander was a busy man and always would be; he'd get around to marriage one of these days. And, too, Alexander had not yet discovered a woman he felt could carry Mother's title of marchioness with as much grace.

He'd only marry a woman who could accept him the way he was and didn't demand he change. So he hadn't married yet. He hadn't betrayed any wife of his by taking a mistress at the same time and ignoring her. That was what Father had done to Mother. She was still bitter about that after so many years a widow.

Alexander would ignore the comparison she alluded to; he was sure she would never be done with the subject until the day he was wed. But for now, Mother was not in any condition to choose her words with any sort of care or tact. "I was not aware that you felt that way about Father still."

"He only wanted me around when it suited him. Just like you do," she complained bitterly. "You helped pack me off to the countryside and forgot we needed you."

He sat up straighter. "I left you to manage the estate because I trusted you."

"You don't trust me," she complained.

"I wasn't the one keeping secrets, Mama."

"Everyone keeps secrets, you most of all." She shook her head and winced. "Fetch me a cold cloth for my head. I have the most dreadful pounding there."

Alexander was on his feet in a flash to wet a cloth.

When he returned, he draped it gently over her brow the way he'd seen Sylvia do it many days ago. "I'll make sure your *real* friends come and see you when you're feeling better."

"Don't you take that tone with me, boy. You're not my keeper." Mama tried to sit up but collapsed, gasping. "I chose to do this to myself, and she chose to put herself through the ordeal to support me. She didn't have to stay. I wish *she* was my daughter, because then you'd pack us both off to the countryside and stop interfering!"

This last was nearly shouted, but then his mother moaned in such a way that boded ill. Panicked, he bounced to his feet and checked for her pulse at her wrist as the physicians had often done. The pulses beneath his fingertips were fast and uneven but her breaths eventually slowed again to a more normal speed. Judging by her twisted expression, she'd done too much, too soon. Moved too much.

He held her hand as she pressed her lips hard together, and he didn't dare ask another question for a good twenty minutes or more. He settled into the chair as he waited, worried, but also relieved beyond measure for the short conversation they'd shared. She might be tired and in pain, but his mother was too stubborn to give up on her life. They would speak again later, when she felt up to it.

But now she was alert once more to her surroundings, he had better start thinking of the future. The nursemaid the physicians had hired was a flighty old matron in ancient rags and a cap, who disappeared the minute Alexander showed his face at the sickroom door. She'd have to be replaced before he could even consider taking Mother home.

When she eventually started to move around without help, the first thing he'd do was remove Mama back to Wharton House. There, he could keep a better watch on her recovery. Together, they would approve his sisters' marriages—when the fellows worked up the courage to ask for his sisters' hands, of course. But this time, when Mother grew difficult about his bachelor state and late hours, he would not allow her to get under his skin again. He'd listen and let her feel confident that her opinion wasn't just important, but without price.

They would work things out, for the good of the family. She would stay with him in London, and he might just spend more time in the country with her, too.

Given his renewed interest in taking care of his family, particularly his mother, he expected that fulfilling their needs would take up the bulk of his time for the foreseeable future.

Chapter Seventeen

Wharton finally disappeared from the house at dusk. Sylvia had watched and waited for him to leave his mother's room, as she'd done for the past three days and nights. The man was not indifferent to his mother, and clearly very worried about Lizzy. If only Lizzy had realized that before the operation, he could have been here with her instead of Sylvia.

Sylvia removed the thick glass spectacles she'd taken to wearing as part of her disguise and rubbed her tired eyes. In her guise of a nursemaid hired by the physician, Mr. Prendegast, the marquess had barely looked in her direction for all the days she'd been living as a servant in the house.

The family were beside themselves with excitement over the marchioness waking up today, and had started making plans for the future. A future far away from this house. But Sylvia knew Lady Wharton wasn't out of the woods just yet. There was always the chance of the wound reopening and infection setting in if she was disturbed too much. A trip anywhere was absolutely out of the question.

But optimism reined for the moment. The daughters, fresh from the excitement of their drives in the park with their suitors, had squealed like little children over their mother's recovery, spoke extensively of their time apart, and of their suitors, too.

One of them had sang and been hastily silenced by the marquess. In the end, in their unthinking excitement, they had jostled the bed the marchioness was lying in far too much and been reprimanded for that, too, and sent away.

At least Wharton was now taking charge, ordering everyone about and smart enough to give his sisters the chore of writing to all their friends with the good news their mama was recovering well from her recent indisposition. Though he'd warned them that their mother's recovery would take many months longer, Sylvia wasn't quite sure if they truly understood how different Lizzy's life would be for the coming months.

She put her spectacles back on, covered her hair with a lacy white maid's cap and quickly made her way downstairs. Sylvia had hoped to have an opportunity to be alone with the marchioness hours ago. But Wharton had confounded her and stayed, sitting beside his mother's bed the whole time. His attention had never wavered, not even when Sylvia, driven to desperation to see more of the patient, had slipped into the room with a pitcher of water that wasn't yet needed. Lady Wharton had been sleeping at the time, her breathing soft and regular in the quiet stillness of the sickroom.

Sylvia had tiptoed past the marquess without him speaking to her even once. Given the paleness of Lizzy's cheeks then, she guessed the fever must have broken sometime earlier that day.

Now, with the marquess finally gone, there was nothing to stop Sylvia fulfilling her promise to Lizzy.

She slipped into the room, shut and latched the door, and moved quietly to stop beside the bed. The marchioness appeared to be sleeping again, so she perched on the edge of the chair, biding her time.

The marchioness gasped, suddenly wide awake, and moaned.

Sylvia edged a little closer. "Lizzy."

The marchioness turned to look at Sylvia, and then frowned. "Who are you?"

Sylvia quickly removed her lacy cap and the pair of spectacles she'd perched on her nose to better hide her features from the marquess and grinned. "It's me. Sylvia. I've come to see you again. I am so very happy to find you awake and talking at last!"

"Oh, you nearly gave me a turn." The marchioness' gaze

flickered over Sylvia and then down at the cap and glasses. "Why do you look like a maid? I hardly recognized you."

"That's the point," she whispered. "Your son was a bit incensed about things."

"As I knew he would be." Her gaze narrowed. "I asked for you, but he wouldn't say where you'd gone. What did he do?"

"It hardly matters."

"It matters to me," she protested.

"He refused to let me see you."

"And yet…" The marchioness glanced toward the door. "You are here dressed as a maid."

"A disguise was the only way to deceive everyone." Sylvia wet her lips. She did not want to get the physician in any trouble, but it was only because of him that she had any chance of getting past the servants. She'd only planned to stay until Lizzy's fever broke and she'd had a chance to talk to her again, and say goodbye. "I can't stay, I'm afraid."

"You only just got here."

"I'm sorry, my lady. It's not possible for me to remain. You see, the marquess does not approve of me right now, and I have to go before he comes back from wherever he's gone." She gestured to herself. "I had to resort to deception to slip past your servants and catch a glimpse of you for the last three days. Please don't ask me to explain how my being here came about. I really don't want to get anyone in trouble. Your son must believe I'm just another servant hired to look after you. A nursemaid."

"An ugly one in that costume, too. I never would have recognized you, and I never forget a face." Lizzie chortled, but then gasped and groaned in terrifying pain.

"I'm so sorry," Sylvia cried, horrified she'd unwittingly been the cause of the lady's discomfort. "What can I do?"

The marchioness subsided against the pillows with a subtle shake of her head. "Oh, that was unpleasant, but it's good to know I'm alive enough to still have a sense of humor to be tweaked."

Sylvia shook her head, in awe of the woman she'd befriended. She'd put herself through so much pain and could still find life amusing. "The weather is *unpleasant*, Lizzy. What you've willingly endured is something quite different."

Lizzy scowled. "Are you always going to contradict me? I'm an ill woman. Be agreeable for a change."

Sylvia moved a strand of Lizzy's hair from her face. "Would you really have me do that to you?"

"I suppose not."

Sylvia got to her feet, opened a deep drawer close to the bed, and rooted around until her fingers touched a thick glass bottle. Sylvia had smuggled the spirits into the room a few days ago, on the off chance the marchioness might need a stronger drink than the wine she had been offered so far. She showed it to her friend. "I thought you might prefer a glass of this to help you with the pain."

"Blessed child, bring that here now. Wine is all well and good, but one must drink a lot to have any real effect," Lizzy said, fingers beckoning urgently. "I don't think I would like you as much if you were proper like everyone else tries to be. You think and act on your instincts, instead of worrying about offending. You are quite the original, aren't you?"

"So, my lady, are you." Sylvia, blushing from the compliment, poured the lady a large glass of the gin and helped her sip it. When the glass was well depleted, she sat back in the chair again for a moment. "You'll feel the effects soon, I'm sure."

"My son would faint if he knew I was drinking that dreadful stuff. Oh, it's awful, but strong enough I hope to give me relief from the constant ache."

"I'm not going to tell on you," Sylvia promised, giving her the rest of the glass. "This is entirely medicinal."

"My father said that often, always after he'd staggered back from the local tavern."

Sylvia's time with the marchioness was short. She measured another glass of gin for the woman and set it aside. "How is the pain now?"

"Constant, but better for seeing you at my side once more," Lady Wharton promised. "I'll have to do something about that."

"But not today. He's gone out, for how long I don't know, and I want to hear about *you*. They say there is no sign of infection, but we cannot be too careful. I know it's hard but you must rest as much as you can bear."

The marchioness pulled a face. "I knew Wharton wouldn't

stay."

"Actually, Lord Wharton has hardly left your side in three days," Sylvia confided, feeling she must do something to avoid further estrangement between mother and son. "This is the first time he's left the house since I began my ruse. He certainly does care."

"For now."

Sylvia soothed the woman's hand. "Give him a chance to change. You gave him a great shock, and he's finding his way slowly. I'm sure he'll be a better son to you from now on."

"He's had plenty of chances over the years," Lizzy insisted, closing her eyes for a moment. Her fingers rose to her chest and settled lightly beside the wound. Fearing any disturbance of the bandages might affect the healing of the wound below, Sylvia gently pulled her fingers away before Lizzy had a chance to scratch.

"People often don't change overnight, and sometimes we don't even see it ourselves, but he has cleared his schedule to be with you. He missed the Fratworth soiree, and a dinner with Lord and Lady Carmichael, and other things to do with his investments, too."

A frown had grown on Lizzy's brow, and she moaned softly again. She wriggled her shoulders as if trying to dislodge a discomfort. Sylvia quickly offered the gin again, and the lady drained the glass quickly. She lay still after that, appearing to grow somewhat drowsy, and then a smile lifted her lips. "How do you know so much about my son's schedule?"

Sylvia smiled back. "He wrote and sent off his excuses to a dozen families from this very room. I happened to overhear the directions he gave to a footman for their delivery."

Lizzy sighed. "While you were skulking about in that ugly gown and glasses?"

She grinned. "Precisely."

Sylvia suddenly became aware of activity on the street outside the townhouse. "I fear the marquess has returned," she whispered.

"Don't go yet."

"I'll try again to change his mind tomorrow," she promised but she clearly heard the front door open and close, and then heavy treads on the stairs coming up. "There's no time, but I will be back as soon as I can."

Sylvia donned her cap and spectacles, hid away the empty glass of gin and bottle, and set her head in her hand, pretending to be dozing in the chair beside Lady Wharton's bed.

The door creaked open slowly, and then closed again. Footsteps drew closer one slow step at a time. When Sylvia risked a peek, the Marquess of Wharton stood beside the bed opposite her, staring down at his mother. He wore a heavy frown, but hardly spared Sylvia a glance as he dismissed her. "You can go for the night. I'll stay with her until dawn."

"Yes, my lord," she muttered in her assumed accent, heaving herself out of the chair as if she was older and wearier, and departing the room with the marquess none the wiser still.

Chapter Eighteen

$\mathcal{A}$lexander hadn't spent much time in the sickroom during his life, but a week after learning what his mother had done to herself, he conceded that he wasn't cut out for the idle tediousness of keeping someone he loved company while they recovered.

Mother, too, was a worse patient than expected.

"Mother, I won't change my mind," he said for the hundredth time.

"I want to see her," she insisted.

He glanced at his mother's face, noting her color and overall appearance had significantly improved over the course of the last few days. If she'd not been swaddled in bandages, she might have jumped from her sick bed to pester him with the point of her finger the way she'd once done. However, Mama couldn't be allowed to exert herself that much. Even a slight shift of position caused her considerable discomfort she couldn't hide.

"If you will not heed me, I shall have to send for your physicians again."

Mama made a decidedly unmotherly sound, almost a curse held under her breath. "Oh, why don't you go walk in the square, or better yet, take yourself all the way to the House of Lords and play at politics again. Leave the nursemaid to take care of me."

"If I could find her," he grumbled.

The one day he'd made plans to go out was the one day she'd apparently found a better position. He'd had to conscript Carmichael into checking on the Norringtons' situation for him. The earl was always at White's on Wednesdays. Today was the only day of the week when he could accidentally on purpose run into the man's wife to see if their situation was still on the rise. Carmichael had grumbled he wasn't cut out for espionage, but he'd do what he could to get the answers Alexander needed.

"You're not getting rid of me so easily, Mama. Whether you like it or not, I will be supervising your recovery."

"You're bored."

"I am not bored." Well, perhaps he was a little, but he'd not admit to it to Mama. He'd already sunken very low in her opinion. "I am trying to make up for my lack of attention to you in the last years."

"I want to see my young friend."

Mother had been asking for Sylvia Hillcrest every day, every time she woke, for two days straight. She demanded to see Sylvia in her sickroom when it was just not possible. Sylvia had gone behind his back, concealed her knowledge of the danger to his mother from him. He couldn't trust her.

On top of that, he'd misdirected all his anger and fear upon her head and not thought enough of the likely consequences. He'd laid all the blame for Mother's actions on Sylvia instead of where they really belonged—on himself. He'd banished her, and the woman had taken her expulsion to heart. She hadn't returned or tried to call on Mother. Not that Mama was aware of that yet.

But Sylvia had certainly done a good job to worm her way into Mother's affections quite skillfully and quickly, too. Not an easy task, actually. He felt bad for Mother now.

"We will discuss this later."

"We will discuss this *now*," Mother demanded. "I'll not have you lord your title over me while I'm on my deathbed. I am your mother, boy. Do as I wish!"

"Yes, I heard you the previous dozen times you reminded me of that fact, and I'm sure you will not die given the way you are carrying on, too." He put his book aside and moved to stand at the foot of the bed. "You will learn to trust my judgment. You need quiet and calm. I don't want to argue with you anymore."

"Why should I be calm when you're being obstinate? When have you ever trusted *my* judgment?" she countered. "I am quite capable of making my own decision, I had to make many when your father was still alive and off with his mistress. Leave me in peace."

Alexander bit his tongue and practiced patience. They'd been going round in circles for days but he was just as stubborn as Mother. "If you had died under the surgeon's knife, what was I supposed to do or think?" he asked, leaning over her. "I'd never have forgiven myself. Should I have thanked Sylvia for keeping me away from you at such a time? Whether you like it or not, I see you now, Mama. I'm here to stay."

She stared at him, her jaw firming. He could tell she was working herself up to launch into another tirade. In any other circumstance, Alexander might have enjoyed a good battle of wits with her. But not today.

Today, Mama would do as he told her to do for once.

He leaned farther over her and dropped a kiss on her forehead. "I would have been devastated to have lost you."

Taken by surprise by his statement, Mother just stared at him for several long moments, and then looked away. "If I had died, I suppose you would have had one less problem to deal with. That is how you think of us. Your family. Siblings and me."

She wasn't going to forgive him easily or quickly. He deserved that, too. Alexander caught up her hand and held it gently. "I have taken excellent care of my siblings while you're recovering, and I will look out for all of you better in the years to come, too. I swear that I will."

Her expression soured. "You only had them under your roof for a week because I tricked you into taking an interest in who they married. A few mournful sighs and talk of your sisters' eagerness for marriage, and you just had to rush in to take charge. Like you always do. Like I knew you would."

He studied the woman who'd given birth to him in consternation. She probably *had* tricked him—playing upon his weakness for order and knowing everything. He'd been too busy to notice when Mama stopped bothering him.

Well, she'd not fool him again so easily, he vowed. "How

would I have reconciled my distraction with them if you had died? You are irreplaceable, Mama."

Alexander ground his teeth to hold back the anguish rising in his throat. He loved his mother dearly, he just never said so out loud, and it hurt him that she'd hidden her worries from him for so long. She'd turned to a stranger, Sylvia, and kept him in the dark.

"I am the head of this family. Only you don't seem to think my opinion matters. You made a reckless decision without consulting me."

"Not everything is about you, son." She took a breath and then closed her eyes. "I have this second chance now to live, to see my daughters married and happy. I chose life over a certain creeping death. You would have stopped me, and I would have died sooner than I might now."

He certainly would have halted proceedings at first until he had all the facts at hand. He wasn't certain what he might have done or said later. The very idea of her operation, of what had been done to her body, turned his stomach even now. He'd not viewed the wound himself, but the idea of it, the pain she'd endured, evoked enough terror to haunt him for years to come. "You chose to tell Sylvia and not me. Your own flesh and blood."

Her eyes opened. "A woman understands better than anyone another lady's fears. She proved herself quite strong-stomached in the end. I want to thank her and make sure she is all right."

Confused, he stared. "What could be wrong with her?"

"She chose to be with me for the surgery."

"Waiting in the hall? Yes, I heard the surgeons talking about what a helpful assistant she'd tried to be."

Mother's expression turned grim. "Not outside in the hall. She held my hand even as they cut into me. She never let me go. Never turned away. I fear in my terror and pain that I hurt her."

Alexander stilled.

Sylvia had not let on that she'd borne witness to the butchery performed on his mother in this very room. It would not have been a pretty scene or fit for a lady. The knowledge of her enduring that, too, made him feel decidedly unsteady. "I'd not thought to add brave to her list of virtues."

Mother's gaze was speculative on him. "I wasn't aware you

were so well acquainted with my dear friend, but you must be. You have called her by her given name. Several times tonight. Why?"

Alexander squirmed in the face of Mama's interest in him just then. "Did I use her given name? Oh, well, she's a friend of a friend's wife. We've shared several dinners, and she attended Exeter's party during the winter, too, now I come to think of it." He forced a shrug, but worried he'd revealed too much knowledge of Sylvia Hillcrest for Mother to overlook. "I thought her like all spinsters. Dull as paint and only interested in needlework."

That last wasn't true. But Sylvia Hillcrest was turning out to be a woman of many talents.

"You always underestimate the complexity of women." Mother was silent a moment but then she said, "When I am well, I intend to help her."

He stared at his mother in consternation. "If you are thinking of giving Miss Hillcrest your pin money, believe me, she doesn't need it."

"Introductions, boy," she nodded, enthused by her own idea. "She would be an asset to any family."

The idea of Mother matchmaking Sylvia to one of his acquaintances raised sudden alarm bells in him. "Do you even know if Miss Hillcrest wants to marry?"

"*Every* woman wants to marry. She just needs the right incentive. We've talked about this already, and Miss Hillcrest will come around in the end, I'm sure." She smiled a little more. "Now that my recovery is in hand, I imagine I'll have the time to do good works for others very soon. Your sisters will have husbands to look after, or they will have husbands to look after them, really, unless you've scared them away. You can return to your bachelor ways immediately. I will have the time later to guide dearest Sylvia in society and eventually see her settled in a good marriage."

Alexander didn't like the sound of Mother's plan at all. She was meddling with a woman she ought not to. "She isn't a charity, Mother. You can't just foist your ambitions on her and expect her not to disagree."

"She *always* disagrees with me. That's why I like her so

much," Mother continued with a soft smile. "Yes, I should like to see Miss Hillcrest catch herself a titled husband, I think. I've heard her speak favorable of handsome men. I must find out if there's anyone she favors already."

Alexander shook his head. Sylvia was…

Not his, but…

"You could do something for her, too," Mother suggested suddenly.

Here it comes. "Do what?"

Mother shifted on the bed, and then groaned. She put her hand on her chest and her fingers flexed, digging into her upper chest. She opened her eyes slowly. "Surely the idea of helping someone we are indebted to comes as no surprise. I shouldn't have to tell you the benefit of helping a good woman catch a worthy fellow's eye. It must be someone we like, of course. Someone important and rich enough, so she might holiday in the country with me when her husband doesn't need her."

Alexander stiffened, insulted by the mere suggestion that any husband of Sylvia's wouldn't always need her nearby. "You're delirious."

"Well, I think you're just the man to help her. She tried so many times to convince me to confide in you. You must have made quite the impression."

A tiny, recently silenced part of his soul thrilled at the news that Sylvia had spoken well of him once. He'd ruined that, of course. Alexander shoved that problem away until later. "If Sylvia cared so much for my good opinion, she should have told me, despite her promise to you."

"Whereas I value her all the more because she didn't, even under extreme distress." Mother clucked her tongue. "I forbade her. She's a good girl, obedient to a mother figure. I swore to never speak to her again if she told you. I'm ashamed to say I used all my powers of persuasion on her emotions to get my way. She must have been worried sick the whole time—and what did *you* do but throw out such a gem! I had no intention of dying, and now I would like to reassure her that I was always right that I would survive."

A maid came in carrying a laden tray. He suddenly thought of the nursemaid who was never around when he was at home. He knew her only by the flare of her skirt as she darted through a distant door. He'd hardly spoken a word to the woman in all the days and nights she's lingered beside Mama's bed. Perhaps he'd terrified her with his presence and driven her out without knowing.

The maid was smiling as she carried a bed table to Mother.

Mother pulled a face. "More stew?"

"Forgive us, my lady. Miss Hillcrest insisted that you must be given the easiest and best dishes to build your strength back up, and everyone agrees beef stew is strengthening. There's diced, steamed greens, too, on the side, the way you like them cooked, and sweetened hot chocolate to sip. Only your favorites, and easily eaten with one hand."

Mother smiled serenely. "You see, Alexander. The gentle, sweet-tempered woman you threw out made sure I would eat well during my convalescence. She's not even here, and I know she's thinking of me still."

Sylvia hadn't been so sweet tempered when they'd argued just before he'd tossed her out the door. Perhaps he'd been too final in his actions that day. Too emotional to behave in a gentlemanly fashion. He was ashamed of that.

After what he'd heard of her loyalty today, he was starting to suspect he'd have no choice but to offer up some sort of public apology for his angry behavior toward her and try to smooth things over. But he was absolutely not having his authority undermined by her again. He was in command of his family. Not her.

The maid carefully placed the tray over his mother's lap. Even so, Mama winced.

"Be careful," he snapped.

"I'm so sorry." The maid lifted the tray up and then down again in a slightly lower position over Mama's lap.

"It's all right, my dear," Mother murmured. "We're all doing our best."

"Where the devil is that replacement nursemaid the physician promised me?"

"Prendegast will find a woman eventually," Mama explained, starting to eat. "I'd much prefer my friend over a stranger, though."

Mama's eyes flashed fire…but then she moved her arm against her bandaged side and gasped again. She ate sparingly but eventually tired, and set her spoon aside. She drank all of the wine poured for her though. "I will speak with her today."

Good grief, Mama was like a dog with a bone about Sylvia Hillcrest coming back. Having that woman around his mother was asking for trouble. "I am not allowing that woman—"

"My friend," Mother said loudly, cutting him off.

Alexander scowled. "She's no such thing."

Mother's expression turned mullish. "Oh, I can see your pride is still smarting at what I didn't tell you, but under the circumstances, I insist you bury the hatchet and thank the stars for Sylvia. You would have prevented the operation from taking place or delayed it so much longer than was good for me. Be thankful, instead. I think if I had confided in anyone else, I would have been entirely alone through my ordeal. You must apologize to her. Sylvia is a kind woman, and she will be around quite a bit in the years to come. I would hate for there to be any awkwardness or lingering resentment on your part. I would also hate to have to choose between you again."

Alexander gaped. She found Sylvia better company than him? Nonsense! "Now, Mama, don't—"

"I can only hope when the time comes that you will marry such a strong-minded woman, but of course, I've always had reservations that any sane woman would have you."

His ears burned. "I'm not ready to marry anyone."

"I told Sylvia the very same, and she agreed you're likely much too preoccupied to make anyone a good husband yet."

Before he could argue how good a husband he would make, eventually, there was a rapid tap at the door. A servant, most likely. "Come in."

The butler appeared, eyes downcast respectfully for Mama's condition and sickbed attire. "Madam, you wished to be notified should Miss Hillcrest call. The lady is at the front door, asking about your health."

Alexander spun around. "Do not let that woman through the front door."

"We never have, my lord," the butler said, stony-faced.

Mother made a choking sound, and Alexander turned back to

her in case she needed assistance. However, she only patted her lips. "This is *my* house, boy, the lease is paid by my widow's pension. These servants you are ordering about now do not answer to you in the end. They answer to me, and if they want to keep their employment, they will remember who will write their letters of reference when I finally leave.

"Send her up, Mitchell, or I will dismiss everyone, from you down to the boot boy, before sunset."

"Really, Mama—"

"I know you threatened them with that, too, my son. You've no right. Not in this house. Not now. I am just as determined to have my way as you often are."

Mother smiled serenely as he discovered the butler had rushed off to do her bidding while they'd been arguing the point still.

"Mutiny," he muttered.

"I will never be under your command, son. I am well enough to put my food down, too. You are always in the wrong when you disagree with me. I am strong enough, and it will be such a comfort to talk to a woman of sense about my recovery and care without having to tiptoe around your temper and masculine timidity."

He set his hands to his hips. "Mother, I don't think—"

She flicked her fingers, dismissing him. "You may return to your bachelor ways now, Wharton."

He was about to argue that he wasn't going anywhere when he heard the rush of tiny feet, and then Sylvia burst through the door. She was so intent on reaching his mother's bedside that she nearly toppled him over to get there.

She stopped beside the bed, carefully reaching for Mama's hand. "I've been so worried about you, Lizzy."

Mother smiled. "I survived to tell you *I told you so.* Now sit down, child, we have much to talk about, you and I."

"You *did* tell me so." Sylvia laughed in delight and seated herself close to the bed. "I am so glad you put your foot down and decided not to leave us."

"Dear girl, you will learn never to doubt the wisdom of my words."

"Never again."

It was all so gushingly sweet that it could have been scripted for a play meant for Drury Lane. Had Sylvia ever trod the boards? He'd have to ask her the next time he found himself alone with her. If he ever was again. But that day would not be today.

He cleared his throat. "Lizzy?"

"Only my closest friends call me that. Not my children," Mother informed him stiffly. "You'd know my opinion about that if you paid the slightest attention to my life."

"Lizzy, please don't be cross today," Sylvia whispered, stroking his mother's hand in a soothing fashion.

He didn't need Sylvia telling Mama to be quiet. He was capable of speaking for himself. "As you prefer, Mama," he said, forcing a conciliatory smile to his lips.

He'd tried once before to change how he addressed his mother. It had seemed a grown-up thing to do to use her given name in private conversation. However, the first time he'd made the attempt to call her Elizabeth had been met with cold silence. But not ignored. Oh, no. He soon learned the error of his ways because his dinner that night had arrived on a plate in his chamber utterly raw, his bath water stone cold, and all his left boots and slippers had mysteriously vanished from his dressing room overnight.

The next morning when he spotted his mother, him limping through the house half shod in search of the missing ones, he'd reverted to calling her mama immediately, and by lunchtime, everything had returned to normal. Never let it be said that the Marquess of Wharton couldn't learn from his mistakes once they were pointed out to him.

Since his mother was definitely on the road to recovery, Alexander studied the back of Sylvia's head a long moment and considered what he could really do about her friendship with his mother. She seemed too cozy with Mama for his liking…and that could change if he confessed to the wild night they'd shared.

Unfortunately for him, he liked the memory too much to share it with anyone.

There was also the problem of what people saw the other day. Throwing a woman from the house was not his finest moment, by any stretch of the imagination.

He willed Sylvia to notice him but she kept her back turned. Was she embarrassed or angry with him for throwing her out?

With lovers, current and former, it was often hard to judge their mood unless they were throwing things at him. His ducking reflexes were excellent when called for.

"Miss Hillcrest?"

Her shoulders stiffened, and she turned slightly. "Thank you for allowing me to see your mother at last, Lord Wharton."

He grimaced inwardly at the brisk, cold tone with which she spoke to him. She was being too polite not to be feeling just a bit put out with him still.

He also noticed she didn't look up all the way to meet his gaze, too, but kept hers respectfully dipped like a shy maiden, or that old nursemaid that Prendegast had foolishly hired. "My pleasure."

"He didn't let you in, my dear, and he is about to leave now." Mother flicked her hand imperiously. "Off you go, boy. I prefer to talk privately with my friend without you glaring daggers at her head."

He cleared his throat. "Could we speak in private for a moment, Miss Hillcrest?"

"I don't think there is anything left to say to each other, my lord." She turned away. "All I want is to know how Lizzy is faring." Then she directed her gaze to the discarded tray of food by the bed. Sylvia surprised him by clucking her tongue at Mama in obvious disapproval. "You need to eat more, my lady. We must build you up, help you recover your strength, so you can dance at your daughters' weddings."

"It will only be theirs, since my son will not oblige me by making a match. I will, however, look forward to dancing at *your* wedding." Mother smiled as she cupped Sylvia's face. "I'll eat so I might see you grace the floor as the wife of some handsome devil you adore."

"I don't think that's very likely," she murmured.

He could see Sylvia's cheeks heating up even from a distance and felt bad for her. He stepped forward, surprising himself by feelings of protectiveness toward Sylvia. "Mother, you shouldn't tease about such things."

"I'm not offended, my lord. It only proves she's feeling better. Have you gotten out of bed yet?" Sylvia asked suddenly of Mama.

"A few steps only," Mama said with a wince, and then lowered her voice. "The maids help me reach the commode. I am so sick of this bed, and what I'm wearing, too. But I suppose a bath cannot be done yet, not for a good long while."

"You mustn't think of getting up without assistance again. Perhaps there is a way to manage it, provided the physician approves the extra movements and we are careful. I'll speak to the housekeeper before I go about how we might arrange a proper wash for you for tomorrow morning. Perhaps a chair over a large waterproof canvas sheet would work. You'll feel better for fresh bedding, too, I'm sure. And you could sit up for a little while each day so you don't suffer bed sores." Sylvia loaded up a spoon and thrust it toward Mama. "Here, eat some of this."

Mother ate, allowing Sylvia to feed her bite after bite like she was a child and helpless, something she'd outright refused to let Alexander assist with, or either of his sisters, for that matter. Apparently, only the last nursemaid, and now Sylvia, seemed the two people capable of bending his mother to their wills.

Made obsolete—by his own lover, no less—Alexander had no choice but to concede defeat for now and quit the room. He did want his mother well again, and disagreeing with her might set back her recovery. If Sylvia was truly good for her, he'd allow her to visit.

But as he strode to the door, he was annoyed that he wasn't needed the way he'd expected and wanted to be.

As he went to shut it, he snuck another peek at the pair to see if they'd even noticed him leaving. Both seemed to have forgotten his existence the moment he'd stopped speaking. They were still discussing how best to manage Mama's needs in the coming weeks, including things he hadn't yet considered, and when she might accept other callers.

Alexander felt he should be involved in those decisions, too. "If you need me, I'll be downstairs going over some papers in the dining room."

"I won't need you," Mother muttered quietly.

"Not for a few hours at least," Sylvia called out quickly. "I'll be sure to let you know, my lord, if anything changes here while you're busy with your work."

"Thank you," he said dryly. "I'll chase up that nursemaid the surgeon was to send us while I'm gone."

Mama laughed, and then complained to Sylvia that she shouldn't laugh.

Alexander shut the door, unsure what had been funny in what he'd said.

Mother was up to something. He could feel it as he walked away—and it had something to do with Sylvia Hillcrest.

Women! He might never understand the contrary creatures for as long as he lived.

He stomped down the stairs because it made him feel slightly better, and he went into the dining room to work for the next few hours. On the way, he passed a female servant on the staircase. Not the new one expected from Prendegast, though. This one smiled warmly, and he recalled that the other, the first nursemaid Prendegast had sent, had always darted off if he got too close.

No doubt a spinster.

When he spread his papers out across the dining room table, he realized he couldn't actually remember what the blasted first nursemaid had even looked like clearly. A lacy white mop cap over brown hair, thick wire-rimmed spectacles, and an appalling taste in fashion was all that came to mind. That one wouldn't be catching anyone's eye, especially not his—

He suddenly looked up at the ceiling.

Or had that been the point?

He swore softly under his breath as he realized his error. He'd thought his control over the household absolute, but he had been deceived yet again!

By both Mother and Sylvia, and now by the pair of them.

Sylvia had been the damn nursemaid, a disguise, darting away whenever he came close so he wouldn't recognize her! Using the servants' entrance instead of the front door—which he'd forbidden her from using.

Alexander sat there a moment, clenched his jaw, fuming. It seemed there were no limits to that pair's reckless deceptions, and determination to have their way and circumvent his authority.

He pinched the bridge of his nose in exasperation. He would have to learn from this mistake, too, if he had any chance to control either one in the future.

Chapter Nineteen

"You could have made him grovel," Lady Wharton suggested a few hours later. "He never apologized."

Sylvia lifted her head from the alterations she was making to one of the marchioness' oldest undergarments and considered what good pressing for an apology would have done her. Expressing an opinion seemed to bring out the tyrant in him. But at least now, they could no longer hear Lord Wharton stomping around outside the marchioness' bedchamber. His going up and down the hall and stairs constantly to check on them had seemed unreasonably peculiar to her. "For what purpose?"

Lady Wharton was holding a fresh glass of gin, a bit unsteadily now, too. But Sylvia was always ready to sweep in and catch it should it slip from her fingers.

"He's gotten too big for his boots since he took the title," Lizzy confessed, "and you need the practice. One day, you'll marry and have a man of your own to manage. It's best to start out as you intend to go on. Don't you think so?"

Lady Wharton was in a talkative mood tonight. Perhaps it was the drink, or just relief that she was still alive to tell her stories to a captive audience. Sylvia found them fascinating.

Her son had been the marquess for almost a decade now, and doing quite well at it, in his mother's opinion. The coffers were full, the family estates thrived, but he had not married yet. That seemed to be Lady Wharton's main complaint with him. Wharton was used to doing as he liked far too much. Bachelors were always like that, in Sylvia's opinion.

"He does wear impressively large shoes," she mused, ignoring the lady's remarks about Sylvia getting herself a husband. It was a subject that would cause friction between them, just as it did between Lizzy and her son. Lady Wharton did not seem to feel that love in marriage was entirely necessary, and Sylvia was a romantic about that sort of thing. Love, and only love, would compel her to the altar. She wondered if Wharton hadn't married for the same reason.

Lizzy snorted. "His father wore much the same size."

"I'm happy for you," she murmured as she bit off a thread and inspected her handiwork. Fair enough to do the job at short notice. Lady Wharton could not move around easily, and, being of the aristocracy, liked to change her clothes often. To help make the job less painful, Sylvia had sliced up one side of a fresh nightgown and chemise so that Lady Wharton would not have to lift her arms at all. Her other outer wear, a pair of loose morning gowns, were being worked on by her daughters down the hall. When they'd come to their mother and seen what Sylvia was doing, they'd instantly volunteered to help.

"Will you have a drink with me now?"

Sylvia folded the soft garments and set them aside. "I shouldn't. When your son returns, I wouldn't want him to think ill of me."

Lady Wharton smiled a little sadly. "What he thinks doesn't matter. I'm glad you are here with me."

"I am too."

Lizzy fidgeted with her bedding. "I can't tell you how long it's been since I've felt this content to lie in bed and let the world move on without me. Not since my marriage have I felt myself in the company of one who wouldn't judge me for not looking my best."

"I'm sure you have a great many friends who would be overjoyed to visit you while you recover."

"I can't think of one."

There were moments when Lady Wharton seemed

uncomfortable with what she'd done to herself. The loss of her breast, a visible sign of her womanhood, seemed to worry her at times. She had so far refused any callers, saying she was too unwell. But she wasn't unwell enough to have Sylvia sit by her bed and talk herself silent. Sylvia believed the company of other women would do Lizzy the world of good. "We should arrange that. Short visits so you don't tire too quickly. I know just who the first caller should be, too."

The marchioness appeared only mildly interested, so Sylvia offered up a name. "Lady Exeter," she suggested.

The marchioness stared at her. "We are not acquainted. How did *you* come to be?"

"I attended Exeter's estate at Christmas, a guest of Lord Carmichael's new wife. We are old friends, and he wanted her to have additional company at her first house party."

"My son was at Exeter's for Christmas."

"Yes, he was," Sylvia said. "I had a glorious time and became friends with the duchess. I'm sure she'd be very pleased to meet you, too. She's not at all top lofty, even though she's a duchess. She has a wicked sense of humor you'll enjoy. I think you two will get along famously."

"I've heard about her, of course. Is it true she grew up running wild on the Grafton estate?"

"I don't know about running wild, but she's as common born as I am." Sylvia worried her lip. "I hope you don't hold that against her."

The marchioness hissed in a breath as she shifted slightly on the bed. "Sylvia, what do you know of my family?"

"Nothing but what you've told me." Sylvia did often discover a great deal about the Hillcrest Academy clients—families and connections and scandals in the end—but had never had any inclination or reason to investigate Lord Wharton or his family.

"My own family come from Wales. We had a little falling-down house above the township and overlooking the distant sea. My father earned his living as a tutor. My mother took in piece work for a nearby seamstress to make ends meet. Our house had three narrow bedchambers, and I had four brothers and two sisters. We were all squeezed in like rabbits in a burrow...quite happily, I might add."

Sylvia gaped. "You didn't come from society?"

"Oh, gracious no. My father had a fortune of precisely two hundred pounds to his name, and too many offspring to support. He did have one passably pretty daughter of marriageable age that he was keen to marry off." Lady Wharton pointed to herself. "Thanks to my father's profession, I was a great reader, but my intellect made me less than desirable to the local gentry, unfortunately. I'm sure you've experienced this yourself. Wealthy men often want a pretty thing between the sheets, but wish for them to have nothing between their ears."

Sylvia nodded. "Wealthy women like that, too, sometimes."

Lady Wharton laughed at that. "Oh, don't make me laugh. But you are right. I have one particular friend whose husband is a complete dullard. She has her way in everything."

"How fascinating," she murmured. "Do you mind if I ask how you met your husband?"

"It's no great secret. I was walking home from church with my sister and the scoundrel was lurking on the path, in our way, and wouldn't let us pass without us offering up a kiss. I slapped his face, of course." Lady Wharton fell silent then, staring off into space.

It might be rude to press, but Sylvia wanted to hear the end of the story very much. "And…"

"I had been brought up to give men like him, scoundrels, no encouragement at all, so along with the slap, I also let him have a piece of my mind."

"What happened then?"

"He let us pass but followed us home, spoke with my father, and began to court me the next day."

Sylvia spluttered. "But why?"

The lady shrugged. "He said he found my disinterest refreshing. I had no idea how important he really was, nor cared, either. I thought him annoying and frivolous from the offset but that hardly seemed to matter to him. He kept coming back, and I kept arguing with him when he tried to steal a kiss. We were married within two months of meeting. He was a good husband for a few years."

"A romantic one, too, I hope, for your sake," Sylvia asked, and Lady Wharton nodded once. "They do make the best husbands."

"The best husbands live a long life and don't die in their mistresses arms." Lizzy sighed. "I do miss our arguments sometimes."

"Probably more often than you let on, I suspect," Sylvia suggested.

Lizzy closed her eyes. "You will come back tomorrow, won't you?"

The need in the marchioness' voice tore at her conscience. By rights, she should begin to withdraw from the woman, her lover's mother. But Sylvia liked her. It was a hard choice to make. She knew what it was like to feel so alone in a crowd, among family and friends. She couldn't turn away. "Tomorrow. One way or the other, and we can discuss you having visitors again, too."

"If we must. But I've a thousand things I want to say to you first, and I can hardly keep my eyes open tonight."

"The drink is working well then," Sylvia noted, climbing to her feet and taking the glass from the marchioness' limp grip. "I'll put this away for tomorrow night, shall I?"

"Bless you, my dear." Lizzy sighed sleepily. "You never told me what your mother's name was."

"It was Millicent."

"A pretty name. Mine was Laurel. I do miss talking to Mama sometimes. What was your father's name?"

Lizzy smiled. "Harold."

"A sensible name for a man of learning. Were they like you? Bold and funny?"

"Both serious and very quiet. It's taken me all my life to find my voice, not that everyone appreciates a woman with an opinion," Sylvia admitted. "Now they are gone, I regret that they never really knew my thoughts differed from theirs."

"I quite like the way you speak your mind."

"So you said before," Sylvia noted as she hid the bottle of gin better under a clean wool blanket and closed the drawer. "Is there anything else you need tonight?"

"A kiss good night, and a promise of more laughter tomorrow."

Sylvia returned to the bed, pressed her lips to the marchioness' outstretched hand and, upon feeling a wave of strong emotion that threatened tears, she straightened the bedding around the woman until she'd pushed the impulse away. "Remind me tomorrow to tell you about the first ball I attended, and how I ended up flat on my bottom in the middle of the dance floor in front of the reining beauty of the village."

"Is it a scandalous story?"

"I don't want to give you nightmares," Sylvia teased. "I'll tell you the whole of it tomorrow when I come back. Sleep well, my lady."

"And you." Lizzy sighed deeply, already half asleep. "Tomorrow, perhaps, I'll tell you of my first ball as a marchioness. Now that *was* a scandalous night to curl your hair."

"I can't wait to hear of it." Sylvia put a little silver bell under Lady Wharton's hand on the bed. "In case you need to call for assistance during the night."

"Shouting is highly undignified at my age."

"Mine, too. Good night." Sylvia snuffed the candle. Using the fire's light to guide her way, she let herself out of the room—and jumped as she found herself face-to-face with the marquess in the shadowed hall.

"She's almost asleep," Sylvia warned quickly, hoping he wouldn't speak too loudly as she closed the door. "She's worn herself out talking."

"Given the late hour, I hoped as much," he murmured, and then gestured for Sylvia to precede him down the hall, away from his mother's room.

She took a few steps in that direction, and he followed. She reached the head of the stairs, and he stopped, too. "Can I help you, my lord?"

"You're on your way home?"

"Yes."

"I'll show you the way."

"I know the way perfectly well, my lord," she promised. He was trying to get rid of her again. He'd made his opinion clear enough already that she didn't want to give him the opportunity to do so again.

"Don't argue," he warned. "It is better to reach home safely than not at all."

"Your escort is not necessary, and inappropriate, too, but I do thank you for your concern." Sylvia pressed her lips tightly together and started down the stairs quickly.

Wharton scrambled to catch up. "I think we left inappropriate behind some time ago," he suggested in a low tone that sent a warning racing over her body. "London is a dangerous place for a beautiful woman alone."

Sylvia struggled not to smile that Wharton thought her beautiful as they started down the next flight together. For a moment, she considered what he might do if she disagreed with him again. Last time she hadn't heeded him, he'd tossed her off the property like a barbarian. Would he sweep her into his arms tonight if provoked, too?

Maybe he'd try to kiss her.

Maybe she'd let him.

But Sylvia quickly concluded that it probably was not wise to risk her reputation further by encouraging that sort of thing with him again. She did want to come back tomorrow to see his mother, and she didn't want Wharton to take her favors for granted, either. She was no light-skirt, too willing and eager to please him.

Sylvia liked Lady Wharton too much to risk losing her good opinion. She and Wharton had had a fling, and that was it. It was over and best forgotten now. They both cared about the marchioness, and her recovery, so Sylvia would behave herself, and he should, too. "I have my maid."

"I had her escorted home hours ago."

"Oh, why would you do that?" she cried.

"She was falling asleep. I was afraid you and Mother would talk all night," he said with a soft laugh.

They might have, too. She did not particularly like walking alone on London's streets, especially not on nights as dark as this should be outside. The moon had been waning in the sky last night, and the shadows of Mayfair's streets could be full of thieves or worse. Sylvia wasn't physically strong and could easily be imposed upon without any hope of defending herself without carrying some form of protection. She didn't even have a parasol with her tonight. He'd given her no choice but to accept the protection of his servants to get herself home.

Wharton took her elbow firmly and guided her across the hall to the door himself. The servants were nowhere to be seen as they swept out the front door very quietly, and Wharton locked it behind them.

Sylvia looked around. "Where's the carriage?"

"No carriage."

The square was eerily dark and forbidding as Wharton escorted her down to the pavement. But her breath caught as a quartet of men immediately surrounded them.

"Never fear. They work for me," Wharton murmured quickly.

She eyed the strangers nervously and edged closer to Wharton. The men nodded and fanned out ahead and behind as they started off across the square, their manner suggesting they were alert for any trouble that might come.

"I thought you might have gone out," she whispered to him.

"I was waiting for you," Wharton whispered back.

Since it was dark, she didn't have to bother to hide her pleasure in hearing that confession. She wound her arm through his a little tighter. "Why?"

"Can you not guess?"

She pressed her lips together, wondering if his thoughts mirrored her own as they had the night they'd made love. Despite his recent behavior, she still thought fondly of the time they'd spent together. He'd been an exciting lover, and she wouldn't mind feeling so well loved again someday.

Wharton's men were thankfully quite a distance from them now, but still she kept her voice low. "I wouldn't dream of knowing your mind," she responded.

"My mind tells me we ought not be seen together."

Sylvia nearly laughed. "We are together now."

"I mean around my mother. When her mind is sharper, she'll catch the scent of any indiscretion between us," he warned.

"Not from me," she promised.

He gave her a long look. "What game are you playing? Cozying up to Mother will get you nowhere with me," he warned. "Nearly weeping over her hand tonight was doing it a bit brown, I should think."

Sylvia gaped. "Do you believe I would not feel genuine affection for your mother? I like her very much, and I am grateful she survived. But I know she has a long way to go before she's out of danger and fully healed. I think I will always worry about her."

"Mother will be herself in no time at all, I'm sure."

"I hope you're proven right in the end," Sylvia told him. "And not just fooling yourself with what you most want to hear. She needs constant care and attention if she is to recover."

"Miss Hillcrest, I assure you, I know my mother's stubborn nature better than you. She will live to bedevil me for many years yet. She has no need for a companion, either. She has her family to rally around her."

Sylvia clenched her teeth a moment. *Here it comes. He's trying to be rid of me again.* "I gave my word I'd return tomorrow."

"You will discover you have other plans and beg her forgiveness."

"I *will* see her."

Wharton shook his head. "Tomorrow you will attend a luncheon at Lady Norrington's home. You will find an invitation awaiting you, which you will accept, along with the others that will come later."

Sylvia stopped. "Why would I do that?"

"I understand my actions have caused people in society to question your reputation. I intend to set things back to how they should be."

She looked up at him, squinting in the dark. "You threw me out."

"Because you failed to heed me." Wharton sighed. "You questioned my loyalty and affection for my mother."

"I know that was wrong of me." Sylvia nodded. "You were afraid and angry, and I was too tired to watch my words. I should never have repeated what your mother had told me in confidence. And you should not have laid hands on me, either, without my permission."

"Obviously not," he said. "I will not make that mistake again. But I will clear the air and ensure people believe there is no cause for lingering resentment between us."

"Thank you."

"Now that's settled...I should inform you that Mr. Prendegast was excused from treating my mother this afternoon."

Sylvia glanced up in surprise and shock. "But he's an excellent physician. The very best in London!"

She caught a glimpse of extreme satisfaction lingering on

Wharton's face in the dim light. "Of course you would think so, wouldn't you? I must warn you that as a result of his dismissal, his especially hired *nursemaids* are dismissed, too," he continued. "Really, Sylvia? A cap and spectacles wasn't much of a disguise."

She stared straight ahead. "I fooled you days longer than I even dreamed possible."

"You fooled me because my attention was where it should be. On my family, and not on a nursemaid with appalling dress sense. Do not cross me again, Sylvia. This is no game you're playing with my mother's affections. I won't have it. I won't offer for you if your plan is to tell her we shared a bed, either."

Sylvia threw up her hands. All the warm feelings Wharton stirred in her that one night vanished. The arrogant, strutting aristocrat thought her sole interest in Lady Wharton was to worm her way into their lives. "Oh, you are unbelievably thick-headed and selfish! I don't want her to know about us, either! And never in a thousand years would I put myself into a situation where I had to marry someone who didn't want to spend the rest of his life with me."

Wharton tripped over his own feet then. "I don't want to marry you."

"Yes, you already made your feelings abundantly clear. Your bachelorhood is perfectly safe from me. So kindly cease your threats and go back to your society amusements, your Madam Bradshaw's, your White's Club wagers, or just pretend I'm invisible again and seduce the next woman in line."

Sylvia forced herself to take a steadying breath. She was getting worked up over nothing. So what if he thought the idea of marrying her abhorrent? How had she ever admired someone like him? It must have been just his looks that had turned her head. It certainly wasn't his personality.

"Now we understand each other, there is nothing more for us to ever discuss."

"Agreed."

Sylvia saw her home was not far away now. "I believe I am capable of finding my way home from here."

"Very well," he replied, stepping back. "I'll inform Mother first thing tomorrow that you have other plans."

Sylvia dropped him a curtsy, her heart now utterly chilled

toward him. She turned to the servants who'd drawn closer as their voices had risen. The men wore a mix of astonishment and approving expressions. They must have heard everything.

Oh, dear. That could be a problem for Wharton.

"Good night, gentlemen. Thank you for the protection of your company. Your discretion would be deeply appreciated, too, I might add."

The servants all tipped their caps to her. "Our pleasure, Miss Hillcrest. It were a lovely night for a stroll."

"What a shame I missed the lovely part," she muttered under her breath, and they laughed. Sylvia pulled her wrap tighter about her, and one of the servants moved ahead of her as she started off.

"Sir?" she called.

"We will see you all the way to the door, miss," he said. "The marchioness would expect it of us."

Sylvia glanced behind.

Wharton appeared to be walking home. His men had not followed after him.

The marquess stopped, seemed to suddenly realize he was alone, turned about in rather obvious alarm, and then he scowled.

Sylvia laughed softly at his confusion, bid the closest man a good night, and hurried up her stairs so the servants would be free to guard the marquess again.

But as she shut the door behind her, she made another promise. She had no intention of abandoning Lady Wharton. No matter what Wharton said or did to prevent her return, she'd always keep her word to another lady.

There were plenty of ways to bend an iron-clad rule if you tried hard enough.

Chapter Twenty

*A*lexander heard the heavy front door shut behind someone and got to his feet. He tugged his waistcoat down on the way to the window and peered out to see who'd just left.

It had been four days now since the night he'd walked Sylvia home and told her not to come back to visit his mother.

She had only tried once, and been turned away.

But he'd seen her every day still.

She was sitting now again in the little garden park outside Mother's Berkley Square home, a book open in her lap, a parasol at her side, and her maid yet again flirting with one of Mother's male servants. She had a clever setup indeed. A regular spy network that would make England proud. Notes passed from hand to hand several times a day, every day, for the last four.

He'd tried to stop them, but she'd trained her agents far too well for him to succeed.

Mother was an enthusiastic participant, too. She had insisted days ago that she was well enough to get out of bed to sit at her writing desk a few hours each day. At first, he'd not understood why she was so keen on the new situation. But on moving to a chair and writing desk at the window, she could see outside. See the square. See Sylvia sitting outside reading the notes she slipped to her maid to pass to Sylvia.

And it wasn't just the servants conspiring against his restrictions, he suspected, either.

Mother's friends, women well-known to him, and apparently Sylvia, were conveying Sylvia's thoughts and opinions, too. He knew this because he'd escorted a few of Mother's oldest friends up to her chambers personally. The first words out of their mouths had included Sylvia's name somewhere in the greeting, and something about sending her love.

He let the butler do the escorting now, mostly so he could keep his eye on Sylvia in the square.

She had done as he'd asked. She'd attended the few luncheons he'd arranged to begin the work of repairing society's impression of her. However, after each one, he found her in the square again, passing notes to her maid that eventually passed into Mother's eager hands.

She was having fun trying to circumvent his authority, and Mother probably was, too.

Each visitor of Mother's today had gone straight to Sylvia in the park afterward, and they all spoke to her for several minutes before finally leaving. Clearly the lines of communication were all wide open. All Alexander had done was put a stop to Mother and Sylvia actually sitting in the same room.

Despite all his best laid plans to keep control of the situation, he was devilishly impressed with Sylvia's tenacity. Would she stay out there when it rained, too? She had the parasol.

He let the curtain fall.

He'd never met another woman like her...and he had to do something about her soon.

When there wasn't a visitor in the house, and Sylvia was elsewhere, Mother was listless. He wasn't entirely sure if his company was lacking or just not what she needed right now. But he couldn't keep his sisters at home to sit with her during the day. She'd go downhill fast if they drove her out of her mind with their constant babbling.

And he was starting to believe that Sylvia's interest in his mother really did have nothing to do with him.

That made him feel foolish in the extreme that he'd been so against the connection. It was not as if he wanted to be Mother's only companion. Dear God, what would happen when she recovered? He wasn't going to escort her about in society every day.

But he couldn't quit the field entirely, either.

He scratched his head and made short work of packing up his papers. He'd promised himself that he could be a better son and watch over his mother. He'd never allow her to make such a dangerous decision about her life again without him knowing about it.

But perhaps he wasn't the only capable person who could take care of her.

If Sylvia was allowed back into the house, at least he was confident Mother would be in good hands if he needed to leave for any length of time. There were a number of matters that required his attention. And not just an hour. He might have to make a short trip soon, too. He was loath to leave Mama alone for a whole night and most of two days.

But if Sylvia came to stay with her, it might well be all right

And if that were to happen, Alexander might just be able return to Wharton House for a few hours every day and tackle the papers still pilling up over his study desk. Not to mention attend the most important society functions at night sometimes, too.

It was a tempting proposition to step back a little and allow someone else to take charge of Mother's recovery here.

Tempting, but was it *wise* to choose Sylvia, given their recent history?

They might be butting heads over Mother, but he was starting to admire the confounding woman. There was a fear in his mind of how much more ground he might be persuaded to give later, too. If he could not hope to dig in his heels now about certain things, he'd surely regret it later.

He glanced outside and found Sylvia's little bench empty. He stood up straighter and leaned close to the window in search of her. She was leaving the garden square, but not heading in the direction of her home, it seemed. And she didn't have a maid with her now.

He headed for the front hall, found his hat and gloves himself, and told the spluttering butler to let Mother know if she asked for him that he'd be back shortly.

Quickly, Alexander rushed down the steps and took off after

Sylvia.

She wasn't very tall, and his longer stride caught up with her very quickly.

He forced himself to walk more slowly so he wouldn't get too close if she happened to look over her shoulder. She was in a hurry, and he was mesmerized by the gentle sway of her body as she slipped down the busy street. When she was far away from the square, she suddenly hailed a hack.

"Now where are you going in that, my dear?" he muttered under his breath.

Without his own carriage to follow in, Alexander had no choice but to hail a hack to keep up with her. He told the coachman to follow Sylvia's carriage.

He hugged the window on the journey, watching with unabashed interest where she went to make sure there was no confusion as to their direction. But when her carriage turned, his did, too. Until she was forced to stop right in the middle of busy Bond Street because of excessive traffic.

Alexander eased back from the window, in case he was recognized by passing members of society. He leaned toward the window every now and then to check on the delay, and noticed Sylvia stepped out of her carriage, was paying the driver, and then she rushed off down a narrow side street.

Only foolish women took such risks in London.

Alexander climbed out quickly, too, throwing the driver a wealth in coin as payment and made to follow.

But of Sylvia, there was no sign now.

The alley she'd slipped into was empty, and thinking that he'd missed her leaving it again, he looked around desperately.

After a few minutes, he was extremely worried. He was almost positive she'd not left the alley to go somewhere else.

Alexander entered the ally at a brisk pace, but had to slow his steps quickly as the cobblestones were slick with filth under his feet. He picked his way more cautiously through the slush and mess of an unswept carriageway best left to thieves and vagabonds, looking for signs of her.

He found no one lurking, and no Sylvia, either.

A tight ball of concern formed in his stomach as he wondered what had happened to her. This area was not fashionable, as much of the shopping district could be called. London was a dangerous place for a tasty morsel such as Sylvia Hillcrest. "She should have a bloody keeper," he growled to himself.

And then he saw her at last. She emerged from a little shop not far away. Her head was down, and she didn't notice him. She seemed to be checking an item off a list of some sort.

As she approached the street where traffic was thickest, head still down, his breath caught in fear. She wasn't looking at all where she was going.

Just as he prepared to shout out a warning to be careful, she finally looked up, hand raised in greeting.

But not for him.

A fine carriage stopped beside her and, after a few moments of conversation, she climbed inside.

Alexander craned his neck to see more of the carriage and discover who the occupants might be. He let out a relieved breath when he got a clear view. He easily recognized the coat of arms on the door, and Sylvia sitting in the rear-facing seat. She was in one of the Duke of Exeter's marked carriages, which meant Sylvia was about to be delivered home in style.

He took one last look, noted her direction seemed to be taking her back down Bond Street, where traffic was still thick and slow.

He should easily reach her home before her.

Alexander grinned and turned his attention to the shop Sylvia had just visited. By the look of it, she'd gone to a modiste, but not one that he had been aware of before today. He'd investigate her business tomorrow.

Alexander raised his hand to hail another hack for himself and gave them orders to take him straight to Albemarle Street in a hurry.

There was really only one thing to do with a reckless woman like Sylvia Hillcrest. She wanted to be indispensable, and so she would be from now on. The woman had no idea of her value to him, but she would before dark. She'd forced his hand with her rebellion and trickery, and he would have to take steps to protect her from herself starting today.

They arrived fairly quickly. Alexander stepped out before the little townhouse, and with a heavy sigh, climbed the steps and knocked on the front door. Sylvia would most likely put up a fight over his plans, but he could be just as stubborn.

An older man opened the door and Alexander gave his card, asking to speak with Miss Sylvia Hillcrest.

The poor man nearly genuflected all the way to the floor. Clearly he was not used to receiving anyone of Alexander's rank, or very rarely. "I'm sorry, my lord, but she is not at home just now."

"She will be soon enough. I'll wait." Alexander gave his hat and gloves over and pushed past the man. To the right of the entrance hall was a library. Unoccupied. He'd heard about what went on in that library. It was where clients of the Hillcrest Academy came for help with their marital woes.

Alexander didn't need that kind of assistance from Sylvia.

He turned for the drawing room instead and made himself comfortable on the settee.

Sylvia walked into the house a few moments later using her own key. A blush formed on her cheeks as she caught sight of him watching her from the drawing room through the still-open doorway. The butler hastily explained that he'd come to see her and insisted on waiting.

He stood, anticipation nearly making him sigh out loud.

Sylvia seemed disinclined to greet him at first.

But then her cousin appeared, and though he wished her away so he could talk freely, he couldn't insist the other woman leave. Still, he felt it was important to come today so Sylvia did not think she'd completely bested him, and could again tomorrow.

"Good evening, ladies."

"It's still afternoon, my lord," Eugenia, an obviously older woman, murmured, and then dipped a curtsy.

So all of the Hillcrest women are bold, opinionated creatures incapable of not correcting a man. "Good to know."

"How might we help you, my lord?" Eugenia asked, taking charge when Sylvia remained silent.

For years, Alexander had done as he'd pleased, spoken as he wished, when he wished, but he could not do that around the family of his lover. He had to tread a little lightly until he'd talked to Sylvia alone. He turned his attention to Eugenia and shook his head. "There is a personal matter I wish to discuss with your cousin," he murmured.

"Ah," Eugenia murmured, glancing at Sylvia in wait for her to say something next.

Sylvia worried her lip, and then whispered to her cousin, "Would you mind arranging tea for the marquess, Eugenia?"

Eugenia seemed disinclined to go at first, but one soft please from Sylvia and she excused herself with a warning she'd return soon with the tea tray.

Sylvia sat stiffly across from him. "How is your mother today?"

"As if you don't already know. You and your network of spies rival anything English forces set to work against the French. You, woman, are a devilishly wily adversary."

A tiny smile twitched her lips. "I haven't broken your rules."

"Only rendered them completely moot," he complained. He sat forward, resting his arms on his thighs. "Now, let's talk about why I've come."

"I think we both know." A blush began to color her cheeks. "You want to again stress my unsuitability for being friends with your mother."

He smiled. "Imagine you're very wrong. I want to speak with you, but not here with your cousin soon to come back. Tomorrow, I want you to visit that modiste you went to today. I'll meet you there at ten to thrash things out."

Sylvia's mouth fell open. "How do you know where my modiste is?" Her eyes widened. "Oh, are you spying on *me* now."

"Seemed prudent since you neglected to take a maid. Mother would be appalled at your lack of common sense." He raised a brow. "Not that I plan to tell her. She'd only become upset, and I'm sure you don't want that any more than I do."

"No, I don't."

"Well?"

She bit her lip. "I don't think it a good idea for us to meet in private again."

"I don't either, but I'd rather not share my plan for managing Mother with you in front of your relative."

Sylvia burst into a huge smile. "You changed your mind about me?"

"I have to a degree, and I like to plan for every eventuality," he said.

"That is wonderful news."

"Well?"

She nodded. "All right. I'll meet you tomorrow, but I warn you, I have a few thoughts of my own on your mother's care."

"Excellent."

"Thank you, my lord," she said, looking up at him shyly.

Eugenia Hillcrest sailed into the room with a footman trailing after carrying a heavy tea tray. "How is the discussion going?"

"Quite well," he told Eugenia, with a half smile for Sylvia. "I have everything I need for today."

"I'm glad to hear it." Eugenia, completely unaware of the real nature of his visit, sat herself down with them.

Alexander stood. "Forgive me, but I must return home."

"Please give my love to your mother."

"Yes, of course," he promised, though he'd do no such thing. This visit with Sylvia would remain as private as their last encounter.

The Hillcrest ladies stood to see him out to the hall. He bowed to them both. "Until we meet again."

"I look forward to it," Sylvia promised, and her eyes flashed a hint of anticipation.

Alexander found he was anticipating tomorrow's meeting, too.

Chapter Twenty-One

Although Sylvia had debated the wisdom of her decision to comply with the marquess' wishes to meet with him the whole night, she had to admit, too, that she was curious to know what more he wanted to say. He had not behaved like a gentleman recently, especially not when it came to his mother's situation. It had been clear yesterday he'd had a change of heart, and she wanted to hear what he had to say for himself.

She alighted from a hack the next day outside the modiste's charming little shop and paid the coachman his fare. She had left her maid at home for this outing again, too, deciding there should be few witnesses to the coming meeting between her and the marquess.

The driver moved off, and Sylvia paused at the doorway to Madam du Clair's shop a moment before going inside. If he was going to try to lay down the law again, she was more than ready to speak up and give some back, too.

The sound of the bell was still ringing in the air when the assistant rushed out to meet her. "Miss Hillcrest, you are right on time."

Sylvia smiled and moved to the back chamber.

Madam du Clair regarded her but then turned to the corner screen. "Monsieur?"

Wharton emerged, a too-pleased-with-himself smile on his lips. He turned to her. "I'll pay you ten pounds to close your shop for the rest of the day and leave us."

The woman frowned and turned to Sylvia. "Only if mademoiselle agrees."

Sylvia shook her head. If the marquess was going to banish the modiste from her place of business, she should be given more than a mere token. "Higher," she countered.

A flicker of amusement crossed Wharton's lips, and a handful of notes appeared between his quickly raised fingers.

Madam smiled graciously as she took his money and rushed from the room. Wharton remained silent until they heard the front door lock behind her and the assistant.

Then he sighed and leaned against the worktable, staring at her. His smile was gone, and Sylvia wasn't sure what to do. He had something serious on his mind.

"Now, first things first," he began. "I trust you are on a warmer footing with society of late."

She nodded quickly. It had felt awkward to be invited to those luncheons simply because Wharton had arranged an invitation. But those friends of his were eager to know how Lady Wharton was faring, and Sylvia had the opportunity to suggest she was well enough for a few ladies to visit to lift her spirits, if they didn't stay too long. "I seem to be accepted again. Thank you very much for arranging those introductions. I found your friends had a great many interesting things to say. You did not need to trouble yourself on my account."

"Of course I did. My actions harmed you. That was never my intention," he promised.

"You were upset."

"To put it mildly," he said, and then shook his head. "Now, we need to talk about Mother."

"Indeed we do." She laced her fingers together at her waist. "I want you to engage Mr. Prendegast to care for your mother again."

He crossed his arms over his chest. "Do you now?"

"Yes. Of all the men attending her, he was the calmest, and he protested that further blood-letting after the surgery was unnecessary, if not downright dangerous."

"That was mentioned as a treatment for her listlessness just today."

Alarmed that he might have given consent, she moved closer to him and set her fingers on his folded arms. "Please, Alexander, don't let them bleed her! She's so weak. It won't help her recover."

Alexander nodded. "I had already refused them."

Sylvia lowered her head in relief, pressing her brow upon his folded arms. "If Mr. Prendegast was still overseeing Lizzy's care, they'd never have bothered you about it in the first place."

"I don't care much for the practice of blood-letting myself." His hand rose to cup the back of her head. "Very well, Prendegast may return if it makes you happy."

"Thank you," Sylvia said, beaming up at him. "He'll make sure your mother is well looked after."

His fingers were warm as they settled on the back of her neck, and he looked down upon her with a soft smile. "Now, given our recent brush with scandal..." he began.

"When you turned all beastly and threw me out," she added.

"Yes, well. Hmm, I have already apologized for that ungentlemanly conduct, haven't I?"

"Yes, you did, but it doesn't hurt to be sure we are speaking of the same brush with scandal," she murmured, patting his arm before stepping back to a proper distance. "Please do continue."

He frowned. "It occurs to me that we must be very careful in how we go about this business of caring for Mother together. Society could easily presume, quite wrongly, that something more exists between us."

"And nothing does," she promised. "What do you propose we do?"

"I think we had best set a schedule for when we will be in Mother's house together. I have a number of business meetings and engagements that I have put off until now, and you, of course, have your business concerns to attend to as well. We cannot both neglect our other responsibilities."

Sylvia had no other business at the moment. Society might have grudgingly welcomed her back, upon Wharton's insistence, but the Hillcrest Academy was still without clients. "A schedule like yours must be complicated to manage."

"Not if we write our commitments in an appointment book, kept at Mother's house, and we consult it each day. When overlaps occur, and I'm sure there will be some, we would negotiate a mutually acceptable adjustment."

She nodded, seeing the sense in cooperation. "You have your sisters to escort about society, too."

"Too much of them in the sickroom tires Mother," he murmured. "I have had no choice but to curtail their excursions until now, but I fear any prolonged decline in their social engagements might prove disastrous."

"If I might speak candidly, my lord." She smiled quickly. "If their suitors love them, they will understand."

He chuckled. "You have more optimism about them making a match than I do, but then again, you are well-versed in understanding the minds of gentlemen seeking a bride. But have you heard my sisters squabble yet?"

She nodded quickly. "Lady Amelia and Lady Jocelyn are just like all other ladies on the marriage mart. A little silly, completive and eager to make a good marriage. I know that while perhaps not as smart as you and your mother might like, they still deserve to make a good marriage. Sir Fredrick is especially patient with Amelia's quirks. I'm quite sure by now he's acquainted with your sister's nature."

"He'd better be, because once wed, I'm not taking her back."

Sylvia laughed. "I know you don't mean that."

"How can you be so sure?"

She held his stare. "I know because despite your preoccupation with your mother, you know exactly where they are at all times. I heard you checking on them at night, wishing them pleasant dreams."

His hand rose, and he brushed his fingers across her cheek softly. "From your short-lived deception as a skittish nursemaid?"

She winked at him, and then blushed. "I couldn't let you see me too closely."

He grunted, and drew closer still. "Very well. I wouldn't turn them away if they needed me. Now, I've taken the liberty and begun an appointment book for us to share. I have added the engagements I would prefer to attend over the coming two weeks. If you could consider them and mark which engagements are impossible with your current schedule, I'd appreciate knowing as soon as possible, so I can decline those invitations."

He handed her a small leather-bound volume and she opened it up. She flicked through the pages, noting his appointments were many but not impossible to manage. "This seems very workable. Shall I mark it now and hand it back to you today or leave it somewhere for you to find?"

"Leave it in the dining room, beside the decanters at Mother's townhouse before you leave her tonight, if you can," he decided. "If all goes to plan, I suppose we shall probably see very little of each other during the coming weeks."

"Yes, I expect so," she agreed, and felt disappointment in that. Sylvia stretched up on her toes to place a kiss his cheek. "Thank you, Alexander."

He caught her arms to steady her, "For what?"

"For listening to me when you really didn't have to."

His arm slid around her waist. "I liked what I heard today. There's no reason for us to be at odds, is there?"

She met his gaze…and that feeling she always had around him stirred.

She liked him still. She liked that, now the shock his mother had dealt him had worn off, he'd apologized a second time and seemed willing to adapt. "None at all. In fact, I think we have returned to where we were before."

He smiled, and his hand rose to cup the back of her neck. "Before or after we made love? I just want to be sure we're talking about the same moment."

A blush swept over her face. "After," she whispered.

"What should we do about that?" he asked softly, bending closer.

She wet her lips in anticipation of his own settling upon her. "Why don't you kiss me again, and we can negotiate that, too."

"Gladly."

His arms came around her, his large hands stroked her body, and his lips devoured.

She kissed him back, threaded her fingers in his hair, and delighted when he lifted her up high against him.

Suddenly, her back was against a wall, and Alexander was pressed hard between her thighs, looking up at her. It felt so good to be in his arms again. He was eager, too, which made her heart leap with anticipation. She hurried to rip off her gloves so she could feel his hot skin against her palms.

He grabbed her by one leg and kneaded her thigh. Finally, he drew back and looked into her eyes. He moved in for a soft kiss. Just one kiss that said so much to her soul.

She'd missed this. Missed him kissing her.

The man was exasperating and clever and devious, and she never knew what he'd do next. He was her one great adventure. Of course, she couldn't tell him that. He'd never wipe the smug smile from his face if she did.

They were good together. Passionate lovers for as long as it lasted.

Sylvia lowered her hands and tried to hitch up her skirts.

A soft smile formed on his lips. "Temptress," he whispered, and then kissed her brow.

Sylvia shivered and fought to bring her skirts higher, but failed. They were too close for more than kissing and touching.

Sensing her eagerness, Wharton whirled her away from the wall and deposited her on the edge of the dressmakers high worktable. His large hands landed flat on her thighs and slid upward, taking her skirts with them.

Then he dropped to his knees and pressed his lips to one stocking-clad leg. "I have dreamed of touching you again."

Sylvia's breath was churning. "So have I."

"Lie back," he commanded, and then began to kiss her knees so gently.

Sylvia crumpled onto the hard table, aware she was being scandalous yet again. However, she could hardly think of the danger when the marquess was rolling down her stockings and kissing her everywhere he shouldn't. His fingers were hot, his lips loving, and Sylvia was in need of release.

At his urging, she parted her thighs for him.

There was a long pause, and then a tortured groan before the marquess buried his face between her legs.

She moaned when he kissed her sex, and bit her lips as he widened her legs more to deepen her pleasure and his exploration. The necessity for pretending modesty was a distant memory when the marquess loved her.

She brought her feet up onto the table, resting them on the edge, as the marquess' wicked tongue teased her to the brink of insanity.

Sylvia brought her fingers to her mouth and bit down to silence herself. Dear God, he'd learned what pleased her so easily the last time. A pity she couldn't have him in her bed for the rest of her life. But they'd be over sooner than later, and he'd find someone else to love.

"Not me," she whispered.

The marquess suddenly stopped. "What's wrong?"

Sylvia shook her head quickly. She had spoken aloud by mistake. "Nothing. Don't stop again."

When she met his gaze finally, she discovered him standing over her with the strangest smile on his face. He reached out and swept the backs of his fingers over her cheek. "You should see yourself lost to passion. There is no better view to be had in this world."

Sylvia's heart swooped at the adoring words, and she bit her lip because she didn't know how to respond to him. She couldn't make the mistake of confusing passion with a deeper emotion. This was only a temporary attraction, not love. She'd be wise to always remember that.

His hands went to his breeches, and his shirt was pushed aside. She caught a glimpse of the marquess' wicked grin.

He swept the head of his cock back and forth across her slit. So hot and so good that she raised up on one elbow to watch him play with her body, and his own. A hot rush of excitement swept over her, and she whimpered softly.

"Do you like the way that feels, love?" he asked, holding his cock away from her quim.

She gulped as her body clenched in anticipation of his next touch. "I do. I want more."

"How much more?"

"All of you," she whispered, and then looked up into his eyes. God, she was a slave to him, and her own desires, too. "Very slowly."

A masculine rumble escaped him. "A woman after my own heart. I'll take care of you."

His fingertips brushed against her clitoris, and then he was pushing his cock into her a little at a time. Sylvia was coming by the time he was fully wedged inside her, even though she'd tried to wait. She turned her face aside, gasping.

"Don't fight your passions. I want them," he told her, fingers still caressing her body.

She opened her eyes and slowly looked up at her lover. She'd never had a more arousing man love her than Lord Wharton, and probably wouldn't again. He took such pains to make sure she was excited enough and thoroughly satisfied by the time he found his own release.

She wiggled a little, but Alexander took her hips between his hands to hold her still.

She met his gaze, saw a wildness in his. He was holding back his passion until she was ready.

Anticipation curled through her again, and she braced herself on both elbows. "Don't fight your passions," she whispered, repeating his words. "I want them, too."

His jaw clenched, and he withdrew, only to slam back into her the next moment. Sylvia gasped, not from pain but from the pleasure of him loving her body. He was eager to be with her, and that excited her beyond measure.

His thrusts were hard and became faster. A sweat broke out onto his brow, and she heard him grunt with each stroke. If he'd not been on the edge before, he certainly was now. Her body responded to the marquess, and she boldly slipped a hand down between her legs to touch herself. His eyes flared slightly but he didn't change his pace or stop her.

She touched herself passionately, became lost in increasing her own pleasure. She silently dared herself to find completion while the marquess found his.

She curled herself higher, and he quickly put a hand behind her neck to support her. All the while, the passionate tempo of his lovemaking never once waned.

The new position brought results, and she peaked, crying out his name louder than she intended. The marquess roared suddenly and slammed into her again and again as he found his release.

Eventually, he stopped, gasping, and his lips found hers for a long, consuming kiss. They struggled to breathe together, huddled close, until he finally released her with a tortured groan.

Sylvia fell back on the table, dazed as she stared at the ceiling with her pussy still throbbing around the marquess' lovely cock.

She closed her eyes as he withdrew and slowly brought her legs together.

His hand caressed her thigh. "Did I hurt you?"

"No. That was wonderful."

"It was, wasn't it? Just like the first time we were together."

"Hmm, yes," she whispered, remembering that occasion fondly. The marquess had satisfied her body for hours. Each end brought a new beginning. The man never seemed to get enough of her then.

Sylvia put her bent arm behind her head to study him. Today he seemed exhausted by just the one release. He remained bent over her on the table. Both hands holding him up. He looked wildly disheveled, too. Like a very wicked man who'd thoroughly enjoyed himself.

He bent down and kissed her curls. "You're just what I need."

He moved back and started redressing himself. Sylvia waited a moment then sat up, too. It was only then she realized the marquess had not withdrawn.

She was so caught up in their lovemaking, she'd failed to notice he'd released his seed inside her.

She jumped down quickly before her gown could be soiled with it and rushed to the ladies' convenience behind the screen to clean herself up. There, she found water and soap and a washing cloth, meant for the clients. A quick wash of her sex would not prevent a pregnancy, however. She might feel old sometimes, but there was still a chance she might be young enough to have the marquess' child.

Had Wharton forgotten the risk, too?

"Sylvia?"

She dropped her skirts into place, and then stepped back around the screen to face him.

He came up to her and brought her into his embrace. "Lovely woman. You've soothed the savage beast in me again."

Again, but for the last time, perhaps. She couldn't lie with him again if they both forgot there were bound to be consequences. "And me."

He stroked a hand down her back. "I'll have a house for you by next week."

"For me?"

"Servants, too. You'll find I'm a generous man."

Sylvia wasn't naive. She knew exactly where this conversation was heading. She just wished they didn't have to have it now. She lifted up on her toes and pressed a finger to his lips. "I have a home already."

She kissed his cheek quickly then turned to the mirror to make sure her hair hadn't been mussed too badly.

He chuckled softly behind her back. "I don't think your cousins will appreciate us making love in your drawing room, nor should we meet here again."

"I agree."

He moved behind Sylvia and slipped his arms about her waist. She saw them reflected in the mirror and dropped her gaze. The mirror revealed a fantasy of a future she might once have had for herself, but she'd known from the start that the marquess had no real interest in her beyond satisfying a fleeting pleasure.

She was not disappointed that he didn't offer her more. But she wouldn't accept less, or any sordid halfway measure that would break her heart in the end. He expected her to be his mistress now, but accepting that offer would truly ruin her in everyone's eyes—including her own.

She turned in his arms and glanced up at him. "I enjoyed today very much."

A frown formed on his face. "I sense reluctance."

"You do." She wriggled from his grip, pressing her palms together before her waist. "I won't move into this house you have for me, and I don't think we can meet again. Not like this."

"What? I thought we were negotiating."

"No, Alexander." She smiled quickly, sad to see he appeared utterly shocked by her refusal. "A fling is all I ever expected with you."

"But you like what I do to you."

"I'm not saying I don't enjoy your attentions. You're an incredible lover, Alexander, and I have no complaints or regrets. However, I don't want to become the sort of woman who sits around all day, waiting for you to come to call."

"Don't complicate things."

She pressed her hand to his cheek. "I'm not the one doing that. You have an abundance of responsibilities, and very little free time for your family. This was only an affair, and now I think it really must be over. I don't ever want to be another person you're trying to avoid."

He caught up her hand and pressed a kiss to her wrist. Desire coiled within her at the brush of his lips and his hot breath upon her skin. "It wouldn't be that way between us."

"It couldn't be any other way," she told him, withdrawing from him yet again. "I'm not saying I wouldn't be interested in being with you again, given the right setting and privacy, like today turned out to be."

The marquess collapsed back against the worktable. "I don't believe what I'm hearing."

"That is your choice, but I can't see how we could have any sort of future together," she murmured, her heart growing heavier by the minute. "I hope you can understand. There are dangers for me—discovery and embarrassment. A pregnancy neither of us want. I respect your mother too much to risk being found out. I only want to see her back to full health, and then, if you prefer, I'll find a way to end our friendship painlessly before she ever suspects we were involved. Will you allow me that time?"

"Yes, but I—" he began, and then stopped cold.

He couldn't see a future for them either, she would wager.

Sylvia returned her hat to her head and tugged on her gloves. Hoping he'd say something to make her feel better. She liked him, but had always known she couldn't keep him. He wasn't ready to marry and, more importantly, he didn't love her.

When he remained silent, and she was ready to face the world, she turned to him one last time as a lover. "You'll see in time that I am right to end things with you before complications arise. Goodbye, Alexander, and thank you for the adventure."

When he said nothing still, watching her with hooded eyes, Sylvia collected her reticule and walked out the door without looking back.

Chapter Twenty-Two

For a whole month, Sylvia and Alexander took pains to never leave Mother alone for long. They were ships passing in the night almost. He'd be going out with his sisters and Sylvia would be rushing in. Their encounters were always very cordial and, by design, brief. It was a good arrangement they had. Mother was happy, and her listlessness seemed largely to be a thing of the past.

Unfortunately, Alexander was the one left feeling out of sorts, even though he had more or less resumed his former busy life. Mother did not need him, but he did visit her room each day and shared more of what he'd been up to with her.

Tonight, he had arranged an evening of leisure for himself, and Sylvia had only been too happy to remain late with his mother.

"Unfortunately," Alexander announced, trying to stand up and failing. "I think I must be going soon."

"You're too drunk to leave yet," Carmichael complained, shoving him back down.

Alexander floundered in a well-padded armchair. At least he thought it was soft. He couldn't really feel most of his limbs as he floated in a pleasant, alcohol-fueled daze after a very satisfying dinner. He hadn't been this drunk in a long time, but they were celebrating.

"If you go to your mother's home in this condition, she'll ring a peel over your head," Carmichael warned.

"She would, too—if she could roam the halls. Thankfully, she's keeping to her room still. Most of the time." He squinted across the familiar chamber, wishing he could be home in the blink of an eye.

But home was still Berkley Square, and he could not be there without running into Sylvia. They were sharing the care of his mother rather well he thought. Or rather, he had given way because he wasn't Mother's first choice for conversation.

"You're just as under the weather as I." He turned to his friend. "What does a wife do to a husband in these circumstances?"

"Mine will probably laugh when I trip over my own feet, and she'll leave me there, too," Carmichael mused. "My wife tends to limit her compassion when there is alcohol involved."

Alexander huffed. "Even if we're celebrating your future son's arrival?"

"Oh, most definitely for that as well," Carmichael promised. His smile turned smug with pleasure for his impending fatherhood. "To the child to come."

Alexander drank deeply. He'd been here several hours more than he probably should have been, and he'd long since lost count of just how many times they'd toasted Carmichael's virility. Alexander had arrived here with Scarsdale in tow at noon, and they'd stayed well past sunset. He squinted across the room at the clock but couldn't make sense of the blurry squiggles on the face.

He dragged out his pocket watch and saw it was only just now eleven. He could have sworn it was later, but it had been a strange month for Alexander. The things that usually happened quickly took an age, and little brought satisfaction. Not even watching the Norringtons drive around with their chins held high because of their improved financial situation had made any difference to his mood.

Mother was recovering well, but slowly. However, she had insisted he get on with his own life…and he had tried. Mama had her new friend, Sylvia, to keep her company during the day, and long into the evenings, too, on most days.

Sylvia.

The woman who'd refused him.

Alexander was not at all used to rejection.

He took another drink and grimaced.

Sylvia curtsied to him, spoke politely to him, but the spark that had lit her eyes when they were alone had utterly disappeared.

Extinguished in the blink of an eye.

Just because he'd wanted more.

It made no sense. Was the occasional tumble all she needed and desired from a man? From him, too?

Discovering he couldn't have her had made Alexander dreadfully out of sorts with everyone. And it wasn't even just the lack of sex in his life, either. He had found himself disinterested in other women; he had no patience for their conversations whatsoever.

Although he knew exactly where Sylvia would be when he was out in society, he found himself foolishly hoping to speak with her, instead.

Discontent that he was thinking of her again, he turned to view Lord Scarsdale curled up asleep nearer the fire. On any other night, Alexander might have laughed at how ridiculous he looked, like a cat on a chair that was far too small for him. "No staying power, that one."

"He did his best," Carmichael argued, raising his glass to study the contents by candlelight. Whatever the earl saw made him toss the contents down his throat. "I think I shall have a very sore head tomorrow."

Alexander would, too, but at least he'd feel something other than frustration. "It's worth it."

"I know why *I'm* drinking, but why are you?" Carmichael poured himself another glass, very unsteadily. "You couldn't be celebrating my future offspring as much as I am. Are you drowning your sorrows out of guilt?"

"I'm keeping you company." He forced his eyes open fully, though. "What do I have to feel guilty about?"

"The Hillcrest Academy."

Sylvia again. Damn. "No, I fixed that," he promised. "It's all settled down."

"For God's sake, it is not. You put them out of business."

Alexander sat up a little straighter, or tried to. "I did not."

"You certainly did."

"But that was weeks ago. Of course I was cross that first day, but I'm not now. I made sure everyone should know it, too."

"How did you do that?" Carmichael tipped his head back against the chair and closed his eyes.

He'd called in a dozen favors and made sure Sylvia had been invited to the most important events. She'd said everything had went well. But he had not asked specifically about her business. He'd just assumed everything would have returned to normal.

"Sylvia should have told me if her problems continued," he complained, scrubbing at his face. "Now, what's all this nonsense about the academy closing? I've said nothing against the enterprise."

Carmichael opened his eyes and shook his head as if trying to keep himself awake. "It's not so much what you said, but *did* that started it all, I understand. Society has taken the view that since Sylvia offended you once, the academy must have, as well. They'd rather stay on your good side than theirs, and have abandoned any connection with the Hillcrest cousins."

"That's ridiculous," he protested.

"I completely agree, and yet every client has sent their regrets and canceled their appointments. Some have even suddenly left Town rather than face them again."

"That is surely an exaggeration."

"Scarsdale, too, and Sullivan both hinted at dissatisfaction over recent events."

"No." Alexander was suddenly stone-cold sober at hearing this development.

His argument with Sylvia about Mother had been a temporary aberration between them. He'd made his position plain, and she'd made hers, too, and loudly. They had made up and made love…and ended their affair. But they were still partners in caring for his mother. There was no reason for her business to suffer.

His relationship with Sylvia was no one's business but his. "What is she—what are they going to do?"

"Sylvia wouldn't say."

His brain woke up the rest of the way. "Wouldn't say or

doesn't know?"

"I think they've decided, but perhaps Sylvia didn't want me and my wife to know yet? Without the business, though, I imagine things won't be easy for them. At least we can offer them friendship and support if they need it. There's plenty of room in Surrey for the trio to set up a new home if London proves too costly."

Concern gripped him. He'd already offered Sylvia a home—and been refused. "They'd not leave London?"

Alexander discovered he'd harbored a fleeting hope that Sylvia would eventually come around, come back to him. With the passage of enough time, perhaps, she might have changed her mind about them, too. She couldn't do that if she left London.

"Perhaps they might go home instead."

"Where is home?"

"They are from Marlow, in Berkshire. Lenore met them there during the time she was a companion."

Berkshire was in the opposite direction to his country estate in Essex. Far from Mother, too. He remembered her suggestion she could withdraw her friendship from Mother eventually, when she was better, but had her troubles with the business been part of her motivation?

He sat forward, concerned that Sylvia's last goodbye truly might have been forever.

He was not ready to give up on her. They were good together. Mother loved the damn woman enough to choose Sylvia's company over her own children's!

They all may never see Sylvia again.

The thought brought him to his feet.

"Where are you going?"

"I just remembered something I have to attend to." Like fixing things, so Sylvia would remain exactly where he needed her to be. Right under his nose, managing Mama in such a way that he had actually stopped worrying when he couldn't be at home. Sylvia allowed him to continue his work, his interests, and still left him feeling confident that he was doing the right thing for his family, even if he couldn't be with her, too.

Carmichael nudged their friend Scarsdale with his toe. The man swatted away the annoyance and went back to sleep. "What shall I do with this one?"

"Well, I don't know," he nearly shouted. How could he worry about Scarsdale when the woman he wanted was about to be driven away from him?

Carmichael scowled. "You brought him with you, or did you forget that, too?"

He looked at his friends sourly. Carting Scarsdale back to his townhouse might mean he missed seeing Sylvia tonight. "Cover him up and kick him out in the morning, like I usually do. I don't have time for him now."

Alexander headed for the door, but had to put his hand out to the wall after a few steps, as the world lurched and rolled. "I need my carriage," he shouted out, hoping a servant was nearby and heard him.

Carmichael was suddenly at his elbow. "Wharton, what's got into you? What's so important?"

"Nothing," he promised, but he couldn't look at Carmichael right now. Not when the woman he damn well had *fallen for* was keeping yet another secret from him.

How stupid he was not to have realized it before.

He was in love—and there was a good chance he could be loved in return.

Or he might have been, if he'd not stupidly offered to make Sylvia his mistress instead of the better position as his wife.

Everything made sense now.

Sylvia was needed right where she was. He wouldn't allow her to retreat from his life, from his mother, anytime soon. She'd chosen them, him and his mother, and he accepted the challenge of making her a central part of his life as soon as he could.

He had a ten-minute wait for his carriage, and when it came, he demanded it hurry him straight to his mother's townhouse. Once there, he rushed upstairs.

Mother was unfortunately alone and asleep in her darkened chamber when he barged in.

"Did your mistress kick you out again, Arthur?" Mother asked sleepily.

Alexander blanched at hearing the question, and Father's name after so long of never hearing it. He wet his lips. "It's Alexander, Mama," he whispered. "Your son."

"Oh, oh," she said, struggling to rise. "I could have sworn you were your father coming home late again."

"No, it's just me. Lie back. I got turned around in the dark, unfamiliar house. I'm sorry I woke you."

Mother huffed. "You've been drinking again, haven't you?"

He didn't even bother to dissemble. "Yes, Mama."

"I knew London would turn you into a sot, just like your father was before he married me. I straightened him out, of course, and then his mistress ruined him for good. I thought I was a good wife…but not good enough."

Alexander approached the bed. Mama had a terrible opinion of mistresses. Father had disappointed her with the way he'd carried on with his. She expected Alexander to be just as weak as his sire, too. But he was far smarter.

"The failure was never yours, Mama," he promised. "Father was selfish and cruel. Everything I abhor about married men."

"And yet, you took a mistress."

He tried to imagine Sylvia in the role of his mistress, waiting for him to find the time to come and see her. He understood now why she'd rejected his offer out of hand. She would have disappointed Mother. His offer wasn't respectable enough for anyone he truly cared about. And he cared about Sylvia very much. "I don't have a mistress now, and when I marry, there will be no need, I imagine."

"Do you expect me to believe you will only marry for love?" Mama asked, frowning.

"Of course. What other reason could make an impatient man wait so long to wed?" Alexander leaned over the bed and kissed her brow lightly. Mother would unwittingly play a vital part in his strategy to bring Sylvia into the family officially, starting tomorrow.

Mother stared at him. Her eyes were the only two small bright spots in the dark room. "A wife you can love and respect is just what you need," she suggested.

Only if her name was Sylvia. A marriage proposal was probably the last thing she expected from him after their last private conversation, but she would have one. Though first, Alexander had something special to collect from home before he started. "I wholeheartedly agree. Good night, Mother. Sorry to have disturbed you."

"Anytime, son. Anytime," she said sleepily. "By the way, I've always hoped you would have a grand wedding here in London, but I suppose it will depend if your future wife and I see eye to eye."

Alexander grinned. Oh, his future wife and Mother seemed to agree on everything so far. He doubted that would change anytime soon.

He backed from the room and went to his, anticipating seeing Sylvia again tomorrow, and forever after that.

Chapter Twenty-Three

The *ton* were out in force in great numbers, prowling Hyde Park, the place to be seen by those who mattered, in their very best carriages and most fashionable attire. Everyone she saw belonged.

Sylvia was here under duress.

The Duchess of Exeter had invited Sylvia to join her for a drive after her visit with Lady Wharton had gone so well. Lady Wharton, keen to please her new acquaintance, had insisted Sylvia must go for the air and exercise.

Sylvia hadn't felt she'd needed any, but protesting too much would have offended her grace. She looked up at the bright sky and forced a smile. "It's a lovely day."

"Indeed it is. I'm glad you could join me. Exeter would have been here, too, but my husband thought he'd ride in the park instead to give us privacy to have a little talk."

Sylvia twisted to look at her. "What about?"

"Oh, don't look so fearful, my dear. There's nothing at all to worry about."

Sylvia subsided. Since Lady Wharton's shocking confession about her health, she'd become a little jumpy when she suspected she'd be hearing bad news soon.

"I merely heard of the problems you and your cousins have had with certain people in recent weeks. I wanted to offer my help if you need it. Why didn't you say something sooner? I was astonished to hear that your name had been dropped from the guest lists for a time."

Sylvia winced. "It hardly matters now."

"But they were your friends, and it isn't right."

"They were fickle. Much too swift to condemn me just for trying to keep a promise."

"I must say, I thought Lady Wharton was looking very well today for what she must have endured. I had honestly expected to meet a sickly woman; instead, I kept thinking she was about to launch herself out of bed at any moment and dance."

"She was in high spirits today, wasn't she?" Sylvia agreed. "I'm not sure why, though."

"Well, whatever has cheered her up, I hope it continues making her smile," Lady Exeter confessed.

"Most days she's a bit prickly, frustrated with her slow recovery."

"She's very fond of you and thinks of you as a daughter, I suspect," her grace murmured. "Do you think she'll move to Wharton House soon?"

"I don't know when she might go, but the physician still warns against jostling her about unnecessarily. The wound is quite large. I would hate for something preventable to cause a setback."

She would be sad on the day Lady Wharton left Berkley Square. She had decided that would be the perfect time to start finding excuses not to travel so far to see her.

"Do you worry Wharton will try to stop you from seeing his mother again?"

"I don't believe he'd do any such thing now," she assured her. They made a good team, really. "He apologized for his behavior, and I believe him sincere."

"Well, if you argue again and he dares try to toss you out, he'll answer to me next time," her grace warned.

"I don't imagine I could give him a reason to resort to such measures again," Sylvia promised.

He was a good man. Generous and kind to his mother, and to herself, too. He hadn't seemed overly affected one way or the other since she'd ended their affair. They had both gotten along with their lives again, had retreated from each other, too.

But she loved having the marchioness living so close by while it lasted. It had been the closest she'd felt to having a mother again. But eventually, Alexander would insist he had to take his mother back to Wharton House, some distance away. At that point, Sylvia would be on her own again with just her cousins. They were still mulling over the direction their futures would take, but the most likely outcome was that they would move from London.

"I am glad to hear it. You must have been very shocked that he would…" the duchess began, and then smiled. "Oh, look. There is my dear husband riding by, and our Teddy, too, is with him. Don't they look a handsome pair?"

Sylvia murmured her agreement as the men came closer. Teddy seemed surprised to see Sylvia but offered a sincere smile nonetheless.

"Miss Hillcrest. Good afternoon," the duke said, and then drew close to his duchess. "Well met, wife."

Her grace extended her hand beyond their carriage to shake his, and then patted his horse, too. "How was your ride?"

The duke looked a little windswept and the horse was almost in a lather. "Quite good. Long enough, I think. May I join you?"

"You're always welcome," the duchess promised, and Sylvia nodded, too. "Actually, we were just about to stretch our legs."

"Then I will be happy to join you," he promised.

Exeter patted his horse fondly then swept off the beast in the manner of a man who had spent a great deal of time on horseback. A groom rushed to take the reins and lead the horse away. Mr. Berringer lingered on his mount, and the duke looked up at him. "Are you not going to join us for a stroll, sir?"

"If I wouldn't be imposing," he murmured.

The duke made a sound like a horse and took the bridle of his heir's mount himself. Mr. Berringer swept off his horse, not quite as smoothly or as lightly as his older cousin, and his horse was taken away to be tied to the back of the carriage, too.

The carriage door was opened by a groom and steps put down for the duchess to exit. Sylvia followed, although she'd not been asked if she wanted to walk about. Her grace went to her husband and the pair started off together down the path. That left Sylvia to walk beside Thaddeus Berringer.

"I'm sorry that our arrival might have spoiled your carriage ride with her grace," Mr. Berringer whispered.

"I was going to apologize for interrupting your ride with the duke," she whispered back.

"It was always bound to happen. As soon as I saw the duchess was in the park, I knew his grace couldn't resist diverting to be with her," Mr. Berringer confessed with an exasperated laugh.

"They are very much in love," she agreed.

"I certainly hope so. What of you?"

"What do you mean?"

"Come now. I think we've known each other long enough not to play games. I know why everyone comes to the park at this hour. I'm sure you're a great admirer of the opposite sex, and are here to admire someone you hold in special admiration."

The only man who fit that description lately was Wharton. She lowered her eyes, determined not to look for him here. "I imagine you come here for a similar purpose, too," she confessed.

"I am very pleased to find *you* in the park to admire," he promised, his expression one of open delight as he looked down upon Sylvia from his greater height with decidedly masculine interest on his face.

Sylvia winced inwardly. She had never wanted this man to imagine there could be anything between them but friendship. He felt…*wrong*, though there was nothing physically about him that repulsed her in any way. She just wasn't attracted to him, or anyone else she'd met of late.

The painful truth was that Thaddeus Berringer just wasn't the Marquess of Wharton, the man she continued to long for in the depths of her soul. Not enough time had passed for Sylvia to imagine herself in another lover's arms yet. If she ever could. "Alas, admiring does not often lead to claiming."

"A pity," he murmured and looked ahead quickly. "I'm not sure you're aware that I called at your home a few times over recent weeks. Your cousin explained on my last visit that you've become indispensable to the Lady Wharton. I hadn't realized just how much time you had been spending with her until her grace explained the arrangement you made with Lord Wharton to both watch over her."

"She's become a good friend, and I'm very fond of her," Sylvia told him. "Her recovery is unfortunately slow and quite frustrating for her. It helps her to have a constant distraction, so I visit often and stay longer than I would normally have visited with anyone. Lord Wharton cannot always be with her, unfortunately."

"I see. When do you imagine the lady will be well enough to no longer need almost all of your attention?"

"I honestly don't know. The surgery and confinement has weakened her, I fear. It will be many months more before she is fully healed."

"Ah," the man said, sounding so disappointed by the news that Sylvia was almost embarrassed she didn't like him more. There was nothing she could do about it though, other than continue to offer a friendly ear and perhaps try to encourage his affections toward someone more suitable.

"So tell me, how many times did you dance at last night's ball?" she asked. "Tell me about the lady that most impressed you? Is she in the park today?"

"I had hoped to dance with *you* last night." When Berringer smiled quickly, almost a wince, Sylvia felt bad. "But where Wharton goes, you are unlikely to be anymore, it seems."

"I was with his mother," Sylvia admitted. "But you are the Duke of Exeter's heir. I'm sure you didn't lack female companionship."

Berringer stopped and looked right at her. "None of them were the lady I most wanted to dance with, but it seems she is immune to the lure of the riches I will inherit…and me, too."

He held her stare, a question in his eyes that she had to answer.

"I'm sorry," Sylvia said, lowering her gaze. He'd all but declared himself in love with her today, but Sylvia just didn't feel the same. She wanted to let him down gently. "I'm sure you will find someone who appreciates you the way they should very soon."

He sighed. "I can't imagine it."

"You will. You must." Sylvia winced again. "Trust me, it is impossible to force anyone to fall in love."

Berringer nodded. "Oh, how I envy Lord Wharton now."

Sylvia froze in fear, but then her cheeks began heating from that remark. "Why should you envy him?"

"Because while he might be forced to live with his mother away from his mansion, he is assured the pleasure of your company almost every day for a good long while to come. It's obvious you hold a special place in his affections."

Sylvia looked away, blushing. "I'm sure Lord Wharton cares only that my long visits make his mother happy."

"It's more than that, I suspect." Berringer sighed again and shook his head. "For you as well, even if you will not admit it."

Sylvia wanted to deny Berringer's claim, but he was correct. She did think very highly of Alexander. Unfortunately, he hadn't revealed such a partiality for her company. He'd tried to make her his mistress, a position which Sylvia would refuse to accept even now.

Berringer pursed his lips, and then turned away. "Shall we catch up to their graces?"

"Yes, I think that would be best."

They met the duke and duchess, now turned back, and headed toward the carriage. They joined the pair in another slow stroll through the park. She and Berringer walked in silence now. Awkward and uncomfortable with each other. She hoped he was not angry with her for not caring about him.

Sylvia climbed into the carriage with a heavy sigh, and was unsurprised when Mr. Berringer declined to join them for the long drive home. Thankfully, he hid his feelings well and displayed no overt sign of bitterness toward her for not loving him back. She waved him goodbye and looked ahead.

She'd fallen in love with Alexander...and she'd keep it her secret forever.

Chapter Twenty-Four

When a man began a courtship, he must have a clear understanding of what he offered the object of his affection. Alexander was a marquess, and his bride would become a marchioness of an old and distinguished English family. He was rich, too, wealthy beyond the comprehension of all but a few in society. He had all his own teeth and he didn't look too bad in bright light, either.

But those were still not reasons anyone should ever choose him as a husband.

He was well aware of his failings. He was proud and vain and secretive. Much too involved in the business of running his vast estate and investments. He was politically minded, loath to miss any session of parliament if he could help it. He'd neglected his family for years and had only just begun the long journey to recapture their respect, and the hand of the one woman he admired above all others.

Only she wasn't in her home right now, while he was.

She hadn't been with his mother, either, so he'd had no choice but to come here and speak with her cousins—women who didn't look at him with too much kindness right now.

The Hillcrest women, the older Eugenia and younger Aurora, wouldn't say where Sylvia was. They appeared vastly uncomfortable right now, especially since he'd insisted he remain in their home without saying why he wouldn't go, until Sylvia returned home and joined them.

"May I offer you another biscuit, my lord," the younger cousin asked, offering him a half-full plate to pick over.

"No, thank you. I am quite satisfied with the cup of tea I have."

Alexander didn't drink tea, but took a small sip now and then to be polite and pass the time, barely managing not to gag on the vile stuff.

Alexander had learned a thing or two about Sylvia's cousins today. Of the pair, the younger was a bit more like Sylvia, bolder, quicker to smile, and smart, too. The older cousin was damn near frightening when Sylvia wasn't here to divert her attention.

At last the front door opened and banged shut. "I'm home," Sylvia called.

The elder Hillcrest cousin rose gracefully and slipped out of the room without another word. He exchanged a quick smile with Aurora Hillcrest and set his cup down as his heart began to pound with familiar anticipation.

When Sylvia sailed into the room, he was on his feet in a second. He bowed and, upon noticing alarm in her eyes, quickly said, "Mama is fine."

She curtsied to him and took a chair to the right. "What are you doing here?"

Eugenia took her place behind the desk again, and Aurora was on his left. He felt himself surrounded and uncomfortable. Was this how they tortured those poor devils without the wits to find wives without help?

Alexander seated himself. "I find myself in dire need of advice," he began. "I know my actions last month have caused the academy to close, but I believe I can help settle matters in your favor again."

"Go on," Eugenia said but she studied him like a specimen under glass until he nearly squirmed.

Sylvia could not have any idea why he'd come to her today, and he enjoyed that look of consternation on her face. But it was not likely he'd ever surprise the woman again after today. If their conversation turned out the way he hoped, he'd never have a secret he didn't share with her again. He'd also be adding these other two women to his life. If they were anything like his mother and Sylvia together, he might as well confide in them, too.

He wanted Sylvia back—and he'd do anything to make that happen.

Eugenia shuffled some papers. "We'd be only too happy to help you if we can?"

He may as well get right to the point. "I have a problem with a particular lady."

Two of the three women sat forward eagerly. "Do you now?"

He did his best to not look in Sylvia's direction for the moment. "Indeed. I'm not quite sure how to reach the conclusion I desire with her."

Two of the three exchanged an alarmed smile, quickly squashed. The moment he ran his words back through his own mind, he caught his double entendre. He caught Eugenia's eye, filled with surprise.

The woman he'd thought prudish was on the verge of laughing at him because she thought he'd implied he could not get a stiff cock. "Not that sort of problem," he chided.

"As you say," Eugenia choked out, looking down with a half-hidden smile. "Did you wish to break from her entirely then?"

"No. I want to keep her. Isn't that what other men come here to get advice for? To design the perfect courtship to ensure the woman they desire becomes theirs forever?"

Sylvia gasped, and then her lips pressed together hard.

Aurora caught his eye. "Never with so much grim determination as you seem to project today."

"Marriage is a serious business."

"It is indeed."

Sylvia's face seemed too pale for the good news he hoped he'd be imparting. He'd honestly expected for some sign, a blush or a welcoming smile, that indicated he wouldn't have to prostrate himself at her feet, pleading to receive the affection that might yet still be his.

But if he had to, he certainly would.

He was going to unburden himself of everything before her cousins whether she liked it or not. "I should probably start my tale from the very beginning. We met through mutual acquaintances, and hit it off straight away—or at least, I saw no harm in her. I was not looking for a serious attachment. My thoughts were as far away from marriage as I could get. I've been so busy, I'd not even replaced my last mistress or had time to look for another."

"How terrible for you," Aurora murmured, sarcasm barely hidden.

He ignored her for the moment. "Anyway, we kept being thrown together, and an opportunity arose for a bit of fun. The sex was incredible," he admitted. "The best I've ever had. She had me hot for her, and reveled in my eagerness, too."

Now it was the turn of the other Hillcrest women to gasp, and for Sylvia to turn a lovely shade of embarrassed.

"My lord, we don't need to know the particulars of your amorous conquests."

"But I don't believe I conquered her. Quite the other way round, actually."

"My lord, please, there is more to making a marriage than intimacy," Eugenia chided.

"But it certainly helps," Aurora admitted, and then quickly added, "or so I'm told."

Alexander looked at the two cousins, women who one day soon would be part of his family, and nearly groaned aloud. Like Sylvia, they were bold, forthright women.

And like Sylvia, they might actually not be the inexperienced spinsters they first appeared to be.

He would absolutely insist that the pair come to live under his roof when he married Sylvia, just so they'd have his protection if they ever needed it one day.

But for now...his first concern was Sylvia and their future together.

"As we became more involved, I discovered she'd make decisions that did not align with my wishes at the time."

"Such as?"

"She meddled in my family affairs."

"Women are, by and large, often unwilling to share their opinions with men who value only their own."

"You see, there is how she misunderstood me. None of us are ever exactly as we seem. She acted quiet and proper in front of everyone else, but underneath, in private, she's entirely a handful. Deliciously wicked and devious, too. In and out of bed, my head is spinning from her tricks. Mark me well, it is the quiet ones that always bear watching."

"Lord Wharton, you seem fixated by the physical side of your relationship with this woman," Eugenia said. "There is more to love and marriage than instant gratification."

"Instant! If you do it right the first time, it should take all night. A very wise woman once said to the wife of a friend of mine that men think of sex all the time, and it's a miracle anything gets done. I tell you now that it is absolutely true. If a fellow is happy at home, he's a better man and far more productive in his business affairs. I haven't been truly happy since she set me back on my heels."

"How long has that been?"

"A day was too long. But in the month that has passed, it's occurred to me, too, that her meddling in my affairs was actually the best thing that ever happened." He glanced at Sylvia finally. "I have reconsidered what matters most in my life, and I can't give up. She might have refused me the first time but I *won't* give up."

Sylvia arched one brow. "If you consider this lady you talk of so essential, do you have any idea why she wouldn't accept you the first time you asked?"

"I haven't actually asked her to marry me yet, but I intend to rectify my mistake today. I went in a wrong direction and have regretted it ever since."

Sylvia inclined her head.

"Husbands and wives can make a formidable team if they worked together instead of apart," he suggested.

She nodded again. "It sounds to me as if you were already working together for the same ends."

"Only I didn't expect it, or appreciate her involvement enough. I reacted poorly to what I perceived as the undermining of my authority. I was an idiot. I'm trying to apologize."

"You are exceedingly arrogant to think a quick apology thrown out would be enough to make up for the crushing disappointment of a second-rate offer."

"Arrogance was the first skill I learned at my father's knee," he said, smiling at how Sylvia was playing along while her cousins looked completely lost to what was really going on around them still. "The next was how to become irresistible."

Sylvia suddenly laughed. "Always so modest."

"I doubt I will ever change."

She sobered. "No, I expect that would be asking too much."

"I have a great many flaws, and I will always be the first to admit them. When I want something, I charge ahead boldly. So do you, for that matter." He fished in his pocket and held out his hand. "I have already picked out a little ring, you see, for my bride. With luck it should suit, or if not, I have many others in the family safe."

The ring was huge, even by his standards. A large square-cut diamond, surrounded by more diamonds, interspersed with rubies and embedded in a heavy yellow-gold surround and band.

Before Sylvia could claim the ring, her cousins asked if they could see it closer up. Alexander pursed his lips, making a show of considering the matter, and then passed the costly piece to Sylvia first.

She held it as if terrified of damaging it. Alexander wasn't the least bit worried. The ring was in the safest hands he knew.

"There's a tiara, necklace and bracelet to match," he murmured. "I did not think to bring them with me today. They'd have spoiled the lines of my coat. But what do you think of the trinket? Will the woman I love like and accept it as her due?"

Aurora took the ring from Sylvia, studying it carefully before handing it to Eugenia to admire next. Alexander couldn't help but notice a look of longing cross Sylvia's face as it moved away from her. She wanted the ring back, he'd wager.

But might she want him now, too?

"This is no mere trinket," Eugenia noted. "Do you believe a fortune in gems is all it takes to sway a woman to accept you?"

"I certainly hope not, but I have a vault full if she likes that sort of thing. I feel confidant the woman I marry will not be swayed by my title, either, impressive as that is, too."

Sylvia met his gaze. "So what recommends you for a husband then?"

"When it comes right down to it, all I can offer is myself. Faults and all."

"And a willingness to share a life," Eugenia Hillcrest suggested.

"Together, yes. I am also willing to be managed," he suggested.

"It must be love, indeed," Aurora said with a shy smile. "For a man to willingly put himself into a wife's hands."

He nodded. "She's very capable. So how should I proceed? How do you usually advise a man on how to perform the perfect proposal of marriage?"

Eugenia nodded. "I would think a little of what you shared today would suffice, perhaps leaving out declaring your deepest amorous inclinations in front of witnesses, particularly family."

He grinned. "I'll consider it, however, the lady I love has always been willing to speak of her amorous inclinations openly to me."

"There is no absolute best way to propose marriage," Aurora told him. "I suggest you consider the setting and try to put yourself in her shoes. Is she at all romantic? Would she really want to see you on both knees or would a tender, private conversation away from her family allow free rein to any emotions she'd rather keep hidden from them?"

Sylvia wasn't watching him now, but her head started to bob up and down.

"Thank you," he said to Sylvia more than to the other pair. He stood. Paused, ready to deliver exactly the opposite. To fall to his knees and deliver a gushingly sweet offer of marriage, regardless who heard him do it.

Sylvia hurried to stand and, one of her hands stretched out, urgently forestalled him falling to the floor. "Do you mean it?"

"Of course." He glanced at her in surprise. "Half the fun of being with me is that I tell a tall tale that's based in absolute truth. I want to marry very much."

"Lord Wharton?"

"Yes, Sylvia?"

She worried her bottom lip "Could I see that ring again?"

"Certainly." He withdrew it from his pocket and held it out to her.

Sylvia didn't take the ring but held out her left hand, fingers spread wide.

"Ah. I see." He slid the ring on her finger. "There you go, my love."

Sylvia held up her hand to admire the piece on her finger.

Eugenia was suddenly at her side. "Sylvia? Is this what I fear it is?"

A shy smile crossed Sylvia's lips as she met his gaze.

Alexander grinned back, waiting for her to say the words he longed to hear.

"The marquess is mine," she announced proudly. "Faults and all."

"Yes!" Wharton crowed, and when Sylvia grabbed his lapels, he swooped down to kiss the woman he loved soundly. Her cousins made some noises around them, but he was so happy to finally be claimed by the woman who never failed to surprise and please him in so many ways that he paid them no mind at all.

He smiled down upon Sylvia when they came up for air. "How did I do with my first ever proposal?"

"Very well, Alexander," she promised, laughing. "No one was more shocked than me when you started talking about your feelings in front of my cousins. Your father did that to your mother, too."

"We will be happier than them, I swear. I saw firsthand how he treated her, ignored her. I don't think I'll be able to with you," he promised. "We should go soon to tell Mother, and I'm sure if we promise her those grandchildren she's craving, she'll get used to having us all around her in time."

Sylvia's brow furrowed. "Don't you mean both?"

"It might be a bit of a squeeze at first, at least until Mother can be moved to Wharton house, but I want you and your cousins to move in with her immediately, if you can. They'd be company for Mother as well when we go out together, and if they are anything like you, they probably have secrets that'll turn some poor gent on his head. They might need us to keep the *ton* on our side one day, if they want to take their place on the marriage mart."

"That will be up to them."

He nodded. "People should really only marry when they are prepared to share their lives, and their mothers too, don't you think?"

Sylvia laughed and pulled him down for a quick kiss. "Indeed I do."

Epilogue

Alexander adjusted his sleeve unnecessarily again as the dull roar of the guests outside rumbled in his ears, glad his long engagement was almost over. It had been many months since he'd proposed to Sylvia. I quick wedding had not been acceptable. "Will you come away from the door," he called. "You know I detest arriving too early."

"Sorry, but you have to see this. It's standing-room only out there," Carmichael noted in awe. "Is there anyone your mother didn't invite?"

"Probably not." He smiled. "Anyone who's anyone would attend my wedding day."

Scarsdale lurched to his feet. "God, you're unbelievable. They're here to see the bride, and not you."

Scarsdale was not taking the news of Alexander's imminent marriage well. He was convinced Alexander had been bewitched. "They'd better be here for my bride. I want her to be the center of attention."

He wanted every good thing for Sylvia. A home, loving family, true friends, endless challenges, and adventures. Passion. Respect. Passion. He glanced up at the ceiling, sent a loving thought toward his future wife, and turned for the door as the bells began to chime the hour. "Now, it's time."

Carmichael wrenched open the door and allowed him to leave the vestry first. He walked slowly along the nave, with his two best friends following close behind. As Carmichael had warned, St. George's Cathedral was full and the sound was overwhelming at first. He noticed his mother's absence in the family pew but was not at all concerned where she might be at that moment. No doubt she was waiting by the door to catch her first glimpse of his bride as she arrived at the church. Alexander had sent a carriage to collect her and ensure she arrived exactly on time.

His brother, Toby, scowled at him from the first pew, while his silly sisters laughed, and their new husbands endeavored to keep them in their front-row seats.

He took his place, and then turned to look up the length of the chamber at all the witnesses and friends who had gathered for this most important occasion.

His mother was just sitting down, and although she appeared serene and calm, Alexander couldn't miss the excitement brimming in Mama's eyes. She turned quickly to nod to friends. Mother wasn't quite herself yet. Sylvia had warned him that she would only dance once today, and only with him because he could be trusted to be gentle when spinning her about.

It was at Mama's insistence that the marriage was happening now and not several more months into the future, when she was at last fully healed. Impatience was the family curse. Mama simply couldn't wait until her eldest child was settled, and they'd agreed to finally tie the knot to make her happy.

Mama inclined her head regally, approving his appearance and letting him know, too, that all was ready for the marriage ceremony to commence.

Somewhere, a violin started playing, and a hush fell over the sacred church.

The violin fell silent then, and he clearly heard the turning of a latch as the church doors creaked fully open.

Everyone turned to face the back of the room on cue.

Mother had such a flair for the dramatic that she'd probably planned that moment years ago when he was still in the nursery.

Alexander found himself holding his breath, waiting for his first glimpse of Sylvia.

Finally he saw movement—and then Sylvia came. She was dressed in sparkling jewels and pristine white muslin. She had never looked more assured or beautiful. He was one hell of a lucky man.

She was wearing Mother's favorite jewels. A high collar of blue sapphires surrounded her throat and encircled her wrists. "Something borrowed and something blue," he murmured, casting a quick glance at his mother.

But Mama was already crying, her hands raised to her lips to control herself. Seeing her like that, so happy and proud, made his own eyes tear up for a moment, too.

Sylvia had styled her hair differently today, and she carried the posy of wildflowers he'd sent over that morning between both hands. Her cousins surrounded her, as they'd mentioned they might do in defiance of usual custom of having a man give the woman away. When he thought about it, Sylvia and her two cousins had walked Lord Carmichael's wife down the aisle, too.

Sylvia met his gaze and then winked, like she had the first time he'd really noticed her.

This time he winked back, unwilling to pretend he wasn't completely besotted with the woman.

The Hillcrest cousins handed Sylvia into his keeping, and stepped back to sit with Lord Carmichael's wife.

"I had a dream about you last night," he whispered as he raised her hand to press a quick kiss upon her glove.

"Tell me later," she said, smiling.

Alexander laughed that she wouldn't be diverted. Not in front of the priest and the whole of the *ton*, but later he'd tell her every wicked detail of what he'd done to her.

He gripped her fingers tightly as the priest extolled the virtues of humility and obedience in a loud, clear voice that should have carried to the far corners. The man obviously couldn't be speaking to him, and certainly not to Sylvia. Their marriage would not be so boring as all that. He expected to be kept on his toes.

In the end, the ceremony was over quite painlessly and he was off the market, if he'd ever been on it, and a happily married man.

Sylvia's husband and devoted lover forever.

They turned toward the guests as a great cry rang out, "Long live the happy couple!"

"Here, here!"

"That was Mr. Berringer," Sylvia whispered.

Alexander was surprised. The man might have been a rival for Sylvia's affections once, but he had conceded the field with little outward fuss. Though Berringer professed to be happy for them, Alexander wasn't sure he would have felt the same if their situations had been reversed, and Berringer had won Sylvia's heart instead.

That's how he knew he'd done the right thing in marrying her. He'd never been at all possessive about his past women.

But he was with her.

Only Sylvia mattered.

They strolled toward the open church doors, or at least attempted to do so. They were waylaid by so many well-wishers, he feared they'd never win free. The Duchess of Exeter hugged Sylvia for a prolonged length of time, sobbing. As did Lady Carmichael, and Aurora and Eugenia Hillcrest, too.

But it was his mother, in the end, who managed to send them on their way.

She put her hands onto their backs and pushed hard. "Don't you dare be late for your wedding breakfast after all the effort I've gone to."

Sylvia smiled. "We won't be, Mama."

Mother burst into tears and hugged Alexander's wife hard, but very carefully. "Such a terrible girl to make her mama cry."

"I know," Sylvia whispered. "We will see you as soon as I'm done with him."

Mama laughed and rushed back to her daughters, chortling to herself, ordering everyone who'd come that they were expected at Wharton house for an afternoon and night of celebration.

He studied his wife's impish smile as they swept down the stairs toward their waiting carriage, and decided not to question her about what she'd just said about being "done with him." There was plenty of time for arguments and making up once they were safely away from everyone.

He helped her in, waved adieu to anyone seeing them off, and fell back into his seat untidily as the carriage suddenly leaped into furious motion. "What the devil?"

"We have a deadline," Sylvia told him as she dug beneath the carriage blanket at her side. She produced a pack of cards and started to expertly shuffle them.

"What? You want to play cards now? This is no time for games, wife."

"Exactly now."

She dealt the cards onto his knee and hers to her lap, and then picked them up. Her expression one of extreme concentration.

He glanced around. "I don't have any money to gamble with."

Sylvia arranged her cards with her usual singlemindedness. "I don't yet have my pin money from my new husband, either, so we will have to give up our clothing to wager with. One piece per round should suffice."

It took him a minute to consider how quickly he'd end up naked, playing against Sylvia's superior skill. When they had played against each other before, they'd usually play twenty rounds before he gave up trying to defeat her.

He did not have a good hand, but Sylvia's knack of turning the game any way she liked made every game's outcome a complete surprise. It was possible their game could go on for some time, since he'd told the coachman to take the very long way home before the ceremony had started.

A smile grew over her lips as Alexander considered what might be possible in this tiny space around them. He wisely drew the blinds down. Things were going to get very heated, very quickly, on their first long journey home as husband and wife.

Sylvia hitched up her skirts but only discarded a shoe. However, the sight of her stocking-clad limb made him groan aloud. Thanks to Mother's interference, they'd not managed to be alone for a whole month. He felt a very deprived man, indeed.

He untied his cravat and threw it down over her shoe, grinning. "A kiss for the winner?"

"I thought you'd see things my way, my lord." She suddenly laid down her cards, showing her winning hand.

All he could do was laugh and catch her as she launched herself across the carriage into his arms to claim her new husband's lips as her well-deserved reward.

———— ♦ ————

More Regency Romance from Heather Boyd...

DISTINGUISHED ROGUES SERIES
Book 1: Chills
Book 2: Broken
Book 3: Charity

Book 4: An Accidental Affair
Book 5: Keepsake
Book 6: An Improper Proposal

Book 7: Reason to Wed
Book 8: The Trouble with Love
Book 9: Married by Moonlight

Book 10: Lord of Sin
Book 11: The Duke's Heart
Book 12: Romancing the Earl

Book 13: One Enchanted Christmas
Book 14: Desire by Design

WILD RANDALLS SERIES
Book 1: Engaging the Enemy
Book 2: Forsaking the Prize
Book 3: Guarding the Spoils
Book 4: Hunting the Hero

SAINTS AND SINNERS SERIES
Book 1: The Duke and I
Book 2: A Gentleman's Vow
Book 3: An Earl of Her Own

REBEL HEARTS SERIES
Book 1: The Wedding Affair
Book 2: An Affair of Honor
Book 3: The Christmas Affair
Book 4: An Affair so Right

MISS MAYHEM SERIES
Book 1: Miss Watson's First Scandal
Book 2: Miss George's Second Chance
Book 3: Miss Radley's Third Dare
Book 4: Miss Merton's Last Hope

And many more…

www.ingramcontent.com/pod-product-compliance
Lightning Source LLC
Chambersburg PA
CBHW031009190726
48286CB00003BA/754